JACK & COKE

JACK & COKE

A NOVEL

JIMMY HAIGHT

NEW YORK

LONDON • NASHVILLE • MELBOURNE • VANCOUVER

JACK & COKE

A Novel

Published in New York, New York, by Morgan James Publishing. Morgan James is a trademark of Morgan James, LLC. www.MorganJamesPublishing.com

The Morgan James Speakers Group can bring authors to your live event. For more information or to book an event visit The Morgan James Speakers Group at www.TheMorganJamesSpeakersGroup.com.

ISBN 9781683507543 paperback
ISBN 9781683507086 eBook
Library of Congress Control Number: 2017916058

Cover Design by:
Rachel Lopez
www.r2cdesign.com

Interior Design by:
Chris Treccani
www.3dogcreative.net

In an effort to support local communities, raise awareness and funds, Morgan James Publishing donates a percentage of all book sales for the life of each book to Habitat for Humanity Peninsula and Greater Williamsburg.

Get involved today! Visit
www.MorganJamesBuilds.com

DEDICATION

To Aimee. Without you, this book would not exist.
How lucky I am to have someone who makes me better
every single day.

PREFACE

We live in an age of decentralization. We are powering our homes with electricity produced without a central utility, using currencies without affiliation to a government, and assembling the largest trove of human information via a worldwide network of contributors. One by one, the gatekeepers of power are losing their relevance.

Jack & Coke is a story of many things, but among them is the destabilizing impact of such a force on our most precious institution—the truth. Any person can now disseminate information to billions of others without the blessing of a central authority figure. There is both great promise and peril in this future. We have the responsibility to ensure that we use this opportunity to promote transparency, fairness, and prosperity for those that come after us. This book is merely one such idea about how we can build the necessary reverence for truth-telling. It is my hope that one of you will take this idea and make it a reality.

This is also the story of youthful ambition. It took me many years to tell the story of Jack Ranger and to articulate what he is chasing. He sees a world where the only certainty is increased stratification, and the only thing he is willing to bet on is himself. As I matured through writing this book, my understanding of what it means to succeed has shifted, and I have no doubt that my feelings will continue to evolve. But right here, right now, I leave you with the story of Jack Ranger, a passionate young man who rages against the world because he believes that his destiny can only be achieved through sheer force of will.

CHAPTER 1

Should I run?

His temples throbbed against his skull. A haze occupied his consciousness where thoughts were supposed to be. A screaming sound rang in his ears.

I need to run.

Jack Ranger lay face-down and discarded.

At the edges of his senses, he felt the dew of the grass pressing up against his skin. He heard the gentle hum of a small suburb going to sleep.

Mostly what he felt was pain. Blinding pain.

Jack rolled onto his back and blinked at the twilight sky. More than anything he wanted to rest. But there wasn't time. He had to move.

Jack attempted to stand. He staggered a few steps and fell on his right hand. His eyes blurred and he screamed out in pain. He couldn't silence it. He couldn't silence himself.

On one knee, Jack looked at his hand as he curled his fingers in and out of a fist. In a stupor, the pain peaked and flowed throughout his body. He had felt the chemicals eating at his skin as his captors held him in place. But now, through glazed eyes, he saw for the first time the bubbles of tortured flesh on the back of his right hand. There was no more blood, but it was still too fresh for scar tissue.

He had to get up. He couldn't stay here long.

Adrenaline kicked in again, giving him another chance.

From his knee, he lifted his head and took in his surroundings. In the gray light of dusk, Jack rose and moved to the house that he had been to once before.

CHAPTER 2

ONE YEAR EARLIER

Jack's fourth interview since his college graduation was going differently than he expected. He followed the man he hoped would be his boss into a poorly lit bar.

Anton raised his credit card in the air. "Liz, how are you today? We've got a new recruit, and I think he needs a beer."

He wasn't sure when the interview had officially started, but he could tell it was well underway.

"So Jack, what makes you think you want to do this?

"Work at the *Tribune*?"

"No—reporting."

He paused. The graduate sat on his bar stool thinking about how he wanted to craft his answer. It was difficult to get a read on Anton. Did he want passion? Was he looking for skill and experience? Or was he a functioning alcoholic who wanted an excuse to drink at 3:00 p.m. on a Wednesday?

"I suppose two reasons. Truth and a mentor."

"A fine answer! But first, who is this mentor?"

"A professor I had in college, Professor Malcolm Ray."

This professor was something of a legend at the university, amongst the journalism school anyways. Malcolm Ray was an ex-*New York Times* reporter. He broke big stories in the 90's and was a lightning rod for political activism in the early 2000's. It was a big deal when he decided to take a back seat from the real world and spend his time influencing impressionable young minds in the hallowed halls of academia. Jack never knew why Professor Ray chose Jack's school or why a journalist would leave at the pinnacle of his career, but Jack suspected Professor

Ray had found himself in the middle of a lucrative bidding war of universities hoping for his services.

"Ah, Malcolm Ray, I know of him. A great guy from all accounts." Anton paused and reflected. "Professors can leave a deep impression on us, Jack. You may owe more to him for this moment than you know."

Anton laughed a bit and raised his glass. "But truth! We have an idealist!" He took a drink and smiled. "You're going to need more than that—tell me why you are here. What about truth?"

The cogs of Jack's mind turned a little easier when greased with a beer. But how could he explain? Jack knew that a bit of desperation was wrapped in that truth. This was interview number four. *New York Times, Chicago Tribune, and Washington Post*—they all said no. Jack's scorecard showed two rejection calls and a pulled job offer. It wasn't a good look. The *Tribune* was his only chance to join a respectable paper, even if it was his last choice. He knew his abilities, and he knew he deserved this. The real truth was that Jack knew he belonged in the arena with the best of the trade.

But somehow that didn't seem like the best way to answer Anton's question. "Truth," he said instead. "Because that's what keeps the world in check. Because the lack of it topples nations and the presence of it exposes corruption. Because truth is what the people demand and it is in short supply."

Another raise of the glass, another smile, and another drink. "I underestimated your idealism."

Anton's face grew more serious as he moved to the next part of his interview. "I'm not sure if you know what I actually do at the *Tribune*, Jack, but there's more to my job than what my title would lead you to believe."

Jack's head tilted right.

"I'm the guy that brings out the truth that you seem to love so much."

Jack was excited although not quite sure what type of offer Anton was framing.

He continued, "I need good people on my team, there's a lot more truth to be told."

And there it was, the implicit sign that Jack was in.

Jack nodded. His impulse was to say 'yes' immediately, but he held back. Something about this was different. He realized that he didn't need to say anything. The choice had already been made. It didn't matter what he said.

The right hand of each met above the bar. A firm shake followed by a deliberate clinking of their pint glasses.

"Who is the next interview with?"

"Jack, it's not a question of who you are meeting. It's a question of what you are doing. And I think you'll like the answer."

With that, Anton reached into his wallet and handed him two business cards. Jack didn't read the second card because he was too confused by what was on the first.

Jack Ranger
Associate Political Correspondent
Tribune Co.

CHAPTER 3

Jack's Bluff

THE THIRD DAY OF COLLEGE

She was perfect. Her sundress, her sunglasses, her suntan—perfect.

Jack walked into the elevator on the way to his new freshman year dorm room. College was a flurry of sensations. The campus, the classes, the girls—everything was a new and tantalizing invitation.

High school had been a breeze, but he already knew college offered something more. Jack loved the thrill of the chase. College could be enlightenment.

His heart skipped when Molly walked in.

The elevator doors closed behind her.

She gave a polite smile and asked, "What floor are you going to?"

Jack felt so lucky in this moment. She had opened the conversation and welcomed him to speak to her. He knew it was his chance to make a first impression. Now was the time to flash his charm. But instead, he froze.

He waited until Molly pressed the button for her floor.

"Same as you," he said, "floor five."

Jack waited for this coincidence to spark a playful remark. It was serendipity that should form the basis for chit-chat.

But Molly was unimpressed.

She gave a shrug and tapped her fingers against the elevator wall. Jack shifted, smiled, and stared at the closed doors.

The elevator pinged and the doors opened. The fifth floor was here. Jack followed her out of the elevator and pretended to tie his shoes until she disappeared around the corner. Jack stood and looked around to see if anyone was there to call his bluff.

He didn't have her name and he didn't have her number. He just had a need to see her again. Jack returned to the elevator and hit the button for the seventh floor.

CHAPTER 4

Leaving college had been a rough transition at first, but Jack was getting along well enough in Boston. He moved to the outskirts of the city, Allston, into a studio apartment. He was surrounded by a smattering of fringe individuals. Allston was known for its magnetic attraction to the eclectic folks who'd prefer a bike to a car, fair trade coffee to a gym membership, and tattoos as opposed to brand names. But it was also home to bright-eyed and newly-minted graduates clawing to make a name for themselves. To put it plainly, the city was expensive and Allston was cheap—for now. Allston served as a foothold for the young and ambitious to stay within shouting distance of their dreams.

The result was that this particular neighborhood of Boston had a serious case of clashing identities.

Jack supposed it was like any gentrification story—the fringe kept it cheap while the yuppies made it more expensive. One of the core characteristics of the modern yuppie, however saddled by student debt they may be, was their unquenchable attraction for more of their kind. Allston was experiencing a swarming of young graduates. They were drawn like moths to the siren light of downtown. But first, they had to pay their dues on the outskirts. Yes, Jack's studio apartment, friends, and insistence on watching Monday Night Football were contributing to the cause. Allston, Boston really, was in a state of flux and Jack once or twice reflected that he might be living at the tipping point.

The routine of work was something he hadn't quite got used to. It was the pace of life more than anything else that was troubling. College was fast. Careers were slow. This wouldn't be a problem if the world itself would decide to slow down. Regimes, ideals, and paradigms were falling and shifting on a daily basis, and Jack was left out. Computers were learning how to drive cars and Jack was stuck editing fluff pieces.

There seemed to be two tracks in the world. Jack and all his friends were not on the fast one.

It didn't help that Molly was in New York City. He missed her more than he was willing to admit. Even his best friend Sean, who understood Jack like few other people, didn't know how much he missed her.

In college, they had been inseparable. Jack Ranger and Sean J. Cosatiri quickly became best friends, a fact that remained unchanged even if its meaning had shifted over the years. It wasn't the same now; there was something magical about the proximity of college. There was a certain allure to walking to meet someone on a whim or sharing a supreme commonality of experience. Whatever allure this was, it gradually eroded in the real world, one crowded subway ride at a time.

He missed his Friday night ritual.

The odd ritual took place nearly every Friday night when he was in college. Before the bars he would head over to Sean's apartment. Before the music, before the dancing, before the girls, there were just the two of them sitting in a room. One drinking rum, the other whiskey. Classes were hard, the week was exhausting, Saturday was a hangover and Sunday was for homework. There existed only Friday evening before the craziness to talk life.

He remembered the night that the ritual started.

Jack had walked into Sean's apartment without knocking. The apartment was classically unkempt, but always within a shade of respectfulness so that cleaning could be accomplished if the situation called for it. He hopped on the couch to find, waiting for him, a cup of ice, and three bottles: Sailor Jerry's, Jack Daniels, and Coke.

They talked about the usual things. "What about Casey?" Jack asked.

"Yeah, I don't know, something about her I'm not really into," Sean replied.

"You mean she's not blonde?"

Sean lifted his glass in acknowledgement.

And then the ideas started to flow: business ideas, political ideas, thoughts about what the future might hold. This was the first of countless times that the future would arise in their conversation. Maybe that was why Jack had loved the ritual so much. Jack was obsessed with the future.

Whiskey and rum worked their way into the conversation. Not overly so, but it fanned the flames.

Sean mentioned that his aunt and uncle had just spent ten thousand dollars to put his little cousin into an 'elite' kindergarten.

Jack marveled. "A good kindergarten means a nice elementary and middle school…. which lets you get into a nice prep school so that you can have a shot at the Ivy League."

They sat thinking about the implications.

Sean offered a thought. "It's weird that the world can be decided for you by the time you're five. You're either in or you're out and you don't have a choice."

"But I don't blame them," Jack said "people are scared. I'd do the same thing. Those on the edge are being left behind."

Another pause and another drink of whiskey.

Sean was a reflective guy. He offered conclusions in the form of observations. He had a way of wrapping other people into his thoughts that made everything seem like a group endeavor. He said to Jack, "When you don't know what the future holds, then you better get to the top while you still have the chance."

Their situation was obvious. Neither had gone to an overpriced kindergarten. No one had opted them 'in.' Their future was a battle of willpower vs. pedigree.

Neither of them fully understood why the future meant so much to them, but they knew it was what had brought them together. "That's why we work so hard, Sean. Because we are our only insurance policy."

Jack lingered on his whiskey as Sean disappeared into his room before coming back out with a fresh shirt. "You about ready to head to Casey's pregame?" asked Sean.

Jack sprang off the couch. "Do you think Molly will be there?"

CHAPTER 5

Working at the *Tribune* wasn't what Jack had imagined. It also wasn't what Anton had promised him either.

"Have you heard about specialization of labor?" Anton had mentioned to Jack one day.

"The internet is great at cat videos, so we let them do that. Our value isn't in cat videos, Jack. It's not in puzzles, and it's not in classified ads either. That's what YouTube and Craigslist are for. We might not be first to report something, but if we say it then people know it's true. It's a big responsibility."

Jack couldn't help but notice the *Tribune* itself didn't seem as convinced about its mission as Anton was.

Newspapers were dying, and everyone working at the *Tribune* knew it. It made for an interesting mix. There were those who were grinding out their final years, those just thankful to have a job, and those who didn't want to give up on their training. With the exception of Anton, Jack had yet to come across someone with a similar conviction for truth.

And yet here it stood, the *Tribune*. Perhaps it was the product of momentum from two decades ago, or maybe it was nostalgia, but the institution itself was still a well-respected fixture in the public's mind. Jack had met the Editor in Chief Pat Flaherty only a few times, but he had heard plenty of stories about him. Conventional wisdom had it that Flaherty was a shrewd businessman who kept the paper alive, first through the coming of the internet and secondly through the downturn of 2008. Some people revered him. Others feared him. As far as Jack could tell, Anton was somewhere in the middle. An uneasy partnership seemed to exist between the two men.

Anton was a hard character to understand. He filled Jack with stories of the importance of journalism. He played the chords of idealism in Jack with his words and simultaneously crushed them with his assignments.

It was as if Anton was purposely assigning the most mundane stories he could.

Unannounced, Anton would take Jack out to grab a beer and talk or bring him into his office to discuss some sort of philosophy of life. But, just as often, Anton would disappear. He would go missing for days or weeks, and no one knew where he was or what he was doing. But, without fail, Anton would always return. He would come strolling back to the office as if he had never left.

Once, after a six-day absence from the office, Jack asked him where he went.

Anton smiled. "I was returning some videotapes."

That was the last time Jack asked.

Jack dug into Anton's past and decided that the man had earned his quirks. He walked with a limp. It was a slight hobble as if his right knee decided on which occasions it felt like fully bending. The knee and its troubles were frequently objects of Anton's cursing, but the cause of the limp was never discussed.

The rumor was that he had once worked for the FBI, but Jack could neither confirm nor deny its validity. What he did know was that Anton had broken some of the biggest stories the *Tribune* had ever done. Corruption, extortion, conspiracy, Anton was no stranger to the darker workings of this world. He had spent time at *The New York Times* and had worked as a foreign correspondent for a number of other outfits over the years.

What Jack couldn't understand was why exactly Anton was at the *Tribune*. Anton was certainly a man with choices, and Jack couldn't imagine a world where the *Tribune* was the best choice. Of the quirks that Anton showed, this was one that Jack could least comprehend.

CHAPTER 6

Jack on the Rocks

SENIOR YEAR OF COLLEGE

It was a fall day. The trees lining campus danced with burnt orange and yellow. It was unfortunate that today needed to be spent inside. Jack was sitting in a chair opposite a desk, waiting for Professor Ray to return to his office.

The professor walked into his office and smiled at the unexpected visitor.

Professor Ray was tall, but not too tall, and distinguished without looking old. The man commanded a presence in a way that Jack had never seen in another professor.

"Hey, Professor, how are you?"

"Fine, Jack, how are you?"

Jack started to respond but held back. It was uncomfortable to bring up what he wanted to talk about. If the professor noticed Jack's unease, he didn't show it. Instead, he filled the pause with his own question.

"Say, how was your internship this summer? Did you like *The Times*? Did you meet Kristen?

Jack nodded. "Yes, it was amazing. I loved it."

"Good to hear. It's always helpful to know someone on the inside."

The two of them had shared many meetings in this office. They had collaborated as Jack cobbled together a resume and portfolio before searching for internships. It was Professor Ray's connections that got Jack's foot in the door to spend a summer at *The New York Times*.

Jack added more to his statement. "I'm still waiting to hear about a full-time offer. But I'm feeling pretty good about it."

Professor Ray smiled. "I'm sure you knocked it out of the park."

Jack thought back to his internship. People at *The Times* remembered their colleague Malcolm Ray. He was still a legend in many circles. Jack hadn't been surprised to hear the stories of his professor's industry prowess. After all, the shelf in his office had enough awards on it to make Jack believe that the professor's old colleagues weren't exaggerating. Even on campus, Jack had seen the professor flex his clout. He ran successful fundraising for new facilities at the journalism school and routinely brought in guest speakers for free that would have demanded a five-figure speaking fee anywhere else.

Jack had taken every class he could with the professor. He had even introduced him to Molly on several occasions. The three of them would grab coffee on campus and talk through life goals. He was a man who had accomplished much and was willing to share his advice to help others get there. Jack admired what Professor Ray had done with his life.

But despite the internship and coffee chats, Jack's most important memories of Professor Ray always seemed to be in his office. Yes, the golden clock, quasi-dark lighting, and framed pictures of front page articles that hung along the walls were a reoccurring back-drop in many of Jack's memories.

There was another pause between the two of them. Finally, Jack brought himself to say what he came to the office to ask. "Were you ever scared by what you published? I mean, were you ever afraid of what was going to happen?"

The professor quickly lost his smile. "What do you mean—are you ok?"

Jack feared that the conversation had escalated faster than social norms would dictate. "Yeah, Professor, I'm fine."

The professor raised an eyebrow. It was an expression that showed he didn't think Jack was 'fine.' He ran his tongue over his bottom teeth as he thought through his next words. "I've made a lot of mistakes, Jack, but the biggest have been when I knew it wasn't right and I did it anyway. I've done a lot of good, too. I also have a lot of regrets, but the biggest regrets aren't the mistakes. They're from the times when I was too scared to act."

Jack nodded with a blank expression.

Professor Ray paused a moment before continuing. "When I was younger I was working on a piece about shady business dealings between two bigwigs at the state level. In my mind, I went back and forth and back and forth. I was going in circles until I finally brought it to my editor."

He lowered his voice and put his hand to the side of his mouth as if he didn't want the bookshelves and picture frames to hear. "There were some people with the paper who weren't going to look good if the story got out."

Professor Ray laughed like an old man reminiscing on the trouble that he and his buddies used to get into when they were younger. "You know what my editor did?"

Jack shook his head.

"The next day I was coming back to my desk, and he flipped my desk over—in front of everyone. And then he laid into me. It was something fierce. I was left with a flipped desk and 25 people laughing at me."

This was standard operating procedure for the professor. He answered questions with stories. Sometimes the stories were short, other times they were winding and confusing. Usually, they made sense.

"You know what I did, Jack? I ate the story, and I regretted it. People should have known, but they didn't. Just like that, the story became another notepad on the bottom of a forgotten drawer."

Jack wasn't entirely sure of the message, but he nodded anyway.

"But, you get over most of those things eventually, Jack." The professor paused again. "Except the real big ones—you don't ever get over those."

Jack suspected the professor was talking about more than writing news stories.

Professor Ray's eyes turned to catch Jack's. "There are a lot of things in life people are too scared to do. The question you need to answer is, 'will the world be better for what I've done?' If the answer is yes—then don't look back and Godspeed."

Silence enveloped the room. Jack took a deeper look at the professor. He always wore jeans and a blazer. Jack wasn't sure if it was the immaculate white and gray speckled facial hair or his often-furrowed brow—but he made it looked distinguished. Not much seemed to bother him. The professor had already made his money, lived his experiences, and acquired his stories. What was left to worry about?

Professor Ray was also his closest mentor, the one that Jack trusted the most. Jack ran the school newspaper and Professor Ray played no small part in his inspiration to do so. Each year the newspaper chose a new editor in chief. This year it was Jack's turn.

But something had come up, and Jack didn't know the right course to take. "I want to publish something, and I think it could hurt me."

The professor offered a question. "And the paper will support it?"

Jack shrugged. "I'm EIC. I can publish whatever I want."

Professor Ray tapped the first two fingers of his hand on his wrist as he thought. "Ah yes, the trump card. That will work."

He kept tapping his wrist and finished, "Although sometimes it only works once."

The two locked eyes for a moment. Jack shifted his stare to the desk in front of him and then moved his eyes to the bookshelves. He looked at the plaques and awards on the shelf. The professor had accumulated a large collection over the years. Jack's mind slipped from his troubles for an indulgent moment. Jack's collection would, one day, be better.

The professor stood up. It was time to leave.

Moving towards the door, Jack lingered for one last question.

"So that story that never got published still gets to you?"

"No, not that piece. They had their day of reckoning eventually. But I'll tell you what nags at me every time I think about it. It's what I would have done today."

His final sentence was delivered with a coy smile, "You see, Jack, kids today are lucky. If that happened to me now... I would have just published it on the internet."

Jack nodded. "Thanks, Professor."

CHAPTER 7

"What exactly is pumpkin spice?"

Jack lifted an eyebrow.

Sean held out his cup of coffee at arm's length. "It's not pumpkin, and it's not spicy… and I don't even drink coffee."

Jack laughed. "Me neither."

They sat facing the Charles River. Today was the Head of the Charles boat race. It was as good an excuse as any to meet up and talk life.

Blue in the sky, orange in the trees, and noticeable steam from their coffee cups.

How long had it been since they talked? Weeks? Months? Too long.

"Is this life, Jack? Wake up, go to work, eat dinner, go to sleep— that's what I do five days a week. The other two days are the same, except I just don't go into the office and I get less email. I don't have time for anything."

Jack silently acknowledged the grind.

Sean sighed. "But everyone does it, right? It's the path."

The two had talked about life after school before. Sean was smart and Sean was a hard worker. He landed a consulting gig out of school. They paid him well, and they made him work hard for it.

"But it's crazy, Jack, I'm the lucky one. I work like a dog and can't see my friends. But I'm lucky because I can actually afford to pay down my student loans AND not have to live at home."

It was true. Jack knew a handful of kids who couldn't afford apartments and more who probably *shouldn't* afford their apartments. He knew classmates who had declared bankruptcy. Jack thought about the people he knew. Sean was the cream of the crop. You didn't have to worry about him. Some people have clothes that always fit just right, some people have perfect pitch, and others are natural athletes. Whatever combination of genetics, luck, and skill these people possessed Sean had it for life. Jack could tell when he'd first met him—Sean was always going to be all right.

But maybe that was the most disturbing thing. Sean was the kid who was always going to win. He worked hard, got great grades, and got a great job out of school… and his life still sucked.

If that was the best-case scenario, what hope did everyone else have?

He took an elongated sip of the coffee. It was mildly sweet and hinted of a distant warmth. It was the chemical abstraction of fall.

Of course, they both knew what the other was thinking. The amount of time they'd spent talking about the future was too lengthy not to have crossed this bridge of understanding before.

Jack offered a bit more, "If life is a party, I feel like our generation is showing up late and all the booze is gone."

Sean looked at his coffee cup. "And the punch bowl has been filled with pumpkin spice latte."

CHAPTER 8

If life needed to be grabbed by the balls then Jack would slap on a latex glove, reach out his hand, and tell the world to turn its head and cough.

Jack sat across the table from Anton. He had more or less demanded a meeting with his boss. Day 127 of working at the *Tribune* and Jack was bored. Hard news and fluff pieces—that was the extent of Jack's journalistic uses. He had felt more important when he was an intern.

He was nervous about confronting his boss, but it had to be done. Without knocking, Jack walked into Anton's office and closed the door.

"I need something more."

Anton looked up from his work and stared at Jack. An unsettling silence filled the room.

Jack's mind flashed back to the words of his father only a day before.

"Hey, Jack, what's up?"

Jack was on his way home from work and called his father.

"I need some advice; I'm telling my boss that I need better work."

His father was never rash. "What do you mean?"

"I mean, I'm dying here. How do I tell my boss that I can't keep doing this grunt work?"

"It's simple, Jack. You don't."

"What do you mean I don't? I could be doing so much more. I'm better than this."

There was an audible sigh on the other end of the line. "Don't be like that. You're lucky to even have a job. Don't be a diva."

"Ok, thanks, Dad. I gotta go."

Jack made direct eye contact with Anton. Jack held his stare even as his father's advice scrolled through his head like the bottom-line of a cable-news channel.

The formula for success in their America was simple. Hard work + Time = Success. Pay your dues and you get rewarded. It was a talk he and his father had many times. The words were often different, but the meaning was always the same. The problem, as far as Jack saw it, was that the equation was broken. Jack had watched the stock market crash from the insulated walls of college. It was a good time to be in school, a shelter from the crumbling world. It was an acceptable four years to learn as the world slowly rebuilt itself. But he had watched his friends' parents get laid off at alarming rates. He saw people who bought into the equation get tossed to the curb. They dutifully followed the rules of the game, but the only prize was behind door number three… and it was an unemployment check.

In the old world—his dad's world—sheep could get rich. Sheep could have a house; sheep could have a family. Just do as you're told, follow the shepherd and you will be rewarded with green pastures. But Jack knew that he worked too hard to let anyone except himself decide his fate. Getting kicked out of the herd was a risk Jack was willing to take, but getting fleeced was unacceptable.

The silence held for another count of breaths. Which world did Anton live in, Jack's or his father's?

Anton's response to Jack's words was different than what Jack expected. He was calm and not the least bit angry. Anton's response was simple: "Please explain."

Jack laid out his case.

"I didn't have an internship at *The New York Times*, go $60,000 in debt, and bust my balls in school to cover town hall meetings."

Jack's delivery was passionate, and he was having difficulty toeing the line between anger and diplomacy. He wanted Anton to know how he felt. But, he also didn't want to get fired.

Jack took a breath and opened his mouth to continue his argument.

Anton held his right hand up in the air, signaling for Jack to stop. Anton smiled and clapped his hands. But he didn't say anything.

Instead, he opened his desk drawer and grabbed a USB drive. With the drive between his thumb and index finger, he dangled it in the air before tossing it to Jack. "I was told that this day would come, Jack. Why don't you have a listen?"

He waved his hand for Jack to leave his office. "Take the afternoon off."

The oddity of what was happening pressed on Jack's mind.

As Jack turned to leave, Anton offered one more piece of instruction. "Oh, and Jack, I'd suggest not listening to that at work. In fact, I wouldn't use your work laptop if I were you."

Jack stared at the tiny device in his hand. How could something so innocuous feel so inherently dangerous? There was a disconnect somewhere between perception and reality. Jack closed his hands around the USB drive and walked out the door.

CHAPTER 9

Straight Up

SOPHOMORE YEAR OF COLLEGE

He sat, eyes closed, sitting on his couch with his head in his hands. The sounds of the apartment door jolted Jack back to the present. He looked up to see Molly walking into the living room.

"You didn't answer your phone, so I figured I would just…"

Jack ruffled his hair, blinked, and stood up. But it was too late. Jack knew she had seen him.

Molly stopped her sentence and tried to understand the Jack that she was looking at. She noticed him holding a single baseball card in his hands.

She spoke. "That's not yours, is it?"

He loved how she could make leaps of understanding that others couldn't. She was right. It wasn't. It was his brother's. His brother wasn't particularly good at sports, especially baseball, but he loved Mark McGwire.

Jack considered his response and then only nodded in affirmation. He walked into his bedroom and reappeared with a new outfit.

He walked up to Molly. "Let's go to dinner."

Whatever conversation she wanted to have was over before it started.

Two weeks later Jack was on the edge his bed sitting silently. It was late; he thought she was asleep. But she woke up and saw him holding the card.

"Tell me what it is, Jack."

"It's nothing."

Jack could feel Molly staring at his backlit silhouette on the edge of the bed.

She responded, "I've seen you holding that four times now. When you think I'm gone, I see you. You just sit there and don't do anything. You don't notice me. You don't notice anything."

He didn't want to talk to her about it. Not here, not now.

Molly continued, "It's not nothing."

For a moment neither of them spoke.

"I was too busy for him." He whispered.

She sat up and waited.

For a collection of moments, he sat in silence. It was like he didn't know she was there. He just sat thinking to himself.

Finally, he spoke. "When you're a kid, you don't think about your brother like that." He paused before continuing. "I was too busy for my little brother. Not in a malicious way. I loved him. It was just that I always thought he would find his own path and everything would be fine."

Molly's complexion changed. "Who? I thought it was just you and Jason?"

Jack didn't address her question. "I ditched him all the time and never thought twice about it."

She tried again. "Who?"

"I took him for granted," he told Molly. "But Mark McGwire brought us together."

He would always remember the summer of 1998. That summer Mark McGwire and Sammy Sosa were caught up in an incredible home run race, battling to see who would be the king of baseball. Jack and his little brother watched. They watched and they watched together. It was the one thing that Jack went out of his way to do with his little brother.

Jack paused as he thought through the meaning of his story.

"Those nights were magical. We watched every at-bat just to see if 'Big Mac' would do it again."

The memory triggered a smile. It was a smile about the past.

Now it was Molly's turn to whisper. "Why haven't you told me about your little brother?"

"He loved to go on bike rides. He went on them all the time." Jack continued his story. His words were well practiced. He had told himself this story hundreds of times.

"I remember one day when he asked me to go for a bike ride. I said no. I wasn't even busy; I just didn't want to go with him. He went by himself, but he didn't come back. Hours passed, and my parents were worried, but they always worried. I wasn't worried at the time. They called everyone we knew. They made Jason and I get in the car and we drove everywhere we could, and we didn't find him. That's when I started to worry. We called the police and asked to be notified if they found anything."

Jack paused for breath.

"It wasn't until 11:00 p.m. that a police officer called telling us that he was in the hospital. We raced there and found him. It could have been worse. He slipped on a patch of sand and hit the road hard. Thank God, he was wearing a helmet. I remember feeling so relieved. He was lost, but we found him. He was hurt, but would get better."

Molly was rigid. She knew where Jack's story was going but refused to believe what it meant.

"But my parents were so upset. They knew I should have been with him. They never said it aloud, but I know they believed it. What if I had been there? I could have done something. I could have steered him clear or at least been there to help him. Instead, he laid unconscious on the road for who knows how long. Now he was in the hospital bed with a sling and a bandaged head."

He continued. "So, I told myself I wouldn't leave him again. Only, I never got that chance."

Jack fully retreated in his own mind. He remembered the days that came next.

The MRI found something disturbing. His brother's bones would be fine, his arm would heal, but the tumor they discovered was a different story. Treatment began immediately—days turned to weeks, weeks to months, and months almost to an entire year. It was the longest year of Jack's life. Jack's brother had only been able to come home for a brief stint.

They tried to live like a normal family. Jack could never get over the feeling that they were just pretending. Near the end, he had to go back to the hospital. His little brother was weak—maddeningly, unforgivably, impossibly weak. But Jack never left his side. He refused to go to school; he refused to go home at night.

Every day for 18 straight days Jack stayed in that hospital room with his brother. He read him stories, and they talked about sports teams. Jack talked to him about anything and everything he possibly could, if only to keep his mind off the inevitable. His parents tried to get Jack to go back to school to make the days seem more normal. But the first day that Jack had been forced to go back to school he left. He walked out of the school and kept walking, five miles until he got to the hospital.

Jack's consciousness returned to the room, and for the first time he looked at Molly.

"One day, right before the end. It was just me and him... those hours together were painfully long because there were so few of those hours left. He was looking at his baseball card collection. I had brought it to him the week before, so we had something to talk about together."

Jack's body went through an involuntary shake. "And then he pulled out his favorite card. It was the 1987 Mark McGwire rookie card. He gave it to me and said: *Keep this one safe, It's my favorite.*"

"I took the card and kept it safe. The one thing I could not do for my own brother."

Jack's head shook. "We... the family... we were different after that. It was just me, mom, dad, and Jason. I knew my father loved me... but my mom. She made it less obvious. I don't think she ever got over losing her youngest son."

This was the closest that Molly had ever seen Jack to crying. They looked at each other for a moment before Jack lowered his eyes. "It's a terrible thing to think. But, I could feel it every time she cried. There was a lot of crying back then. Every time I embraced her she cried. I couldn't help but think she wished it was me instead. Every tear, every sob, I could feel her reaching furiously for someone who could never come back."

Molly broke her silence. "No. No, that can't be true."

There was more to it. Jack couldn't bring himself to speak it to Molly. It created a rift with Jason as well. Jason was older and more responsible. When their brother died, he became closer to his parents. It was a pattern across the years. While Jack drifted, Jason stayed. College, jobs, girlfriends—Jason stayed even when he should have left. Jack left when he should have stayed. There was a resentment that they never talked about.

Molly seemed to understand that Jack's story was finished for tonight. She didn't try to say anything. Nothing would make the situation better, and she seemed to know it. They sat in silence. Together they shared that moment—a moment that Jack never wanted to share.

CHAPTER 10

The topic of how Jack almost got expelled came up a number of times with Anton. The topic seemed to surface every so often. Anton liked these sorts of stories. To him, there are no better stories to recount than those of catastrophes barely avoided. He shared many of them himself, and said on more than one occasion, "What good is almost screwing everything up if you can't get a laugh out of it?"

Jack still could remember himself sitting alone in his dorm shaking, just waiting and wondering what would happen. He remembered, too, the visits to Professor Ray's office.

One afternoon with Anton, Jack relived the story in its full painful glory as he retold the tale of his biggest undertaking while working at the school paper.

Jack remembered walking into Professor Ray's office and placing a piece of paper on the desk in front of him. The paper was a copy of an expense report. The name "Joseph Haleson" punctuated the copied piece of paper.

Jack looked over at Anton. "I had serious dirt on the president of the university. I remember the first thing I found was an expense report for a $3,000 dinner with only him and his wife."

Jack was getting excited as he retold the story. "But I found a lot more. Dinners were just the start. There were parties, limo service, and nepotism. I mean this guy was doing it all. The school had raised tuition by 8% that year, and the president of the university was spending tens of thousands of dollars on the school's dime."

"And you found this out how?" Asked Anton

But Jack continued without acknowledging the question. "President Haleson's son-in-law worked at the university. You know how much he was making? $175,000 a year. His title was 'Chief Department

Administrator' Administrator of what? It was insulting how stupid it was."

Anton already knew how the events would inevitably unfold.

Jack remembered that Professor Ray seemed to know how things would go as well. He had asked Jack *how much do you have?*

That day the professor sat in his chair and looked at the student before him. It was Jack Ranger, a kid who was terrified to discover that his actions could have power. Jack wouldn't forget his mentor's response that day either. *You need to leave, Jack. I cannot be a part of this.*

Jack remembered feeling a confusing mix of disappointment and fear. Obviously, the professor couldn't have ties to this story; Jack couldn't blame him for that. But he couldn't help but feel that he had followed Professor Ray to the edge of a cliff only to find himself staring over the edge with no one by his side.

"So you published the story, and…" Anton knew the final destination but clearly wanted the particulars.

"Of course," Jack said with the assurance of someone who had the benefit of knowing that his audience was taking his words at face value. "It had to be done."

Jack remembered the exact moment he knew he was going to publish the story. He had been getting the mail from his apartment. It was a strange occurrence, for no other reason than simply because he never got mail. Packages from Amazon—sure, but a letter—never. The letter was addressed to Jack Ranger with no return address. He told Anton what happened next. He told him he opened the letter to find a single hand-written sentence in the middle of an otherwise blank white piece of paper.

Don't look back, Godspeed.

Anton smiled. Professor Ray was a clever man who knew how to push people.

What Jack didn't tell Anton was how deciding to publish the article pulled him apart inside. He was talking to his boss after all. It was good to show confidence. But truth be told, Jack almost didn't do it. The decision cost him sleepless nights.

Looking back, he didn't worry about the lost sleep as much. He could get sleep back. What made him wince inside was the thought that it might have cost him Molly, too. It didn't cost her immediately, but something changed.

Jack learned a lot about himself when he decided to publish, and he thought Molly learned a lot about Jack, too. Publishing had flipped the switch and flooded the room with light—the real Jack Ranger was there for both to see. It was a new understanding, one that couldn't be shaken.

Jack laughed in unison with Anton. Jack knew that one of the two laughs was fake. That was the version he liked to tell. He didn't tell his boss how it had unraveled his relationship with Molly. Jack could remember that night. He didn't think he could ever forget it.

CHAPTER 11

No Chaser

SENIOR YEAR OF COLLEGE

The two of them sat up together at night. Jack's nights had been sleepless, and so had Molly's. It was quiet outside. Talking with Molly was easy. It always had been. Moonlight was coming into the room—enough to make the room an eerie shade lighter than pitch black.

"I'm not sure I can do it."

"Who else knows, Jack?"

"Just you, me, and Professor Ray, I think."

Do I publish? That was Jack's internal debate. His mind's eye could see it being played out. He could be expelled, or President Haleson would be forced to resign. Maybe the school would be better off. Maybe it wouldn't. Maybe the president would resign, AND he would be expelled. Or maybe nothing would happen. Maybe the accusations of administrative overspending would be tucked under the rug and dismissed with earnest denials of any wrongdoing. The president would raise the specter of doubt that maybe someone had an axe to grind... like an angry, misguided student. After all, you didn't get to be the president of anything without having a politician's knack for deflecting wrong-doing.

But what if it worked? What if he exposed the truth and things changed for the better?

It would be a thrill. Not for the notoriety, not because it would be a great story for his resume, but because it felt right. But getting expelled wasn't an option. He was too deep into his degree. Jack knew it was a risk. People who had done lesser things had paid greater prices.

"You know they'll come after you, Jack. They won't want you to come up with more."

This was perhaps the tenth time they had the conversation. Molly was scared. Jack was, too. It would be too obvious for Jack to be kicked out by the president himself so soon after the piece published. But what about cheating on a test? This fine academic establishment, like so many of its fellow prestigious New England schools, had a precariously high punishment for what they liked to call 'academic dishonesty.' A tap on the right shoulder and it wasn't hard to see Jack being put on the spot for cheating on some exam. What about his scholarship? The president of the university had many ways to make Jack's life more difficult.

"It's your life," she said, "but what am I supposed to do? What if you get expelled?"

"What do you mean what are you supposed to do?" Jack said, "It's not like I'm going to die."

"But I'd miss you Jack—you know that."

"I don't have to go anywhere."

They looked at each other. He was right. Whatever happened he didn't have to go anywhere. But that didn't change their fear.

"Sometimes…" She paused.

What words was she looking for?

"You don't need to break the next Watergate. I just need you to be a good guy."

Jack got up and walked to his desk. It was late, but he didn't feel tired. He opened the desk drawer and pulled out four stapled and typed pages of paper. He turned on the light in the room.

Molly was annoyed. "What's this?"

Jack took two steps toward her and tossed the pages onto the foot of the bed. He sighed. "It's a compromise."

Molly looked at the emboldened words at the top of the paper. It was a draft of the article.

"President Haleson's Curious Use of School Funds: Embezzlement, Nepotism, and Fiscal Mismanagement"
—By No Man

Molly read the headline once and the by-line twice. "No Man?"

Jack smiled, "Plausible deniability." He reached for the lights and turned the room back to its not-so-pitch black color. He slipped under the sheets of his bed.

The two were silent for a moment as each pretended to go to sleep.

Molly rested her head on his shoulder. "You promise you're going to publish anonymously?"

He lay there in the semi-dark closing his eyes and wishing he could fall asleep. Thoughts bombarded his mind. Was that enough for him? Could he just be unknown?

He knew that Molly was waiting for a response. He could almost smell her desperation. A nod, a grunt, any affirmation was all that she needed from him.

But it never came. Just silence.

CHAPTER 12

Jack took his boss's advice and took the rest of his 127th day of work at the *Tribune* off. At home, he took out his personal laptop and spun the drive around in his hand between his fingers. It was marked simply 'graduation' in black sharpie written along its side.

On the memory unit was a single audio file that was 25 minutes long. Jack began to listen. It began innocently enough. It was a recording of two men talking. They were someplace quiet without background noise. As best Jack could tell, the man whose voice sounded closest to the microphone was named Ronnie.

The conversation continued across drawn-out exchanges and was followed by silence. Whoever this Ronnie was, he was obviously upset. Whoever the other voice belonged to didn't seem apologetic. They were talking about a woman who had been killed.

Jack checked around his apartment for anyone who might be listening. He knew no one was there, but he checked just the same.

He couldn't tell what they were talking about, but he understood one important thing. The unidentified voice did not know this conversation was being recorded. The two were talking about an ongoing project. It was a status check of one kind or another, and the name "Zeke" came up enough times for Jack to notice.

Twenty-one minutes into the recording the conversation shifted, and the man whose voice sounded closest asked a question that sent Jack reeling. "Why'd you have to kill her?"

There was an excruciatingly long pause.

"Listen, Ronnie, sometimes… she was dangerous—her being alive. You can't know what she knew."

Ronnie's voice rose as he called this bogus explanation what it was.

"She was a good woman; you can't go around killing good people."

The response was chilled, "We don't like loose ends."

Jack heard a knock at a door. He was startled, thinking it was his own apartment, and he turned around to see who might be there. But, in the same split second, he knew it was from the recording.

The two men greeted an unidentified third figure. The recording continued for a minute longer. There was a string of trivial three-way banter, and then the recording stopped.

Jack didn't know why it stopped. Did Ronnie hit pause? Was the battery dead? Was it something else?

Jack wasn't sure what to think, except that this wasn't how he expected his afternoon to start.

CHAPTER 13

"What was that?" Jack had gotten to work early and was sitting in Anton's office by the time his boss arrived.

The door closed and Anton hushed his voice. "That's what we call a big deal."

The two talked. Jack wanted answers and Anton had some of them. No, he didn't know when the recording was taken. No, he didn't know what lady had been killed. Yes, he did know who took the recording.

Anton pulled out a hand-written note from a file marked 'city hall meetings' and read it aloud. It was a simple note, only a few words. It could only be from the voice in the recording.

Listen first. I will be wearing green. George Washington Statue at 7:00 p.m. tonight. I have more.

Jack's mind flashed back to the voice asking why a good woman had died. He pictured Anton meandering around in the shadows waiting for an unidentified man.

"Did you meet him?"

"Yeah, I met him. Listen; let's take this on the road."

The two walked to Anton's car and drove out of the parking garage. Jack listened as Anton explained the story of how he got the letter from Ronnie. Anton had received a manila envelope containing the note and the thumb drive addressed specifically to him. He had met him for the first time in the shadow of the great stone monolith that was General George Washington standing guard at the entrance of the Commons. That was almost a year ago. Anton had met with Ronnie on multiple occasions. He wouldn't divulge everything, but he was angry at something.

Anton explained, "He kept telling me it couldn't be traced back to him."

"Where is he now?"

"I don't know. The trail's gone cold. I haven't been able to get in touch with him for months."

"What about the police?" The question was too obvious not to be asked.

Anton's reaction wasn't swift. He paused and tapped his hand on the wheel of his car. His voice changed, it was lower now. "Jack, I'm sure the police know. But they can't know that we do."

Anton made a check of his rear-view mirror. His voice maintained its deeper tone. "I have friends on the force Jack. Something's not quite right. Don't go asking questions yet. Promise me that."

Jack shifted in his car seat.

Anton continued. "I have friends there. You don't. Don't ask favors from people who are not your friends."

Jack nodded.

The car radio was on low. As the conversation stopped, bits of the chorus overcame the sound of the car's engines. Jack sat still in his seat and stared at the car in front of them. It occurred to him that he didn't know where they were going.

Anton drove a large SUV. The car rode smooth, and if Anton felt it that it was too large for the tiny streets of Boston he never mentioned it.

It was part of the charm - or frustration - of the city. Roads were mostly winding, usually too narrow, and always crowded with traffic and double-parked cars. City planners in the 1700's just didn't have the foresight to account for Land Rovers.

They made a turn leaving the Back Bay neighborhood and towards the North End.

Not asking questions wasn't going to get them any closer. Jack wanted to press Anton on this.

But Anton was already on to a new topic of conversation. He was talking about something Jack didn't bother to understand and he was making jokes. Anton was laughing at himself to compensate for Jack's lack of attention.

They crossed Canal Street, and Anton made a gesture pointing out the window. "Our office used to be there you know." Jack neither confirmed nor denied his interest in Anton's conversation.

Anton laughed. "We could just walk a block during lunch, and we could get to the best food in the city. There's got to be a hundred restaurants in this neighborhood. Nothing beats good Italian food."

Jack was still thinking about Anton's approach to Ronnie and he didn't like it. He was silent as Anton steered the car into the heart of the North End. There was traffic, of course. Anton muttered something about a shortcut and veered into a street that would have been called an alley in any other city. The road was cobblestone and just barely wide enough for people, let alone their car. Jack would have been nervous if he had been driving his own vehicle. But Anton didn't seem to care. They took a left turn, and Jack heard a sound as the side mirror scraped a light pole. He winced. They were now in a parking lot, and Anton parked the car. He made no mention of the scrape.

They got out of the car and walked towards a door with a single neon sign hanging over it.

"This used to be my favorite lunch spot. The best buffalo mac & cheese you've ever had. Lucky you."

Jack wasn't sure what to think. Why had they left the office? Was this about secrecy or was this about lunch? The restaurant was underground, so the two walked down the stairs, took their table, and ordered food. Jack turned the conversation back to what he thought the matter-at-hand should be.

"What's the next lead?"

Anton refocused on Jack and grinned.

"That's why you're here. We need to break this open from another angle. You're here to help me find what's next."

Jack didn't know what his boss meant by this, but he nodded and cracked a smile at a future of uncertainty.

CHAPTER 14

To: Gary J. Vincent (GVincent@TribuneCo.com); Amir Maxwell (AMaxwell@TribuneCo.com)
CC: Jack Ranger (JRanger@TribuneCo.com)
Subject: Jack Ranger's Work Availability

Gary & Amir,
Effective immediately you are to cease assigning Jack asinine busywork. Jack is now my direct report and will no longer be spending time on non-essential (i.e. your) assignments. If you have any questions, then please re-read the previous two sentences.
Respectfully,
A

Work from then on was different. The 7:00 a.m. email in Jack's inbox this morning was the subject of today's conversation.

"If anyone tries to put you on any work just ignore it."

"I can't just ignore my assignments." Jack was standing in the doorway to Anton's office.

"Yes. Yes, you can." Anton was grinning. He had the grin of a clever seven-year-old. Jack was trying to decide if Anton needed Jack to devote all his time to the new case or if Anton just enjoyed overstepping work boundaries.

Anton motioned for Jack to leave the room.

As Jack turned to go, Anton said, "You work only for me now, Jack."

Obsession is a funny animal. It looks much more obvious from far away than it does up close. When you're too close to obsession it has a habit of distorting itself so you don't notice it. To the outside world, Anton could be considered obsessed. To Jack, he was just hard at work.

Calls started coming in at late hours in the night. Both ways, Jack called Anton—and Anton called Jack. Code words were used on the phone, but all real communication happened in person. At the bar, at a restaurant, in the car. Yes, Anton was obsessed with this case, and Jack was along for the ride.

Obsession also has a funny habit of pulling others in, especially when that person has a void to fill. The night after Jack first listened to the recording of Ronnie something new happened. When he was alone at night he thought about Ronnie. Who was he? Who was the woman that died? Jack's mind raced as he thought of all the possibilities.

As Jack walked across his room that night, he glanced at a picture of Molly that still occupied space on his desk. For the first, time he realized who he hadn't been thinking of.

It was a welcome distraction. Thinking about Molly was as unpleasant as it was compulsive. Getting a girlfriend wasn't on Jack's 'to-do' list when he went to college—for all the reasons you might imagine. But there was something more, too. Something akin to a fear of accountability played a part. It wasn't that he didn't want to be tied down. It was more that he didn't want to be responsible for another's unhappiness. You wouldn't invite someone you loved on a dangerous trip from which you might not return. Jack didn't know what his future held, but he knew himself. The trail of ambition was only wide enough for one traveler at a time.

But she changed that.

He didn't know the exact moment it changed, but there were scenes that contributed to the bigger picture. The memory of one spring night played again and again in the theatre of his mind.

They had sat on a park bench each eating ice cream. Molly reached out and grabbed his hand. "I need to know you're serious, Jack."

He looked at her and laughed. "About what?"

"About us."

He rubbed her hand and softened his voice. "Of course I am."

She smiled. He couldn't tell if she believed him. "I've heard those words before."

That's how Molly was. She demanded more from him than Jack had given to anyone else before. It took Jack a long time to get himself to that point.

The memories never existed in isolation. Jack's mental film flipped to the next scene.

A summer on a lake.

A friend's cabin and a boat. There were ten of them.

They were all friends recapping the memories of their first full year of college. That night they traded stories, tired from a day in the sun and relaxed while staring at the orange glow of the fire before them. Molly and Jack stayed up late looking at the stars. It was a warm night with a slight breeze. Jack's hand traced the constellations in the milky sky as the last embers of the fire pulsated and faded. That was happiness. That was what Molly demanded of him, and Jack didn't regret it at the time.

Maybe that's why he still texted her even though she didn't respond. He thought again of the picture on his desk of the two of them. Was he angry at her? He had changed, and she didn't seem to care.

But for now, at least, he was free.

That night, after listening to the recording, Jack didn't feel compelled to steal another look at the picture or replay his memories. His mind was free while trapped in a new maze.

CHAPTER 15

The investigation went on for months. Those were some of the most intense months he could remember. His energy was refocused on digging up whatever it was that Ronnie had wanted them to find.

Jack knew that Anton had been working on this case before he joined, but he didn't know to what extent. After all, he did already have the recording. But that wasn't the whole story. Anton had done his own digging; he had even pieced together a potential identity of the murdered woman.

Sometimes, the discoveries that Jack made were new. Others, it was as if Anton was waiting for him catch up. Jack was on a train and Anton was the conductor who knew every stop.

Every stop except for the final destination. This rabbit hole was deeper than Anton had thought. Jack was certain of that.

Jack didn't mean to start making contacts in the police force. It just happened. Maybe Anton didn't want Jack snooping around and asking questions of the police, but as far as Jack was concerned it was a false logic. If you need answers, then you need to find people with information. Ignoring this truth wasn't going to cut it.

He asked questions. Not directly, but he asked them just the same. He asked for police records for certain date ranges, and he tried to learn as much as he could about the way the city investigated murders. In the age of the internet, it was odd for Jack to make so many trips around the police station to find information. But, he doubted anyone would make a big deal out of it. He was just a reporter doing his job. He'd watched enough movies to convince himself that fact was true. Anton was a movie buff. He would understand.

His name was Samuel. Samuel was a youngish officer with curly hair, brown eyes, and a confusingly strong jawline given his slender build. He was nice though. He was a friendly face that Jack took to talking to on his trips to dig up information.

It was just small talk at first. Samuel had noticed Jack's presence over the weeks and took to asking questions. The two were compatible enough. Samuel was happy to help. Jack suspected that the young officer liked to help, but wasn't called upon very often to do so. He was over-qualified, under-appreciated, and eager to please.

He was the perfect friend to have on the inside.

Jack pushed the boundaries. He asked more questions. Samuel knew that Jack worked for the *Tribune,* and he was chasing something, but it wasn't until their third conversation that Samuel got Jack to tell him what he'd been waiting for all along.

"What are you doing here?"

It was the middle of a Thursday afternoon. Jack was asking to see records that Samuel knew Jack had already seen.

"Going through records."

Samuel was looking at Jack waiting for him to make eye contact. "Why? Why these?"

The eye contact never came. "It's my job." Jack's answers were never as short as when he wanted to avoid a subject.

Samuel put his hand on Jack's shoulder. Contact. It wasn't aggressive, it wasn't a sign of friendship, but it was a brief physical connection. "Tell me what you're doing."

Finally, he lifted his eyes to meet Samuel's.

Jack looked around. No one was here. His mind fought over the decision of telling Samuel the truth. Perhaps the most important person absent from earshot was Anton. The left corner of Jack's mouth turned upward in a crooked grin.

Jack motioned his arm in front of the two of them down the hallway. "Shall we?"

Samuel obliged.

As they walked, Jack wrestled with how much he should share. "Does the name Ronald Sinclair come up much around here?"

Samuel paused for the briefest of seconds at the top of his gait. Then he recovered. Jack saw the hitch in his step, and he heard the protracted silence as Samuel's brain went down its mental checklist of which answer he was authorized to provide. Jack had picked up the scent.

"How much do you know about him?"

Samuel paused. It was his turn to look around. "It depends on what sort of things you need to know."

The reporter considered the response. He himself didn't know the answer to the question.

Before he could answer, Samuel made his intentions clear. "The exit is this way, Jack." He pointed to the opposite end of the hallway.

At first, Jack didn't move but Samuel held his pose. Jack nodded and turned to the exit. He took a business card from his pocket and extended it to the young officer.

"In case you change your mind."

Samuel took the card and shook Jack's hand. There was something behind the handshake, Jack could tell. "You know people wouldn't want us talking about this."

Jack's grin broke into something a little larger. "That's exactly what makes this so important."

CHAPTER 17

Chilled Over Ice

SENIOR YEAR OF COLLEGE

There was no hiding from it: sources, hard evidence, and one undeniably obvious by-line. Jack had published his story in the school newspaper, and it didn't look good.

"President Haleson's Curious Use of School Funds: Embezzlement, Nepotism, and Fiscal Mismanagement"

—By Jack Ranger

Jack got phone calls from some of his friends; he received emails from professors. The least interesting was one from a science professor he had freshman year that simply said, "Good Work."

When he went to class that day, everyone was staring at him. True or not, he felt like everyone had the story top of mind. Jack walked a little taller that day. But he didn't go back to class that week. No, he decided it would be best to watch things unfold from the relative obscurity of his room.

He remembered the first days of being holed up in his apartment, hoping something—anything—would happen. He had worked too hard for this just to blow over. How could business as usual go on? He kept feverishly checking online newspapers for something new.

But it never came. No mention on the news on TV, nothing in the papers.

He remembered now the revelation of his mistake. Why hadn't he given the story to the other outlets himself? Why didn't he let them know? Jack had just assumed that the truth rose to the top as a law of nature. In the same way that hot air rises or ice cubes float—the truth would prevail. But that wasn't the case. A week went by and students were angry, alumni were grumbling, and faculty denounced careless spending. But the disgust never seemed to leave the confines of the campus. Was the outside world deaf?

And then Jack was summoned by the school. He couldn't tell Molly. She would cry. He couldn't call his parents. They might do the same. There was only one person that he could talk to, so he sat outside his office for three hours until he finally came in.

"Jack, you can't just walk in here."

"You seem to be busy every time I try to set up a meeting."

They both knew the situation. Their partnership, the worldly advice that Jack so desperately craved, had to happen off the books.

Does that make me dangerous? Jack wondered this more than once. It was an odd feeling, to feel 'dangerous,' but it was certainly exhilarating. Jack couldn't help it—it made him smile.

"I'm being called into an investigation around academic misconduct, professor."

Jack had received an email, a letter, and then a phone call from the administration. He was to appear before a panel to investigate some alleged wrongdoings. Jack was a good student, certainly not a perfect student, but also not one to warrant such an investigation. He didn't even know the university conducted investigations. This was new. This was scary.

The professor leaned back. Each of them knew what was behind the letters. Each knew what it meant.

"You're going to be expelled, Jack. You know that right?"

Jack knew, but hearing the words aloud from a man he trusted was a new level of understanding. What would his parents think? What about the money he already owed the college, what about Molly? What about a job?

Professor Ray stood up slowly. He walked around the room and closed the door. "Jack, in these types of situations you need to ask yourself why things happened the way they did and what can still be changed."

He was talking lower now. Was it for effect or was it because he genuinely didn't want anyone to hear? The professor sat on the corner of his desk and leaned in.

"President Haleson is a well-connected man. Staying at the top requires damage control. Power, favors, and money are awfully good at damage control."

CHAPTER 18

"And yet, here you are. Gainfully employed and, I assume, with a piece of paper framed on a wall somewhere that says you graduated."

Anton and Jack were talking during one of their car rides that Anton had a habit of taking the two on.

Jack replied as he described a memory he didn't quite understand. "The story leaked."

It was true, a week before Jack's hearing the story got picked up. *The Boston Globe*, a local daily publication, and even the *Tribune* started raising questions. Jack wasn't sure what to make of it, or if it would do anything. He even got asked to interview with a news station as the "student who broke the story."

"A lot of the faculty were indifferent—I mean it didn't really affect them—but a lot of students started to make noise." Jack continued his story to Anton.

A lot of students did get angry. He never understood why they didn't act out when he first wrote the story in the school paper. He figured the bigger attention from other sources legitimized the claims. Maybe the fleeting shine of the limelight galvanized the anger.

But regardless, Jack's hearing was still scheduled. What Jack hated most in that week leading up to his hearing was that he didn't control his own destiny. He sat up late at night for three nights in a row. It's hard to sleep before your pending expulsion. Molly was the only person he talked to during that time. She cried. She cried for both Jack and for herself.

"And then two days before the hearing I couldn't take it anymore," Jack told Anton.

Those days were a fusion of fear, hate, and uncertainty that couldn't let Jack think about anything else.

Jack remembered his showdown with the president of his university.

Every weekday, President Haleson made a point to eat lunch in the main dining hall. It was a "man of the people" stunt Jack supposed. Whatever the purpose, he had staked out the President.

President Haleson placed his food on a table in the corner of the dining hall. Just as he was reaching into his pocket to take out his phone, Jack came up and sat directly across the table. He had no food in his hands, no smile on his face, no small talk on his lips.

"President Haleson," Jack had said.

"Mr. Ranger. I wasn't expecting to see you until Thursday."

That was the scene. One old man and one young man staring at each other, separated by the width of a table. Jack placed a section of *The New York Times* on the table between the two.

"Well, sir, neither of us has that kind of time."

Jack had pointed at the newspaper between the two of them. "*The New York Times* is running a series on the broken higher education system."

The president remained silent as Jack finished, "Their next piece is on rising costs in the face of overspending." He paused. "They need a few more quotes to round it out."

The president sat back crossing his arms. The offer was clear. Jack didn't know much about President Haleson's past. He was an accomplished man, no doubt. Jack couldn't remember exactly his background, but corporate success had preceded his current tenure as the school's president.

The president was a relatively unremarkable man to look at. His most noticeable physical trait was not his height, well-kept hair, or his sloping nose. It was his right eye.

Or rather, it was his lack of a right eye. Jack watched the older man scan the copy of *The New York Times* that he had laid out before him. His left eye tracked the headlines from left to right and top to bottom. His right eye was lifeless. It was a perfectly crafted glass replica that resembled its counterpart in every way from its light brown hue to its milky white—except that it didn't move.

This was the first face-to-face conversation between the two of them and Jack tried to get a read on the man who was sitting across from him. They say that the eyes are the window to the soul. But this eye betrayed nothing.

President Haleson had started the conversation again. "I never thought I would live to see the day where I was threatened by my own student."

He had sat there further considering Jack.

"I wasn't sure I was going to expel you, Jack. I might have gone easy on you. A one-semester probation and an apology might have sufficed. But I do appreciate you coming here and making up my mind."

Jack didn't move. What did boldness look like on the outside? What combination of facial expressions shows that you don't have fear? Jack tried to translate his thoughts into the right words that might save his situation. "I have more. Much more than what I published."

These words were a surprise to both men at the table. "And what if I call your bluff?"

"And let me give my interview? Then I suspect it will be hard for you to keep your job."

"How old are you, Jack? Twenty-one? Twenty-two? You could have a lot of good years in front of you—it's not smart to cast them aside so willingly. But even so, I think I might call your bluff."

Jack focused on the face he was projecting. "With all due respect, President Haleson, in this situation one of us has a whole lot more to lose than the other." Jack met the President's eye. "My interview is at 5:00 p.m. tomorrow." And he walked away.

After leaving the dining hall, Jack went to his room and lay on his bed. He wasn't hungry. He wouldn't be hungry the rest of the day. He watched the second-hand tick on the clock hanging above his desk. Jack scratched an itch on his head and blankly stared at his hand. It was salty and wet. When did he start sweating? Jack put a pillow over his face. When did the lights get to be so bright? His eyes burned and his head throbbed with every rise and fall of his pulse knocking against the inside of his skull.

He replayed the conversation with President Haleson in his head thousands of times.

He thought back to the moment he decided to publish the story. Why? Why did he do it?

After several hours of torturing himself, he called Sean and Molly to come over and keep him company. He didn't want to be alone.

Both Sean and Molly had one question, the same question.

Molly asked it first. "Why didn't you just publish it anonymously?"

Sean agreed, "Yeah, Haleson would still be screwed. The only difference is that you wouldn't be."

At this point, Jack was rocking back and forth in front of the two of them. He was only half present. He was caught replaying decisions in his mind and wishing things were different. He wanted to put on a strong face for the two people that he had grown closest to at college, but it was hard when you hated every single decision you've ever made leading up to this moment. Why hadn't he published anonymously? The truth would still be told either way.

To Sean, Jack's decision was a miscalculation—a tactical error. Molly had her own thoughts.

Sitting in a chair across the room, Molly looked at Jack. Her slumped shoulders spoke to the words that came out of her mouth. "But you promised."

Jack remembered looking back at Molly without words. They both knew that she spoke of a promise that was never made. He remembered looking at her eyes as she started to cry. Jack wondered who those tears were meant for.

But the worrying was for naught. That day passed, and a notice never came. Jack didn't get expelled. In fact, the hearing was canceled.

This is where Jack's recantation of his story picked back up for Anton. His boss didn't need to know the struggle in between his showdown with President Haleson and its outcome.

Listening to this story, Anton was grinning ear to ear.

Jack looked directly at Anton, "And it worked like a charm."

"So how much extra dirt did you have on the guy?"

Jack shook his head and laughed. He had no extra dirt. Anton understood the implication, "How about the interview?" Jack laughed at this as well. "That was made up, too."

"That takes some balls, Jack. Some serious balls."

The two of them simmered for a minute.

Anton spoke. "Then I guess you're lucky that the story leaked."

Jack nodded. That part was true. The story getting picked up finally, after weeks, may have been the only reason Jack graduated. He didn't know for sure how it happened, but he had his guesses. Coincidences like that don't just happen.

Anton began his next thought, "How do you suppose that happened?" But he paused as he reached the only obvious conclusion.

"Our friend Professor Ray."

"He's quite the guy, huh?"

CHAPTER 16

The butterflies in Jack's stomach were something that was perhaps befitting of a child. Jack was nervous, an interesting nervous. He had something he knew he needed to tell Anton. Jack knew it was the right thing to do; he just didn't want to do it.

Jack was nervous about the consequences of his words.

Anton was at his desk hunched over his laptop screen.

"Hey, boss." Jack walked into the room and shut the door.

The door closed and Anton put on a bemused grin. He could read Jack. "What'd you screw up today?"

"I… well…"

Jack knew the exact words he had to say. He was flustered. His boss already knew that he was walking into a confession. It was as if Anton could smell it. There wasn't much point in sugar coating the news or dancing around the subject. So, Jack spoke without sitting down.

"I have a connection on the inside who can help us."

Anton closed his laptop. He still had the grin. "What do you mean by inside?"

This is where Jack paused. He involuntarily looked down.

Anton lost his grin.

"You little prick." The tone was calm, but his expression was not.

"One thing, Jack… the one thing that you can't do."

Apologies weren't the answer. "He can help us."

"Can he, Jack? Can he? You know what the police can help us do? They can help us get dragged into this. They can help make sure that the bad guys, whoever they are, know exactly what we are doing."

Anton's voice was escalating now. Jack hadn't seen him like this. The nerves gave way to something more primal. Jack knew he was in the right; there was only one way to get Anton to come around to his way of thinking.

Jack returned with fire.

"Maybe you're right. Maybe they will find out, but at least I'm doing something. At least I'm actually looking for the answers. Your genius plan of talking to everyone EXCEPT the police hasn't gotten us very far. *Sir.*"

The "Sir" was short and overemphasized.

Anton rolled through the implicit insult. His voice was calm, unnerving. "Do you value your life, Jack? Because if you do, then don't ever do that again."

They stared at each other. Anton stood. "And if you don't value your life, then please think of me. Don't raise issues to people who don't need to know what we are doing."

The two were about six feet apart making direct eye contact. In Jack's mind, something clicked. His anger gave way to an unfriendly nervousness. The young reporter arrived at an understanding.

"How much do you know that I don't?"

Anton's response was not immediate. He pursed his lips. Finally, he said, "There was a lot you weren't ready for."

What came next wasn't what you would call a revelation, but some cousin to it. Ronnie's recording had been just the beginning.

"About 12 months ago I went to my own contact in the police."

Anton continued, "Rumors were swirling about a swing of power in moving drugs, and I had seen in the police logs there was a rise in murders. I asked my buddy in the force about it and he said he hadn't heard anything either."

"Isn't that a little fishy, Jack? If *I* could see it then they *must* see it. It's their *job*."

Jack's boss had raised his voice to a level slightly too high for comfort. He looked around to see if anyone had noticed outside the office.

Anton carried on, "I kept looking, I kept asking questions, and I requested a lot of information from them. But things got lost, things were delayed, things didn't exist. That's when I got curious. Something was wrong."

Anton paused for a minute. "Have you ever been tailed, Jack?"

Jack shook his head as Anton continued, "They made it obvious. They were unmarked cars, but they were obvious. For two weeks. Everywhere I went someone followed me. Grocery store, work, home, gym—they were there. They weren't trying to hide. They wanted me to know. I'm sure of that."

Had that happened to me, too? Jack's mind flicked through the last few days. Had anyone been following him?

"There's something deeper here, Jack. It goes beyond a couple murders and some drugs. People know things and are scared to talk. Someone big is involved, Jack. This is political."

"Why are you telling me this now?"

Why didn't he know these things? He and Anton had been working together so closely, and this was the first he had heard of Anton being tailed? Why was this the first he heard of some deeper connection between murders, drugs, and what must be hush money?

"Because I needed you to care."

And there it was. Simple psychology. A dog always wants his bone, but if you show him a glimpse of it, if you dangle it in front of him—if you make him sit, stay, and roll over before he can have it—then he *needs* the bone.

Jack had been hooked.

"So, if you know so much why don't you publish?"

"You don't play poker with your cards facing up. Tipping your hand is how people get hurt. When this comes out it needs to be irrefutable, I can't be a lone voice on this. Too many ways to shoot me down."

Anton looked up. For a moment, he was knocked off his soapbox.

Anton quickly stepped back up.

"Public opinion is a shouting match. Whoever yells louder is telling the truth. I publish this and watch how fast I become a dissident. See how long it is before some information surfaces that I was holding a grudge, or some doctor comes forward saying that he's been seeing me for mental disorders."

The two paused and considered this. Anton's argument was clear. When this broke, everything needed to break simultaneously. The news needed to come from more than just a single voice at the *Tribune*. More importantly, proof was needed. A single irrefutable piece of evidence would win the shouting match of public opinion.

There was a system that they were up against and the system didn't become what it was by being easily defeated. The system always preferred to deny the reports, refute the allegations, and keep the status quo. Self-preservation is the name of the game, no matter how sick an individual part may be.

Public pressure must reach a certain tipping point before change can occur. Only under fear of certain defeat will the system make the surgical decision to sever the infected appendage and save the body.

Jack knew that it would be fear of displacement that makes the system walk out of the operating room, face the cameras, and say things like 'taking responsibility' and 'reform.' Jack also knew that Anton was still searching for something. Was it the single irrefutable piece of evidence, or was it a way to make it known to the world? Or was it both?

"I have a family, Jack; I can't let that happen."

Jack watched for any clue that Anton's otherwise stoic expression would provide.

The tension was settling between the two, and a calmer conversation evolved. "All right, Jack. Since we can't go back and stop you from being a moron … tell me what you have."

Jack told him about Samuel. He told him about what Samuel might or might not know. Jack posed a question to Anton. "When was the last time you saw Ronnie?"

Anton didn't answer directly. "Why does it matter?"

"Because I know how we can find him." Jack took a piece of paper from his pocket and handed it to Anton.

Anton looked at what amounted to less than ten scribbled words and numbers. There was a date, time, and location.

"What's this?"

"You told me to treat investigations like a puzzle." Jack pointed at the paper. "This is our corner piece."

Anton considered the information in his hand. "This is a meeting?"

Jack nodded.

"Set up by this guy you've been talking to?"

Jack nodded.

Both stood pondering the moment. Jack could see Anton's brow turned upwards as he weighed the outcomes. It was a risk vs. reward analysis. Both men in the room could tolerate risk. But it wasn't a question of risk tolerance. It was a question of how much they yearned for reward. The air in the room was still.

"Do you trust this guy?"

Jack didn't hesitate in his answer. He didn't like to lie, but right here, right now he needed to.

"Yes."

"Well, then it's settled." Anton clapped his hands. It was an emotional pivot that few men were capable of. The decision was made. The phase of anger was over. Time to move on, logic and opportunity prevailed.

But neither man moved.

Jack was unsure what role his words had just played in shaping his future.

Anton sensed the hesitation and extended his arm to Jack's shoulder. "Look, Jack, all of this is real. People are dead; people don't like what we are doing. I've been through this. Trust me, Jack. If you follow my lead, I will get us through this."

These were nice confident words, but were they true?

The younger man shook his head. The reality of the situation was fanciful. He was too far down the rabbit hole to turn back now.

His response was sarcastic. The biting reality of the situation rolled up into three words: "Aye aye, captain."

Anton let out an involuntary laugh. He escorted Jack to the door of his office and turned. He walked slowly with his limp back to his desk and his chair.

CHAPTER 19

"Where did you get these?"

Jack was holding a tiny microphone in one hand and the small coil of wire attached to it in the other.

Anton laughed. "I've been around for a while."

Jack looked at it further. He clipped it underneath his shirt and ran the wire across his body.

"It looks a little clunky to me. Don't they have things without wires nowadays?"

Anton laughed again, "I've been around for a *long* while."

If Anton's heart was pounding, he didn't show it. Jack knew that this wasn't the case for himself, as he could have counted on two hands the number of times Anton told him to calm down.

Today the two of them were conducting what Anton called 'primary research.' Today was the date of the meeting that Samuel set up. Today they were supposed to meet Ronnie.

Before they left, Anton suggested that they go to his basement to suit up with the proper equipment.

The wires were for recording the conversation they hoped to have. Jack was swaying side to side uneasily as Anton bent over a supply closet. He was rummaging through several pieces of equipment. He sorted through flashlights, backpacks, and camping tools, telling stories about adventures with each. Anton held up an old camera. "This bad boy... he got me through a lot. A few political careers were ended with the help of this guy."

Jack just nodded and continued to sway. Finally, Anton pulled out what was unmistakably a bullet-proof vest. He held it up in the air and admired it while Jack's mind raced, trying to figure out why Anton had one.

"I only have one. Here you go." Anton handed over the vest. "It looks like you need the peace of mind more than I do."

The vest was made of Kevlar. It was meant to stop bullets—a true marvel of human ingenuity. But that didn't make Jack feel any better as he slipped it on.

Jack made a face and tugged on his bulletproof vest. "Do you think I'll need this?"

Anton replied, "I'll tell you after we make it back."

The information they were going on was spotty to say the least. Only the absolute minimum was shared; location, date, and time. Although there was one other piece of context that Samuel had divulged.

Jack recalled Samuel's words. *"He came to me looking to rat out the new drug runners. He's been burned enough not to trust them anymore."*

Jack and Anton were ready to go. The two drove 25 minutes outside of the city to an old industrial park. It was broad daylight. Jack couldn't ever remember being this scared in broad daylight. Anton had refused to use his own car for the meeting, and so he parked their rented car at the far end of the lot of the abandoned factory.

They waited for 20 minutes. The building before them had the familiar graffiti markings of bored adolescents honing their yellow, red, and white craft. Two of the garage's loading doors were rusted and crooked, no longer flush with the ground. A few of the windows were intact and held daylight reflections of the two men sitting in their dark blue Chevy sedan.

Jack's leg bounced restlessly in the car. Both men breathed heavily as they waited.

"All right, I'm going to get out." Anton opened the door and stepped outside of the car. He walked towards the nearest door to the derelict building in front of them. Jack froze as Anton opened the door and slowly extended his right hand into the building while keeping his face and body outside.

Anton's voice was muted to Jack's ears from the inside of the car. "Friends of Samuel. We are here to talk."

No answer.

Anton slipped his face around the door to look inside. "Ronnie? Ronnie, are you here?"

Nothing still.

Dust kicked up around the parking lot as a flurry of wind came through. Distant sounds from the highway were finding their way to the lot as well. But there was nothing from inside.

Anton went even further into the building, and Jack realized that he had stopped breathing. Then Jack's pulse spiked. The world stalled and a white haze blocked everything except what he saw in front of him.

Anton burst through the door and immediately collapsed holding his chest.

Jack threw the door open. He rushed to Anton and in four steps was by his side. He went to one knee and grabbed Anton.

But something was wrong.

Anton turned over and was smiling. Laughing in fact. First a few intermittent laughs then a small string of full laughs.

"Nobody's in there."

Jack looked at his partner's eyes. They were more mischievous than he thought.

"What?" It wasn't a question.

Anton stood up and dusted himself off with a few pats on his leg. "I needed to know how you perform under stress. I needed to see what kind of man you are."

Jack stood for a minute. Adrenaline was ripping through him, but now his fear was mixed with embarrassment. It was not a pleasant combination. Without thinking, without saying a word, he swung and punched Anton in the face.

The punch connected with the older man's cheekbone. He grabbed his face and bent down to fight the pain. But Anton didn't fight back, he didn't scream, and he didn't say anything in return. Instead, he chuckled.

His laugh was slow at first, then faster. It was contagious; Jack started laughing, too. The two of them stood laughing together. Their situation was absurd. They realized that now. Laughing seemed oddly appropriate.

When the laughing stopped, Jack paused to better take in his surroundings. Part of the parking lot extended around the far corner of the building. He pointed and Anton followed his finger. "Think there's space for someone to park around the side?"

Anton shrugged and tossed Jack the keys. "Bring the car around."

Jack slowly drove the car to the far side of the building as Anton jogged ahead of him. It was a long building with unkempt bushes around the side. Anton turned the corner first, and Jack slowly rolled the car to a stop when he saw another car parked on the side of the building. It was a silver sedan and looked empty.

Jack parked and stepped out. He joined Anton, who was moving toward the new car carefully waving his hand. As they stepped closer they saw shattered glass on the driver's side of the pavement. They both began to jog to the car, knowing too well why it appeared empty. They circled the car and Anton opened the driver side door. Jack was a few steps behind and saw the dead body slumped down in the seat.

Anton shook his head. "That sucks."

Anton turned to look at his partner. Jack was doubled over vomiting.

The three bodies, two warm and one cold, didn't move as the wind sent another flurry of dust scattering.

Anton looked at the shattered glass; the man had been shot through the window.

Jack gasped for air that was too hard to find. He managed the start of a question.

"Is it…"

"Yeah, it's him."

Anton took a step closer and inspected the rest of the car. There were bags. Clear bags with white powder, lots of white powder. Most were neatly stored in a lunch box sized container. But one was open and the substance was strewn across the backseat of the car and on the chest of the slouched dead body of Ronald Sinclair. Anton took one more step and opened the back door of the car. He extended his right hand across the back seat and picked up a trace of the powder between his thumb and forefinger. He drew it to his nose and snorted.

He shook his head like he stepped into a cold shower. He whistled slowly from high to low.

"That's a lot of cocaine."

Anton barely registered Jack dry-heaving in the background.

CHAPTER 20

He was a ghost the rest of the day. It was his first murdered body. He imagined that most people felt that way when they saw their first. He didn't go home that night, how could he? He needed to talk to someone. But aside from Anton, there was no one else. So, he spent the night on Anton's couch.

"You need a drink."

Jack nodded. Anton could have said anything and Jack would have nodded.

He went to the kitchen and came back with two dark fizzy glasses. He offered one to Jack and held up his glass to cheer. "Your namesake," he said, addressing the glass.

Jack sipped the drink to taste it, but he already knew what it was.

Anton continued, "When I'm short on words I often seek the advice of wise men."

He took a drink, and Jack mirrored him. Anton admired the drink in his hand. "A very wise man indeed."

Jack could feel the infusion work its way through his body. He could feel the edge subside and his thoughts release from their paralysis. He took another sip, life returned. So much had been written about men and their search for a magic elixir. And yet here it was, a simple two-part concoction.

"I've never seen a body like that before." Jack hadn't spoken this much in hours. "I've seen a dead body; I saw my younger brother die. But that was different." His face was distant.

"He didn't have bullet holes."

Anton pressed his lips together. He'd seen this before, but there was no advice to give. Even the wisest of men didn't have advice for this.

Jack sipped more, maybe too much, but it didn't feel like enough.

"Could that have been us?"

Anton nodded again. "It's a dangerous world."

That didn't sink in. Jack bit his lip. He was not satisfied with the answer.

Anton moved the conversation to a point he had been considering. "I need you to break all communications with Samuel. Tell him you stopped the case, tell him you got fired, or just stop telling him anything at all. He's dangerous."

Jack had not thought this way. "You think he's in on it?"

"No, but maybe. The question isn't whether or not that could have been us, but if maybe whether or not that was *meant* to be us."

Jack thought. Could it be that Samuel had tried to set up a hit on them? Is it possible the gunman just got the wrong guy, not realizing two more were on their way? Was Samuel in on the operation and trying to get rid of anyone who might interfere? It didn't make sense, not in this world.

Knowing the truth was far more difficult than he liked.

Anton reached for his TV remote and turned on the first show he could find. Jack wasn't paying attention; he was still thinking. Finally, he spoke out again. "It's still weird to think that could have been us."

Anton looked at Jack.

"I'll tell you what we don't do. We don't stop. This is more important than we thought."

Anton went once more to the well for advice. He finished his glass and paused before finishing his statement. "Nothing great was ever accomplished from safety."

The young man nodded his head. He got that.

CHAPTER 21

First Taste

SOPHOMORE YEAR OF COLLEGE

Jack always drove his car with one hand on the wheel. His right hand was tapping nervously on the shifter.

Molly laughed. "Relax, it will be fine."

Tonight, was an important night. Jack was meeting the family. Every semester Molly's family made a point to come down and take their only daughter out to dinner.

It was a nice little tradition, and Jack liked it. He also liked the idea of becoming a part of the tradition. But that didn't mean that he wasn't going to be nervous.

They were the first ones at the restaurant and followed the hostess to their table. The two sat smiling at each other as they awaited the family's arrival.

Molly stood and moved to the front of the restaurant. Jack's eyes followed his girlfriend as she nearly jumped into the open arms of her parents. He could hear the excitement and laughter from across the restaurant.

Mr. Bingham, or Jeff as he insisted, was a man with a kind disposition. The same could be said for Molly's mother, although there was another quality immediately apparent but difficult to pin down. Lillian Bingham was still beautiful. Every decade has its type of beauty; there was the salacious inviting curiosity of the 20's, the confidence and radiance of well-anticipated 30's, and the glow and distinction of the 40's and beyond. Jack instantly saw Molly in 25 years. She had the same blue eyes and the same smile that made you thankful to be looked at and hopeful that you had caused the smile. Lillian had navigated each decade of her life embracing the look and reality of each; there was wisdom to her presence.

They made small talk. Jack was immediately invited into their lives. "We've heard so much about you." Jack blushed, had they? He didn't know he meant that much to Molly. It was a thrill to be intertwined in their story. Soon, Molly's brother showed up. He was a minute or two late and made a quick comment about traffic. Christopher, not Chris, Bingham shared the same softly angled nose and closed earlobes with the rest of his family. He immediately came over to shake Jack's hand. "Jack, it's great to meet you. Molly tells me that you and I would get along, that we are a lot alike."

The dinner proved this. Jack shouldn't have been surprised. Molly was seldom wrong when it came to personalities. It was a gift she had. They all talked and laughed. They asked questions about Jack's work at the school newspaper and what he was planning to do after he graduated.

"A bold move, considering the way the world is today," the eldest Bingham said.

Christopher stepped in, "Yes, bold, but I like it. Chance favors the bold, Dad."

Jack responded with questions about what they did for work. Molly's father worked for a modestly sized accounting firm, and her mother ran a non-profit. "That's where Molly gets her love of helping people."

Jeff nodded from Molly to his wife, Lillian.

Lillian responded, "Yes, we Bingham ladies are the ones who have all the heart."

Everyone chuckled.

Christopher was high up in a government consulting business and business was good judging by the watch on his wrist. He had a fire and ambition that was apparent in the way he talked. Jack liked him.

Christopher stood up and excused himself to take a call.

Lillian shook her head, "Probably another one of his politician friends."

While Molly and her mother were more dismissive, her dad was clearly proud. "He plays golf with some of the biggest names in Massachusetts, some real movers and shakers."

The conversation shifted and continued. More laughs, delicious food.

After about ten minutes, Christopher came back to the table.

"Welcome back, hot shot," said Molly.

Christopher laughed a well-rehearsed laugh before changing the subject. Jack noticed that Christopher was preoccupied; he had the look of someone present in body but not in spirit. He had something more important on his mind.

Molly had snuck her hand under the table to rest on Jack's leg. Things were going well. Her parents liked him. Jack liked her parents. Molly loved Jack.

A chime from a cell phone went off, a text message. Jack checked his pocket to turn off his phone, but it wasn't his. Christopher instinctually pulled a phone from his pocket, silenced it, and put it back. Business must be really good; Jack couldn't help but notice that Christopher had two different phones.

On the ride back to her apartment, Molly was all smiles.

"Did I pass the test?" Jack asked.

Molly giggled, "Yes."

Jack nodded. It was a big scary world out there, and Jack couldn't think of anyone else he would rather face it with.

CHAPTER 22

When Samuel knocked on Jack's door at 11:00 p.m. on a Thursday night with a bag on his shoulder, Jack knew something was wrong. Jack skipped the obvious question of how Samuel knew where he lived—he was a cop after all.

"How much is this worth to you, Jack? This story, how far are you willing to go?"

They sat down, and Samuel continued, "Because it's worth a lot to someone."

Under the best conditions, Samuel was not a master raconteur. Under these conditions, he couldn't string together basic sentences.

Jack followed the fragments. He gathered pieces of Samuel's last two days.

Someone had taken notice. A guy Samuel never knew, high up somewhere in the Boston police, had paid him a visit. People knew Samuel had been asking questions and digging.

"They planted this in my car." Samuel took the bag off from his shoulder and tossed tightly sealed bags of cocaine onto his table. Jack ran his hands through his hair. Samuel stared at Jack's face looking for a signal.

"What do we do?" Jack asked.

Here stood two twenty-somethings in a dingy apartment wondering how they got so far in over their heads. Neither had an answer. It came back to Samuel's question. How much is this worth?

"They know about you, Jack. They know who you are. He asked about you tonight."

Jack exhaled a single long forced exhalation followed by short, shallow breaths laced with ice. Of course, they knew about him. Jack wasn't an idiot. Of course, he knew that people take notice when you start asking questions. But this was different. Someone cared, and they cared a lot—certainly they cared much more about their secret than they did about Jack.

"We can't talk anymore."

Jack nodded, he understood.

"I'll help if I can, but from now on we don't know each other."

Another nod. Jack pointed at the bags on his table.

Samuel repacked the bags. "For me this stops here, but I know I'm right. I know we are right. But what good is proving something if you're dead?"

Samuel was about to become a reluctant bystander. Jack sensed that the opportunity to get anything more from him was slipping away. This was terrifying, but this was exhilarating. They were on to something much bigger. Samuel made motions to the door. Jack's mouth felt numb. Forming words was taking a supreme act of will. He needed to know how far this stretched.

"How far up does it go?"

A million questions boiled down to six words.

Before exiting Samuel looked at him and shook his head.

CHAPTER 23

Jack found a peculiar sanctuary at the *Tribune*. He wasn't sure the precise reason, but he felt, at the very least, he was less likely to get unexpected cocaine-wielding visitors while he was in the office.

"No more mysteries. What else don't I know?"

Anton over-emphasized the chewing of his gum. It was as if each jaw movement gave him another moment to formulate the answer. "I've been tracking the governor for a while. This isn't his first rodeo."

"The Governor of Massachusetts?" Jack was irritated as he asked the question; he hated playing catch up.

"How else do you think it got this big? This has his fingerprints all over it."

The logic was simple.

Anton explained. "The money is big and the police are obviously complicit in covering up whatever is going on. That level of orchestration can only come from someplace high-up in the food chain. Between drug distributors, police, and politicians, there are substantial amounts of money greasing the wheels."

Jack listened but was still unconvinced. "That doesn't prove anything."

Anton was still chewing his gum. There was no way it could still have its flavor. Jack was convinced the man was just chewing to chew.

The boss sensed his opening.

"Let me tell you something, Jack. I haven't always been here at the *Tribune*, but I have been following the governor for a while. This is how he operates. This is what he does."

"We're not in the business of making unsubstantiated accusations."

The point, although naive, was fair. Anton circled around and walked to his desk and opened his drawer. Jack wondered what collection of obscure documents called that desk drawer home. He pulled out a series of papers bound by paper clips. Jack stretched out his hand as the exchange was made. Thumbing through the pages, he could get the gist of their purpose. There were headlines, news stories, paper clippings, printouts, travel logs, diagrams, headshots, and scribbled notes. Everything seemed to center around one man. Jack knew this man, albeit by a different title.

Anton explained. "I've been following him long before he was the governor. Trust me when I say I know how this man operates."

There was no obvious response to such comments, so Jack stood without words as Anton took back the pile of documents. Anton continued, "This man owes his power to lies and extortion."

Now there was an obvious question. "What was that?"

The drawer opened. The papers were stuffed back in. The drawer closed and the two looked at each other. "Years of unfulfilled work. Jack, when I tell you that man is a slippery bastard, I mean it."

It was clear that Anton was thinking back to past events. There was anger in his expression as he looked up and to the left as if conjuring memories from the ceiling of his office.

Jack took time to process what was happening. How was Anton so certain? "Ok, so let's say it *is* the governor. We certainly have enough to hold his feet to the fire."

There was a laugh. A condescending laugh.

"First, Jack, it *is* him. And secondly no. No, we do not." The words were said in such a manner that each was elongated and overemphasized. "We're missing the piece that ties this together. He's a difficult man to pin."

Anton continued with his logical calculations. His tone was less harsh, more conversational. "The governor is not stupid. He uses other people to insulate himself."

It was an interesting consideration. Jack had learned a long time ago from Professor Ray that important orders were made face to face.

You don't email things you don't like pointing back to you, you don't text words you'd rather not be discovered. Jack remembered a lecture in Professor Ray's class where he was describing the art of investigating cases without communication trails. The professor hadn't mentioned specifics in class, but he did mention that looking for "travel patterns" could yield unexpectedly helpful clues. He also mentioned that such research may or may not have contributed to a Pulitzer that his team shared.

The governor was too savvy to leave a paper trail himself.

"It's the inner circle where we have a shot, Jack. They are the ones who might slip up. That's who we need to find."

Jack agreed.

Anton again looked pained. The memory that he was drawing back was clearly not a fond one. If there was a third-party observer listening to their conversation, they would have trouble knowing if Anton's next words were meant for Jack or for himself. "I won't let him slip this time."

"What?" Jack's voice wavered. "What does that mean?"

Anton didn't respond directly. Instead, he offered a borderline sequitur: "Being better prepared is essential."

"What are you talking about, how are you better prepared?"

There was a smile. "Well, for starters, I have you."

This was confusing, and it did nothing to make Jack feel better about the bag of illicit drugs that had found their way to his apartment less than 24 hours ago.

Jack tried to understand if he was asking the right question. He wasn't sure, so he asked two more. "What did he do to you? And what is that stack of papers about?"

Anton tapped his fingers on his desk. He was in the limbo of a decision. The decision was made and his good mood returned. "You'll find out when I need you to know."

The comment was wildly interesting for all the wrong reasons. But there was nothing that followed. That part of their interaction was over.

It was almost lunchtime—hunger was weighing on them. All they ever did was talk about the case. Even Anton looked like he needed a break; it was time to step out of the office for some food.

Anton went to pick up his keys. He adopted the tone of a colleague asking a coworker about upcoming weekend plans. "How are things going otherwise? Life is good? Any ladies?"

Jack was relaxing now. He looked back at his boss. The quirks were real. He was an odd fellow. An exceptionally talented, wonderfully driven, odd fellow.

"Since when do you care about my social life?"

"Come on, Jack, I think you'd be surprised how much I care about you."

Jack decided he would give it a shot. Anton as a boss? Sure. Anton as a friend? It remained to be seen.

But it was a good question. Jack was a single guy in his early twenties living in a city of full of other single twenty-somethings. Life shouldn't be so bad.

"It's tough. I guess I'm just having a hard time getting over this one girl."

"The one who got away?"

"Ha, yeah you could call her that…"

"I can see in your eyes that you haven't given up on her. Don't give up on her."

Jack thought about this. Of course, he hadn't given up on her.

"You should get her back, Jack… it will help you."

Help me? What did that mean? Jack wouldn't give up, but he was unconvinced that this would help him. It was strange advice. Anton, though, was a man who never seemed to give up.

"Why do you care?"

"Maybe, I don't. I just think it would be helpful."

CHAPTER 24

Paranoia is a funny emotion; yes, that's what he wanted to call it. Something that descended over you and stayed there, always waiting to bubble up. That white van that was sitting too long outside of his apartment, how long had it been there? The situation was bugging Jack out. This was not the type of bugging out that he and Sean used to experience in their dorm rooms on the occasional weeknight. This is the bugging out that moves the center of your pulse to your throat and makes you jump when something moves in the side of your vision.

He didn't want to admit it, but it was dragging on him. The more he worked on this case, the more paranoid he became. No coincidence was too small. Everything was interconnected. Was his phone tapped? What did it mean that he saw the same man at the grocery store and the train stop?

Being a prisoner in his own mind wasn't something Jack liked.

"Can we talk?" Those were the words he had written in a text to Molly, but he hesitated before hitting send. He read them and changed them four times. He reread the words five more times before sending. He hated it, but it was all he could come up with.

The only cure to his tortured insides was to inflict more pain on himself. He sent the text—a single, simple question.

Jack imagined Molly reading his text, telling her friends, and complaining, or maybe worse yet, ignoring him completely. Had she stopped caring enough about him not to even complain about him? Was he just an accepted part of her past? Was she so dispassionate that it didn't even warrant a passing complaint to her friend? How long had it been? Six months, a year? Life in the rabbit hole was good for keeping memories but wasn't good for keeping track of time.

What came next was surprising—a phone call. Jack wasn't sure what assemblage of fate aligned to compel Molly to call him, but she did.

"Hi, Jack."

"Hey."

"You wanted to talk?"

And they did talk. Not for long, but they talked. Neither said anything real, just the usual "how are you" and "what's new," but the act of having a conversation meant everything. As the words died down, there was a silence that hung.

"I miss you," said Jack.

"I miss you too, Jack."

And then she hung up.

The phone call ripped him back to a moment from his past.

He wasn't sure why the memory meant so much to him, but it haunted his thoughts from time to time. It had been in college, and it had been just Molly and himself. Things were new and different that day.

They escaped one late spring weekend before finals for a hike. The drive to New Hampshire was long but not too far. Hiking was an escape for Jack—he and Sean had done it a few times. In some ways, it was the sober counterpart to their Friday night ritual, but unlike Friday nights, hiking happened far less than once a week.

The trail they hiked had been easy. Spring is an incredible time; the earth is reborn beneath your feet, and the sun is illuminating possibilities that were cold only a few months before.

The two had held hands walking along the trail. It was something utterly inconvenient as they hopped over rocks and navigated roots that stuck out. But they couldn't help it. They were alone, they were happy. If the leaves wanted to snicker at how foolish they looked, then so be it. It was a foolishness shared by the two of them, and he loved it.

They talked, and they laughed. He was still getting to know Molly and the flow of her answers to his questions. He found everything she said to be intoxicating. This is where he learned that her dad had been in politics when he was a younger man and before he left for a more stable and less public career. It was an unfulfilled legacy her older brother was on the fast track to redeem. But Molly had rejected politics and found her own path. She was a photographer by hobby, a writer by passion, and an aspiring marketer by college major. She wanted to work for a non-profit when she hit the real world. When Jack asked her why, she simply said, "There are a lot of people who just need a little help."

He couldn't get enough of her. They walked under the leaves, winding their way up the mountain. They talked and they talked, and the layers came peeling off. Molly was scared of spiders; Jack once got a detention for pulling a prank on his 8th-grade teacher. Most importantly, boiling beneath the layers was a passion for the future. They shared a yearning to know how the world could be shaped by their efforts. There was a fire to see what could be made of the world as soon as they got the chance. That's when Jack knew he loved her. The trees and the mountain were silent partners in his discovery.

They laughed and they hopped over rocks. The two took a break in a clearing and stared at the blue sky and the powdery clouds it held.

A pile of rocks marked a smaller spur trail off the main path. The two considered their options and adventured to whatever this alternate encounter might be. As they walked, faint reflections of sun came dancing into their eyes. The trees began to thin and a metallic reflection grew stronger. Molly saw the American flag planted in the ground first. Both saw the crash site at the same time.

There before them were the remnants of tortured World War 2 era aluminum and steel. Pieces had been looted, scrapped, or removed, but the remainder was the unmistakable wreckage of a plane.

The two of them stood looking at the twisted skeleton before them and thinking of the lives it must have held. Jack walked to the plaque; it was accompanied by seven small wooden crosses behind it. One for each life betrayed by the aircraft. As Molly walked up behind Jack, he read the engraved words aloud.

To the men who served our country. They were willing to give their lives protecting those who could not fight for themselves.

Neither knew what to do, so they stood, stared, and wondered how this came to be. Jack had heard stories of training missions gone wrong. He knew of a mountain in Maine where a plane had crashed, and a memorial to its memory was now a destination for curious hikers. He had heard similar stories of a mountain in New Hampshire. Here it was.

They reflected on how terrifying that moment must have been for the men as they realized their fate. They noted the unnerving tranquility of their current surroundings. Over half a century had doubtless brought hundreds of friends, lovers, and adventurers to where Jack and Molly now stood alone. All the while the wreckage had been guarded by the same silent trees, standing as tall as they had at that moment when the plane came crashing down.

There wasn't much to say between them. They stood, and they stared. They eventually got back onto the trail that they had left. They had stumbled upon a memorial to seven lives—a wondrous and haunting metallic discovery that they would never be able to shake from their minds.

CHAPTER 25

He could handle it.

He would rise to the occasion. He always had.

Jack sat at his desk sweating. It was 2:00 a.m. and the light from his desk lamp glowed an unnatural yellow. But he sat transfixed at the task before him. Sleep was nothing more than an afterthought.

He had talked to Anton about the implications of their case. Jack traced the possible fallout scenarios if and when they published. Exposing political ties to corruption didn't always end well for those who did the dirty work. He knew what happened to whistleblowers. Expulsion would look like an easy punishment by comparison.

He had voiced his concerns to Anton.

Anton smiled. "Welcome to the Big Leagues," he said. "This is a shot to grab the wheel and steer your career towards greatness."

For a moment, Jack wondered if Anton had positioned this statement so that it would ignite his ambition. No matter. It worked. Jack sat at his desk and wrote furiously. He wrote about drugs, police bribes, and political influence. He connected the dots and included all the discoveries that he and Anton had made over the past months.

Jack stared at the collection of his notes. There was enough to raise eyebrows and certainly cause some questions to be asked. Not enough to convict anyone, but maybe enough, if push came to shove, to save Jack from prison.

He looked at the beginning of his journal: *My name is Jack Ranger. I have been investigating the death of Ronald Sinclair and his ties to political involvement in illicit drug trafficking. I fear that through my investigation I have uncovered circumstances that many in a position of power would prefer not to be made public. I fear that physical harm may come to me. I have detailed the findings of my investigation to this point within the pages of these notes...*

The next morning, he woke and gathered his collection. Jack got in his car and drove to a place he hadn't been in over a year. He was going to see a man that he hadn't talked with in two.

The professor was sitting at the same desk in the same office that Jack remembered. It was a weekday afternoon, but the professor didn't ask whether Jack should be at work. Jack placed a sealed package on the desk filled with his notes. "It's best if I don't tell you what's in here, Professor."

Professor Ray picked up the package as if he was weighing it and nodded.

"If something happens to me, I need you to send this to people."

The professor leaned over his desk. "So herein lies the truth? I've written more than one of these in my life."

The two looked at each other as he continued.

"Luckily, I never needed it, but they are always nice as a backup. I assume there are multiple copies each addressed to different newspapers? Or is that why you gave this to me?" The professor laughed quietly. "It was really just a matter of time. Whatever Anton has you working on is deeper than you thought—I can see that."

Jack tried not to act surprised. "How do you know I work for Anton?"

The professor measured his response. "The real mystery is why you think that I *wouldn't* know that."

The point lingered, but dissolved.

Professor Ray stared unblinking at Jack.

Jack didn't blink.

The professor smiled. "This is what will make you great, Jack. Don't back down."

CHAPTER 26

Jack on the Links

JUNIOR YEAR OF COLLEGE

Getting good at golf was always on Jack's to-do list. The reasons behind this were just as much about personal pleasure as they were about acquiring a necessary business skill. When Molly suggested that Jack go golfing with her older brother Christopher, he leaped at the chance. He felt like the game could kill two birds with one stone. Although the more he thought about it, the more Jack came to think of it as a playdate.

Jack was trying to get to know Molly's family better. At this point they had been officially 'together' for a while. Both agreed, it was time to start making a bigger effort. What better way could there be to bring two people together than golf? Jack couldn't think of any alternatives worthy enough to refuse the invitation.

"Beers?" It was a rhetorical question.

Christopher came walking out of the clubhouse holding four cans of beer. He lined them up in the golf cart they were sharing.

They played the first holes talking about the usual ice-breaking topics. Christopher was better at golf than Jack, but it was still close enough to be enjoyable. "You're still studying journalism, right?"

"Yes."

"Weird." Christopher paused, and Jack looked up. "You seem like a smart kid, too. Molly tells me you're smart. Journalism is dying. Tough thing to be studying these days."

Jack wasn't sure how to respond, so he didn't. Instead, he walked to his ball for another shot. His ball was sitting on the fairway. After multiple practice swings, he concentrated and hit his second shot. Not great, but not bad. He was just a few yards short of the green—Jack would take that all day.

"You know, next week I'm golfing with Congressman Graham. Me, him, and a couple guys from the office."

Jack remembered Molly's words about how proud her dad was of Christopher's rising stardom in that world.

Jack pressed, "How'd you swing that?"

Christopher continued, "There's no 'swinging.' It's what I do. My job is to make things like that happen."

The two continued to play and by the back nine it was going well. The two of them were similar. They were both ambitious, and they respected that about each other. They were also both connected by their love of Molly, albeit different kinds of love.

11 holes into their round, things were smooth. Each was a little looser now. The conversation eventually headed in its inevitable direction.

"So, you two are serious?"

"Yes, Molly is a great girl."

Christopher bobbed his head in approval. "She is a great girl. She means a lot to me."

Jack's ears scoured the words for traces of a threat. Was Christopher the intimidating kind of big brother, or the big brother who wanted to be your friend too?

"It's a big deal dating Molly. I don't like seeing people I care about get hurt."

Definitely traces of intimidation.

Jack became interested in the scorecard and pencil he was holding in his hand.

Christopher continued, "She's such an innocent girl."

Jack smiled. That's one of the things he loved most about Molly. She was an extremely innocent girl.

Until she wasn't.

Christopher kept talking, and Jack's mind danced back to a moment from the previous semester. He remembered walking between classes in the journalism building when Molly snuck up behind him and grabbed his hand. He turned and saw her smile. Her smile was highlighted by her blue eyes—eyes that knew what was going to happen long before you did. She had this subconscious tick where her nostrils flared ever-so-slightly. It was like a tell in poker—a twitch that gave away her hand. Jack knew what happened when he read this tell.

She grabbed his hand and led him around a corner to an empty office and closed the door. She held up her right hand seductively dangling a set of keys. It was the office of the professor she was the research assistant for.

Apparently, he didn't come to campus on Tuesdays.

She pushed Jack down on top of an empty desk and slowly pulled her shirt off over her head. She stood there giggling. Jack watched as she moved closer. She was smiling, beautiful, and somehow innocently mischievous.

"Did you hear me? Christopher spoke louder.

"Yeah." Jack's mind returned to the moment where he physically belonged.

They continued to play, but Jack's concentration was shaken. Molly was a drug for his mind. Just a taste was never enough. In between putts he saw her dimples. He heard her laugh in his backswing and he wished for her body as he walked to his shots.

Christopher laughed. "Yup, I was the troublemaker. Molly was the one who never did anything wrong."

Jack's mind's eye flashed to a smoke-filled dorm room. Music was playing in the background; both were giggling.

Christopher continued. "Daddy's little princess…"

Jack thought about the necklace she often wore and how it skirted the neckline in her shirt. He thought about how daddy's princess always kept that necklace on, shirt or not.

The round was winding to a close. All things considered, it was a success. Jack kept the match close enough to be respectable. Christopher was tallying up the scores for a final count. "You know Jack, if this journalism thing doesn't work out you should give me a call. We can always use guys like you in politics."

He was mildly flattered. "How do you mean?"

"It is a great business to be in. It's where men can be men. There is an art and there is gamesmanship to everything that you do."

"I'll consider it."

"Do more than that. I can see it in you. It's a thrill that I know you'll enjoy. The world's not just about knowing people. It's more about knowing the right people." Christopher smiled.

Jack smiled in return.

The two shook hands.

Jack was certain that each of them was returning to their car happy with the outcome of the day.

Molly would surely hear about the occasion from both sides. She would be thrilled.

CHAPTER 27

Metal screeched as the subway train took its turn. It was the same screech that Jack heard every day on his way back from work. He wondered how many times a day the subway car made this screech? How many times a day did the train make its obedient trek from downtown to the outskirts of the city, only to turn around and retrace its steps?

Today was not a good day to be riding the subway. It was hot, it was loud, and it was crowded. There must be a home game tonight. Eighty-one times a year the Fenway faithful pushed rush hour from the intolerable to the excruciating.

Jack had a headache, and the screech of outdated metal on underfunded tracks was not making it better.

He stared at the subway map. Each station's name was placed over a dot on a green line representing the track. He stood counting the stops until he could relax. The train shook as it started, and stopped, and turned. Passengers swayed with the movement of the train and Jack tried to pretend that he didn't feel the man behind him bump into his leg. He also tried to pretend that his arm wasn't tired from clutching the standing-room-only pole. His elbow hovered inches above the head of a short woman dressed in hospital scrubs. Jack liked people, but he didn't like "T people" as he had come to call them.

Jack noticed the tiniest idiosyncrasies in his commute. He did it in a way that is only possible from doing something so routinely that your brain's threshold for excitement reaches its lowest levels. He noticed little things about the T people; who the regulars were, who the weirdos were, and who were the people most similar to himself. There was 'Gameboy,' a 30-year-old man who played a fantasy game on his phone every morning. There was 'The Professor,' a prematurely balding guy with glasses that Jack had played pickup basketball with, although neither had made an effort to speak of this aloud. But most infamously of all was the "T Humper". The T Humper was a special case. He was approximately five foot one, Asian, balding, and of dubious employment.

The T Humper, as Jack had explained to his friends, had two defining characteristics. One, he always wore wind pants. No matter the temperature, no matter the weather—the man wore his wind pants. Two, he stood close to people. More accurately, he stood uncomfortably close to people. Empty car, partially filled car, or full car—the concept of personal space did not exist. With every fast turn, quick start, or short stop that jostled the train's passengers, the T Humper earned his name one unwelcome bump at a time. Jack hated the T Humper.

Today the T Humper was nowhere to be seen. That was a good sign, although Jack conceded that he could be lurking beneath the sea of people. The train pulled into the stop where the Fenway faithful unloaded and breathing room returned.

Normally Jack did not have meaningful interactions with people on the train. But fate had decided today would not be a normal day. A man in a baseball cap was making eye contact at Jack. From across the car, he looked at Jack and stared without making any attempt to hide it. He wanted Jack to notice him. The train rolled to a stop, and the man approached.

"Mr. Ranger?"

Jack just looked at him. He was silent.

From a pocket in his jacket he took out a single white envelope. He held it between his thumb and forefinger and motioned for it to be taken.

Jack didn't move. The man was unremarkable in several ways. From his height to his hair and clothes he seemed plain. When Jack didn't move, the man took the envelope and placed it in the pocket on the left chest of Jack's shirt.

The young reporter tilted his head as he followed the envelope being placed in his pocket.

The stranger spoke. "A friend wants you to have this."

With that, he nodded his head in acknowledgement. The man's purpose had been achieved. He walked to the open doors of the train and out onto the platform. Jack stood still, trying to process what had just happened.

He waited until he got to his apartment to open the envelope.

The message was simple. It was only three words on plain white paper. "Please Forgive Me."

Jack didn't know what it meant, but he knew it was bad news. He called Anton.

"What does that mean?"—Anton's first reaction.

Then silence. Anton asked who the letter was from.

"Samuel."

Jack could hear Anton's tongue clicking as he thought.

"What a nice gesture to apologize right after you screw someone." Sarcasm was an unflattering strength of Anton. "Maybe the snake suddenly grew a conscience."

Anton tapped his thumb on the desk. "This forces our hand."

Jack's logic was trailing Anton's. "What do you mean?"

"I'll see you in the office first thing Monday morning. It's time to publish."

CHAPTER 28

It was Sunday, and Anton was preparing the story to run in the week ahead.

Jack stuck to public places when he left his house. Samuel's note had spooked him. But it was the inflection in Anton's voice that terrified Jack.

In a failed attempt at normalcy, Jack sat across his friend at the dinner table. Meeting with an old friend seemed like the right recipe to take his mind off the case and to calm his nerves before whatever was about to happen. But the conversation was terrible. His friend, Ashok, didn't notice when Jack had asked to be seated at the restaurant with his back against the wall. But Ashok did notice that Jack couldn't keep a conversation. He kept looking past the table searching the room.

"When did you start answering questions with a yes or no? You all right, man?"

Jack's answers to personal questions were replaced by head nods and half-hearted smiles. Jack took prolonged drags of water from his cup while his eyes never focused on anything for more than a few seconds. The charade of dinner came to its end.

Jack walked to his car and started to make the drive back to his Allston apartment. It was still dusk out. Jack turned on his blinker taking the unusual U-turn that he always took to shave three minutes off his drive home from that part of town. There was nothing out of the ordinary except that today, just now, Jack wasn't the only one making the U-turn. Jack looked in his mirror. A black SUV had taken the turn as well.

But it's a fairly busy road. Jack's mind played out the obvious counter to his paranoia. His hand reached to the volume as he turned down the music in his car. Jack's car rolled to a stop at the next street light. He was fighting off hurried breaths.

The light turned green. Jack's car moved again. He had a plan. Jack drove another 30 seconds. He didn't use his blinker. Jack took a swift hard left, cutting from the middle lane to the left to make a turn that was completely asinine for anyone who was concerned about getting to their destination on time. No one would take this combination of turns; unless of course, you were so thoroughly paranoid that your compulsion forced you to do just that. Or, as it turned out, unless if you were following someone.

Jack looked back. The SUV was there. It had taken the turn. Jack's knuckles were white; his foot pressed further down on the gas. Jack didn't care about the speed limit.

But no, this was stupid. If you feed your compulsion your mind demands more of it. Jack had come to understand this. Jack had never talked aloud to himself before this last month.

"Don't be an idiot, Jack."

"This is just in your head."

"Slow down before you kill yourself."

Jack was polite to most people, just not to himself. So, he slowed. This was the test. There was one more hurdle he would force himself to go through before he gave in to his paranoia. One last reality check.

Jack put on his signal to turn right. He slowed down; he telegraphed the turn. He took the next right onto a residential street. He drove down the street and pulled over to the side at the intersection 30 yards past his latest turn. He watched in his rear-view mirror seeing what the answer to his final test would be. Jack watched to see if the black SUV would turn and dictate which reality would come into being.

It passed.

The black SUV rolled passed the turn. It disappeared.

"Okay, okay, okay," he said. Jack wondered when he had stopped breathing. His lungs burned and sucked in new air. He put his head down on the wheel; he closed his eyes and tried to concentrate on his heart.

"Breathe Jack, breathe."

In. Out. Deep breaths.

He counted to ten. Jack picked up his head and leaned back in his seat.

Big out breath.

Outside sounds returned to Jack's senses. He was calming down. He shook out his hands, adjusted the visor to account for the setting sun, and heard the rev of an engine. He turned. But it was too late. A streak of black was upon him from his left. The black SUV smashed into the broadside of Jack's car slamming it into the light post on the sidewalk. Jack's head whipped with the impact. The airbag exploded into his face. Shrieking metal, powder in the air, and pain flooding his consciousness.

There was slow motion. There was white.

Then there was darkness.

Three men walked from the colliding vehicle. They walked with measured steps. No one rushed; they were taking steps that they knew well. The men sported slacks, collared shirts, and ties on their body. In their hands they held rope, handcuffs, and a cloth bag. The point-man cleared away the remaining glass from what used to be the driver side window and unlocked the door to expose Jack's slumped body.

CHAPTER 29

Voices. Yes, he could hear voices. But he couldn't see anything. Jack didn't know how much time had passed, or if any time had passed. He could tell he was in a car because he could feel it rolling to a stop and he could hear the doors opening. His mouth was taped shut and his hands were trapped behind his back.

Hands grabbed Jack's shoulders and forced him out of the car. Where was he, what was happening—these were questions he couldn't comprehend. He was being marched. Forcefully pushed by figures on each side, Jack staggered step after step. He was still in shock. His head was swimming from the impact. It wasn't Jack Ranger that these men were leading along; it was a dumbed, muted, dazed shell of the man operating on a primal and submissive level.

A chair. Jack was shoved into a seat. He could feel arms grappling with his handcuffed hands. A forearm took hold on the back of Jack's neck and pressed him forward until his neck was twisted and his face was pinned to the table in front of him. Air was difficult to find in the cloth that was surrounding his face. Jack knew nothing of the men around him. He could not see them, and when they did talk it was too low or far away to understand their words. He could feel them as they removed his handcuffs and removed the forearm from the back of his neck.

Then the unmistakable sound of duct tape. The long drawn out sound of removing tape from the roll. Jack's hands were forced onto the table in front of him onto some fixture. The duct tape was spread across his wrists and whatever his hands were resting on. Jack jerked his hands. There were laughs. He was stuck.

And then there was a sensation on the back of his right hand. The blackness of his environment was maddening. There was a liquid on his hand and then there was burning. Soon, there was a smell.

The pain cut through his dulled senses like no other feeling he had ever experienced. It was a pain beyond his imagination. The smell was flesh, his flesh. From his right hand came a singular sensation of panic. He sat writhing in his chair, pulling, twisting, and desperately willing his body to break free and end the pain.

"Does it burn, Mr. Ranger?"

The first words Jack could understand. Jack screamed, but it was muted by his taped mouth.

Jack twisted, and thrashed, and willed for it to end as the sensation continued to ramp. Bubbling raw flesh silently wailed for mercy. He was losing consciousness again.

And then a new sensation. Liquid. Cooling.

There was more laughter. The same voice was next to Jack's ear now. The man whispered.

"I'm the one who decides when the pain stops."

His hands were cut loose from the table and then handcuffed behind his back.

The men had marched Jack back to the car. His hand hurt like nothing he had ever experienced. It was throbbing in an unnatural way. It was screaming and pleading and torturing Jack's mind. His head was still covered as he sat in the backseat of the car. They drove and then stopped.

The door opened. One man held Jack down in the back seat with his hand on his throat as another man unlocked Jack's hands from behind his back. They loosened the knot keeping the cloth bag over Jack's head. He was thrown from the car.

Jack was out of the car with his hands free. He heard tires digging into the road as the car with his captors took off. The young reporter clutched at the cloth bag, peeling it away from his face. Sight. The most illuminating of the senses returned to Jack. He looked around and crawled from the street onto the lawn.

He collapsed face-down on the grass.

CHAPTER 30

Should I run?

Jack Ranger lay face-down and discarded.

He exhaled as his body calmed.

He hurt. His body was rejecting his existence. The numbing effects of shock were subsiding. His neck, his head, his legs, and his hand called out as if someone listening could make it stop. Exhausted, he sprawled out, face up, staring at the sky. Jack shivered, and Jack ached.

Sometime later he picked up his head. Jack looked around as a moment of understanding crawled into his brain; he had been here before. Whoever these men were, they knew a lot about Jack.

Jack stood slowly and gathered his legs. He began staggering across the lawn towards Anton's front door.

CHAPTER 31

"Please tell me you're drunk, crashed your car, and need a ride home."

Anton spoke as he opened the front door. Jack shook his head.

Anton looked harder at Jack. He could use much more than just a ride home. He ushered Jack through his front door and sat him down at his kitchen table.

Without a word, Anton reached out and grabbed Jack's wrist. He examined Jack's hand. The skin on the back of his hand had a red, bubbling streak of burnt flesh from his second knuckle to the base of his wrist.

The look on Anton's face told Jack that he knew what a chemical burn looked like.

They talked, or more accurately Jack attempted to communicate his circumstance.

His wits were returning slowly. He was putting pieces together. He was stammering. "Here, they dropped me off here."

"Awfully nice of them, don't you think? Especially considering you don't have a car, or money, and I'm assuming they took your phone."

Jack turned out his pockets. Empty.

"But they know you."

Anton continued without acknowledging Jack's point. "Honestly, no one else would give a ride to a stranger with a black eye and hair as messed up as yours." Anton paused. "Especially at this time of night… and with a nasty thing like that on your hand." Anton twisted his own hand absently in the air.

How was this funny to him?

"I can't do it. I can't do this."

Anton sat down across the table from Jack. He put both hands on the table. "Yes, yes you will."

How much was his life worth? Was it worth this story? Was his life what was on the line?

"This isn't mine, Anton."

Anton laughed and pointed once again at Jack's throbbing hand. "Oh, Jack. This will always be part of you."

Jack was shivering. Everything was colliding. How could he do this? How could he keep going? He couldn't do it.

Anton looked back at him. His voice was softer now. "You're tired. Get some rest. I'll drive you home." He paused for a second more. "I've told you this before Jack, but stick with me and I'll get us through this."

"I can't keep doing this. I can't."

"Don't be weak, Jack. Quitting is for weak people and that's not who we are. Don't do that to us."

His neck was too stiff to turn his head. His body was transitioning to a new normal of pain. He was tired. He was sore. He was unhappy. Jack rubbed his neck. He'd never been in a car crash before. Jack thought about his car. Where was it? How do you explain that to your insurance company? Did they steal it, or was it still there on the side of the road wedged up against the sidewalk and lamp post? Sleep. That is what his body demanded. Sleep would be first, everything else needed to be second.

"Look at me. Look at me, Jack." Anton stood from his chair. He reached out and put both hands on Jack's unscarred left hand. It was a mix between a handshake and a plea. "We are going to publish this. They can't touch you once this is out there. When the world knows, you will be safe. The most dangerous thing is to keep it a secret."

They walked towards Anton's car and Jack fell in. He was going home to sleep. "Tomorrow we will set this straight. Tomorrow I'm going to break the news."

Jack wasn't paying attention to much else besides the throbbing in his head. He looked over to the driver's seat of the car with eyes that were fighting to stay shut.

Anton was in thought. He looked over at Jack and made no effort to hide his smile.

CHAPTER 32

The cycle of the sun pays no mind to the lives of people.

Why would it care? It has better things to do.

Momentous, trivial, stressful, or happy—the sun rises and falls without consideration for the events of the day. The clockwork sun greeted Jack the next morning just as it had any other. But for him, today was not to be a day like any other.

The pain in his skull was splitting. In the haze of last night, he didn't close the blinds in his bedroom. The morning light made its way through the window of the old apartment and woke him in concert with a car honking its horn. The noise was incessant; not a good start to the morning. Next, the doorbell. Finally, a knock on the door.

Jack found his way to the front door of his apartment. His eyes were puffy, the front of his head hurt in a way that he could hardly describe. Opening the door, Jack saw his boss standing and smiling.

He walked in. "Morning sunshine. I brought you breakfast." Anton had never been in Jack's apartment before, but he wasted no time getting comfortable. He took out plates from the shelves and put them on the table.

He placed a brown grocery bag down and ruffled through. Paper crinkled and Jack was staring blankly.

"I hope you like sesame bagels. I got you a sausage egg and cheese on a sesame bagel."

He pulled out two sandwiches and slapped them on the plates. He reached into the bag again and pulled out a small plastic bottle of pills. "I also brought you painkillers." Anton rattled the pills to make a noise that coincided with his words. He tossed the bottle at Jack, who instinctively caught it. Turning his attention back to the bag, he pulled out a bottle of champagne.

"Champagne?"

"Like I said, I brought you painkillers. Only this one is for later."

Unsure of what else to do, Jack took a seat at the table and began eating his breakfast. He chewed on his food. "Thanks, Anton."

"You can thank me by putting on some real clothes and getting ready for work. I'm your ride today and in 20 minutes we are going to be late."

There was an understanding. Anton was taking no chances in getting Jack to the *Tribune's* office today.

CHAPTER 33

Jack walked into the office and to his desk. But he would not be there for long. There was a note on his desk. He had been summoned.

The legendary editor in chief, Pat Flaherty, had requested Jack's presence.

The door to his office was already open. The editor sat leaning back in his chair. He was expecting the arrival.

The editor stood, asked his assistant to leave, and then closed the office door. There was an absent-minded motion for Jack to take a seat.

Jack sat in the empty chair that was too obviously meant for him. He looked on at the editor. He was a man in his fifties who wore his hair slicked back and talked with a measured confidence. He wore suspenders over his expensive French-cuffed shirt and Jack guessed that he was a man who had an affinity for fine cigars.

"There are only a few ways that this can end."

"What could end?"

The editor was pacing alongside the broad window on the far side of the office. They were on the 15th floor, which offered a sweeping view of the city. The room was well-lit and modern. Yet the space was filled with artifacts of a better time—it was built on the fortunes of a decade ago.

It was the office of a company that wasn't ready to announce that it was a shell of its former self.

"The choice is yours of how you want to do it." The editor motioned to the door. "But I'm going to need your resignation before you leave my office."

The editor was silent for a moment.

Jack froze. How many other people had sat in this exact chair in this exact office receiving the exact same fate? Why? That's what Jack needed to know. Why would I be fired? But as Jack sat there absorbing the words that would surely change his life, he already knew the reason.

It was plain to see. The timing was precise. Jack stood from his seat and spoke in a loud, searching, tone. "This can't be about…"

The editor countered with only a calm expression. The answer was "yes". Yes, that is exactly what it was about.

"What is wrong with you? This is the biggest story we've done in years. You can't fire me over this."

"You're right, Jack. That's exactly why I need your resignation."

Silence followed. They both stared. And they both knew how things were going to be. "You can't keep this down."

"Sure Jack, tell whoever you want. I'd love to get this story out to the world." The editor motioned like he was rubbing money together, "But you'd be surprised how many people can suddenly go deaf."

But Jack did not move. He wouldn't quit, he couldn't quit. He responded. "I can't… I won't."

Pat Flaherty had convinced men of stronger conviction to his way of thinking.

"Won't you, Jack?"

The two stared, daring each other to make the next move.

"I know what you're thinking. But there is no safety in publishing this story. The *Tribune* will not be your shield." The editor looked at Jack from top to bottom. He lingered on his neck, which had bruises rising above the collar on Jack's shirt. He shook his head.

"It's a shame what they've already done to you."

Jack's next thoughts didn't leave his mind. He devoted too much time to this story. There was too much behind this story. Too many people needed to know what was going on. He had suffered for the truth. This was his story.

Or was it Anton's?

Could the editor read internal conflict by looking into Jack's eyes? Regardless, Jack felt the pain of the next well-chosen words.

"You've been wrapped up in something that isn't your own creation. It's not your fault that you're here. I respect your commitment, but it won't end."

The editor held up his right hand and sequentially moved his fingers into a fist and then opened it again. "It won't stop when you publish. There is no glory in this. The people that you think you are saving will forget. They always forget. The people that you're scared of… and I can see that you're scared… well, they won't forget. They never do."

The whiplash of yesterday's car crash came back in a sheet of white. The unseen whisper in his ear played repeatedly.

Pat Flaherty opened both hands, palms upward. "Unless there is a reason for them to forget."

Jack knew the arrangement. He knew what it must be.

"I'm offering you a way out, Jack."

His resignation was a peace treaty.

The reporter's head bowed. He chewed on his lip. The silence of the room was broken as the editor slid a paper document across his desk. After a pause, he took a pen and placed it upon the document. No words were said.

Jack took the pen. He clutched the instrument of his fate in his freshly scarred hand. His skin was still red and raw. It hurt to close his hands. But just now, gripping this pen, there was no pain—almost as if the metallic ink-filled cylinder was absorbing the hurt. Jack could feel the transfer of pain from his hand to the ink.

He signed his name.

Jack dropped the pen, its duty done, onto the floor. He shook his head and grabbed his hair.

Pat Flaherty watched and nodded. He approved.

"This can't be over."

The editor laughed. It was a loud, constant laugh. "This can't be over? Don't be naïve, Jack. It's been over for twenty years." Jack turned and walked to the door. The editor was now raising his voice. "Don't take it personally. How do you think we're still in this building? We do what we have to. This is an old man's game."

With each step to the door, his voice grew louder. Jack opened the door.

The editor spoke. "You're welcome."

Jack turned and paused for the briefest of curious moments.

"You're better off getting out while you still can."

CHAPTER 34

And that was it. He was done. Just like that. He stood outside of his apartment angry, sad, and unemployed.

Anton called. Jack ignored. He couldn't face him. He knew Anton was fired. He would never have folded like Jack. A dog with its tail between its legs doesn't want confrontation. Jack didn't want to talk to Anton.

He always wondered how many people still bought the newspaper. Not people like, old people, but people who still had the fire. Jack knew he was in the minority of this. He got it; people liked their traditions. If you've been reading papers for 50 years, then there was no point to switch. The feel of paper and its black and white was a comfort that Jack thought was admirable to hold on to.

It was a shame though, papers were dying and the entire world was accepting this fate. No one who mattered, or was *going to* matter, still got the hard paper. "Except for me," he thought. "I was the last one."

He held the *Tribune* on his back porch. It was spring, the season of love, rebirth, and the end of his career as a journalist. It was as good a day as any to start a fire. He fished in his pocket for a lighter and held it to the front page of the *Tribune*. He crumpled it and put it in the basin of his charcoal grill. Birds chirped as wisps of orange spread. The paper was transformed from black and white to just black ash. He took the second page and did the same. Jack watched the headlines burn. *City to see a 5% tax increase, Teacher's Union on Strike, Hospital receives Federal Grant.*

He spoke out to no one. "This is where my story should be." He burned the pages one by one. He stood staring at the newspaper that could be used for so much more than just smoke.

CHAPTER 35

The Last Drop

SENIOR YEAR OF COLLEGE

The day Molly told him that she would be moving to New York City he would always remember. It was their senior year of college. Jack had avoided being expelled from school, but that wasn't how Molly judged him.

She had brought food over to his apartment for dinner. A move that, in hindsight, was a preemptive apology. They sat to eat. She didn't say much. Molly always got quiet when she was uncomfortable. Looking at her, Jack knew something was coming. Molly's eyes shook, betraying the words she was about say.

"I got the job, Jack." He knew what job that meant. It was a non-profit in New York City. They sent books, teachers, and just about anything else across the world. They built schools; they changed lives; they were a great cause. But they were in New York. Jack was not going to be in New York.

"That's amazing. I mean it's your dream. I'm so happy. You should be happy. It's not far. I can bus. I can drive."

He was speaking fast, as if the flurry of options might somehow cheer her up. "It might be tough. Boston's not too far."

Molly's face was soft with grief. Tears hovered at the corners of her eyes.

Why was she sad?

Air from the open window lifted her hair in front of her face. She brushed it away. Molly looked down. "I don't think we should do that, Jack."

He went through all the objections. *But it won't be for too long. What about the last three years? But I love you.*

Her frame shivered for an instant as if she were suddenly cold. She was holding off the first tear. She needed something new. He knew that. But how could he be a part of the issue?

She wanted to break away from Jack's world. "This job is a chance to be a good person. To do good, for the sake of good."

Molly looked at Jack still holding back the first tear. Even when she was sad Jack couldn't help but think she was beautiful. She looked up at him as if he might have some answer.

"But Molly, you can still live that life, and we can be together." He put his hand on top of hers.

But Molly just shook her head.

CHAPTER 36

Jack looked up from his phone to make sure the street sign matched the direction on his GPS. He took a left onto England Street amidst the brownstone homes that lined this part of the city. Here, away from the traffic, the streets were quieter. Coffee shops and cafes sat nestled on street corners and the wind rustled leaves in the alleys. But Jack had no appreciation for the solitude. It allowed unwelcome thoughts to expand into his consciousness. The memory of Molly leaving him became stronger with each footstep.

Today was the day that he finally caved and decided to meet again with Anton. The two circumstances were reminiscent of each other.

Losing your job was like being dumped. When you give so much to someone, or something, only to have it ripped away—that hurts. With every footstep, his future became his past.

Forty steps into his past he ducked under an awning and into his destination—Café a' la Mar. His former boss was waiting for him.

Anton had been fired. Or that's what he said. He would be fine though; he had a lot of friends in places where it was good to have friends.

"I'm just kicking around some opportunities at the moment. I'll be fine." That's how Anton described his situation while holding a coffee in his hand and leaning over the café table. "But that's what I wanted to ask you about. Come work with me, Jack. There's still a lot to be done."

But Jack didn't say yes. Student loans and no job dictates a 'yes' in these situations, but instead, Jack didn't acknowledge the offer.

"Are you still going to work on the case?"

"When something is worth seeing through, I see it through." Anton had been gnawing on a toothpick in his mouth which he took into his right hand. He circled his hand above the plate where what appeared to be a macaroon lay untouched.

"Think about it Jack. The governor is out there behind this whole thing. The hush money, the drugs, all of it is happening under his watch, and he is getting away with it. He's shaking hands, kissing babies, and lining his pockets."

Anton paused and made eye contact with Jack as the two shared a common hatred over a cup of coffee, blueberry scones, and coconut cookies.

"Look at us. I mean this guy seriously screwed us over, Jack. I'm not stopping until I pin him, expose him, and grind him into the ground."

With too much force Anton drove the toothpick into the bleached white coconut macaroon on his plate, harpooning the pastry before it crumbled under the weight of his hand.

He looked up, "I could use you, Jack."

Jack pondered this. He wanted to say yes, but this wasn't his to chase. He wanted his own vision. He'd walked in midway through someone else's quest. He wanted more than to be just an accessory to triumph. It was Anton's mission to finish.

Jack thought through his current situation. He was broke, broken-hearted, and likely still on someone's hit list.

"I can see your love of the truth, Jack. I can teach you how to do good in this world." Anton spoke softly, "I can show you how to stand up for the people that need it. But I can't teach you not to be scared. I can't help it if you don't have what it takes."

What was he implying?

Anton continued, "Don't hide by convincing yourself that this isn't your responsibility. You know what's right and what you should do. I'm just giving you the chance."

These were unwelcome words.

Anton had spent enough time with Jack to read his delayed response. "It's all right, Jack, I didn't expect you to want to come along again. I will keep going until I finish it or until it finishes me. But I'll wait for you; I don't think this story is over for either of us."

The elder ex-*Tribune* reporter threw money down on the table. "Coffee is on me today."

As he stood and walked to the door, Jack couldn't help but notice that Anton was struggling increasingly with his limp.

CHAPTER 37

What do you do when you're 25 and unemployed? Jack wasn't sure, but he'd never accept just sitting around. Not now. Not ever. He applied to a handful of small-time local papers, and he started writing for a number of different blogs. But he knew that those could be nothing more than temporary. He had no interest in dead-end jobs with such a low ceiling. He knew he needed something more, much more.

By this time, he had spent more days than he cared to count in a Starbucks crawling job listings on his computer. He considered just about everything. Some of his friends had good jobs in consulting, insurance, and finance. They were all fine jobs, steady and lucrative—certainly more lucrative than almost anything out there in the realm of journalism.

What was it that he couldn't quite give up about journalism? It wasn't the pay. Was it the writing? No, it wasn't the writing in itself. It was something more. *Change*, that was closer to it. He needed to be able to create change in a way that was bigger than changing a few decimal points on a bottom line.

Why was he this way? It was a question Jack cursed every time he looked at his bank account. He was smart and ambitious; he was talented… so why was he broke?

He supposed that he could thank the great Edward R. Murrow.

When he was a kid he had read a book about the man. His father had given it to him on a rainy day during a family vacation at the lake. The pages were folded and slightly yellowed. Jack was never one to much enjoy reading biographies, but as the rain pounded against the walls and the winds whistled past the windows of the Ranger family vacation home, he opened the book and began to read.

It was the story of the rise and fall of an American journalism icon in the time of the cold war. He was fascinated. The 'Red Scare'—how could a time like that exist in America? We were afraid of our own citizens. But it was McCarthyism that made him think the most. Senator Joe McCarthy had managed to scare America. He rose to prominence on a wave of fear and accusations. Political opponents and dissenters were swiftly labeled communists. He made blind and wild accusations, and no one would speak out for fear of being called a communist themselves. This is just human nature—in the face of tyrants if you are not for them, you are against them. Fear and paranoia was the ruling ideology. It took someone to make a stand to make a change. That was the journalist Edward R. Murrow.

He put the senator on trial in the court of the public eye. His broadcast was in the early days of broadcast television and profoundly affected America. He discredited the senator with statements from his own speeches and urged for sanity to return. Murrow didn't convince the public, he empowered them. The senator was forced out.

Jack knew that McCarthy would have eventually fallen out of favor; he was an inevitable culmination of fears. McCarthy would have faded with the ebb and flow of the crisis of the moment. But how much more damage would he have done; how much longer would Americans live in fear? For that Jack respected the legend of Murrow.

Something in that story was the reason Jack wasn't ready to give up on journalism. There was something from that rainy day spent trapped in a lake house that wouldn't let him quit. As he sat there staring at his laptop on the wooden countertop leaching free coffee shop Wi-Fi he dug into his pocket. He took out the baseball card that he had been keeping in his wallet as of late. He looked at the card of Mark McGwire. Protecting the helpless was a compelling cause.

It was a peculiar position to be in. Journalism, especially investigative journalism, was something that the public needed and yet nobody was willing to pay for. Newspapers were dead men walking, and so, too, was his choice of a career.

CHAPTER 38

Inspiration can strike anywhere, and in this case, it came on the side of a bus. Jack was walking out of his latest interview for a position that he secretly hoped that he wouldn't get. On the side of the bus was an advertisement for Kickstarter. That was all it took to get the wheels in Jack's mind turning.

He pieced together the parts in his mind. Jack got the giddy light-headed feeling that happens when you know your idea has a chance to be more than just an idea. As Jack got back to his apartment he didn't eat dinner; he didn't call his mom like he said he was going to do. He just wrote, researched, and thought.

The next day at 7:30 p.m. Jack was waiting outside of Sean's office.

"Hey, Sean."

"Jack?"

Jack knew how weird it must look to show up somewhere without giving Sean a text or call ahead of time.

"What's up, Jack?" Sean paused as he examined Jack standing there with a notebook under his arm, waiting for him. "Dude, have you slept?"

"Let's go shoot some pool. I need to talk to you about something."

The two of them had many conversations over the years, and yet Sean had never seen Jack quite like this. He was excited, almost strung out, but excited nonetheless. Whatever the reason, it probably had nothing to do with playing pool.

At the bar, Jack set up the pool balls neatly in the triangle as Sean placed the cue ball at the opposite end of the table. "How's the job search going?"

"The best thing that's ever happened to me."

Jack circled around the table and got ready to break and start the game. "Journalism isn't dead, Sean. It's just that the way we fund it is stupid. Newspapers make all their money from advertising. That means eyeballs are what matters."

Another few turns went by in the game. Jack lined up the cue ball and smashed it into a striped ball harder than he had to. "The system doesn't work."

The striped ball went into the pocket, and Jack continued talking without looking up or taking his eye off his next shot.

"We can't have good journalism because we need to write stories that get the most clicks. We can't publish some pieces because they might upset advertisers."

"So, what are you saying?"

"So, I'm saying, let's change it. Let's flip it on its head."

"What do you mean *let's*?"

Jack picked up his notebook from a stool and tossed it to Sean. "I mean, let's change the model."

The notebook was filled with scribbles. Sean flipped through the pages.

Sean tossed the notebook back to Jack, his face betraying his confusion. He stood there waiting for the hook.

"I'm going to build it, Sean. I'm going to build a platform to crowdfund investigative journalism."

The two-kept playing. Sean had never heard Jack talk so fast.

Jack was excited. Sean was skeptical. "But Kickstarter has already done journalism."

"True, but it's awful."

Sean laughed. "What about other sites, you can't be the first to think about this."

"I've checked out the other guys. They're crap, too. You don't need to be first. You just need to be better." Jack pressed his point, "They all do it wrong, no one is thinking big enough. There needs to be a brand, we need big name journalists, we need big name donors, we need to tackle stories that *actually* matter."

"Who is the 'we' in this, Jack?"

"To start? Me and you. Who knows how big it could get."

"And why would I want to do this?"

"Look Sean, I know you. There's no way you're going to miss out."

CHAPTER 39

And so, they started. Sean didn't quit his job, but he did donate his weekends and some nights. Jack knew that Sean wouldn't give up his consulting gig so easily. He was getting paid too much and worked too hard to just walk away. Jack knew that he could get Sean to work with him. Of course, their friendship played into it, but that alone wouldn't be enough to get Sean to give up what meager hours he had outside of work. Sean, like Jack, wanted to change the world and so the trick was selling him on the idea of what Flint Media could become.

"Flint Media?"

Jack looked up from his laptop and replied to Sean. "Yeah, just Flint for short though."

The two hadn't discussed the name before. Jack didn't have a good reason for why he wanted to call it Flint Media, but the name was fixated in his head.

Sean pressed, "Flint, like flint and tinder?"

Sitting in Jack's apartment, the two traded looks of amusement. It was a warm summer afternoon; the windows were open and the various sounds and smells of Allston worked their way in.

Sean shook his head. "Sounds like a stupid name to me."

Jack took the comment. "Sean, 'Google' is a stupid name."

Sean shrugged and filled out Flint Media on the form online. Today Jack and Sean were officially going into business. They were incorporating. Two-hundred dollars, an idea, and an internet connection were all it took.

There was probably some story to be drawn from the simplicity of starting a business with the internet as the great equalizer—an indiscriminate force that displaced and replaced entire industries with no regard for tradition or tenure. The barriers to entry were smashed.

With a few clicks, two beer sipping kids threw their hats into the ring and declared war on the world of their fathers.

But that wasn't so apparent to them at that moment. The company was founded, and the two of them sat across the table from one another, peering over their laptops. Jack cracked a beer and tossed an unopened one to Sean. "For brainstorming."

Sean lay back in his chair and relaxed. "Why am I here? I get that we're friends, but it's not like I know how to build this. You could do this without me."

Was it true? Maybe it was. Flint Media could be built without Sean. But could it be built as well as it needed to be without him? Jack doubted it. Sean had an intangible mix of something which Jack felt that his company needed.

Jack's response was more direct than the meandering thoughts in his mind. "Because you get the job done, and that is what this company is going to be all about."

Sean nodded; at least that much was true.

Jack took a moment to reflect as he looked over Sean's shoulder at the filled-out form on the screen. "You always sign things Sean J. Cosatiri. What's up with the 'J'?"

"Ah, it's stupid. It's one of those old-world names. I just sign my middle initial because I think it looks more professional."

Jack didn't press. He didn't really care. He was just curious. The two of them lingered and then moved on to the more important things at hand.

"So, what's next?"

Jack smiled and moved his head as if he was listening to a song. "Now we build."

All the ambition and dreams in the world can't substitute for an absence of a product. Flint Media needed to be created. The two of them could handle the business and journalism side of things, but they needed a website and neither could build that.

Jack let his words linger and then added, "Sean, we're going to need someone who can build us a world-class website."

Noise from the streets ebbed in intensity inside the apartment. The two co-founders sipped on their beers as they thought through the question before them. The new CEO of Flint Media closed his eyes and thought. He was motivated, naive, and broke.

CHAPTER 40

It was the sort of town that boasted a farmer's market and a cautiously optimistic population that was excited and scared about the possibility of their town being 'on the rise.' High school fundraisers, craft fairs, and strip malls were all a thing. Welcome to 'Middletown-ville, USA.'

Jack's hometown was a town of small dreams and reasonably ambitious expectations. Prosperity in moderation was plentiful. There was a reason Jack had left.

But he had returned. He may be broke and out of a job, but he was ambitious. Jack didn't know who else he could ask. He needed money to get Flint Media off the ground, so he was asking his dad.

Intangible ideas are hard to sell to someone whose livelihood is in building physical objects. Jack was sitting across the table from two builders.

Sitting at the dining room table was Jack, his father, and the oldest Ranger son—Jason. Trying to explain what Flint Media was and what it could become was difficult. Jack didn't fully understand it himself; it was still just an idea. Jack was trying to summon Flint Media into being through a sheer act of willpower. And yet, no matter the passion, desire, and drive he possessed—it was still just an idea.

Jack's father was successful. He ran his own contracting company specializing in building homes and storefronts. Business had been steady for 20 years.

Jason didn't buy the idea. "Jack—forget it. Come work with us. Dad and I could use a hand."

Jack shook his head.

"Why not? Give me a good reason."

A million reasons came to his mind, but none of them could be said aloud.

"Unless you think you're too good for that?"

It was clear that Jason knew the filtered words behind his brother's silently shaking head.

"Boys." Jack's father laughed. This wasn't the place to renew rivalries. "Tell me again. What exactly will you use the money for?"

And so, Jack explained. Again. But they didn't get it. Jack painted the vision. He told them it was an opportunity to make right in the world, the chance to build something great—to become someone great.

Jack knew his father didn't understand the idea. But Jack also knew that his father wasn't trying to understand the idea so much as he was trying to understand his son. His father could see that Jack was burning to do this. He knew it was a burn that wasn't easily satisfied.

Jack's father stood and left his two sons shifting awkwardly at the table as he left to retrieve something from the home office. Jack's father came back with an old-fashioned passbook from a bank.

"Your mother and I have been putting a little bit of money aside for each of you boys."

He put the booklet on the table, and Jack opened it to see what was inside.

"I'm not sure when we were planning on giving this to you, but now seems like as good a time as any."

Jack skimmed to the last page. The balance was nearly $15,000.

Jack looked up and his father nodded.

The oldest Ranger son didn't say anything. His face reflected something between curiosity and disappointment. His concern was less about the merit of the idea than it was about money frivolously given away. The three Ranger men shared a moment reflecting on the gesture.

The next day was Sunday and Jack was to return home. He was excited, $15,000 could get Flint Media rolling. His father dropped him off at the bus station.

"Do well with it, Jack."

"Thanks, Dad. I will."

Father and son shook hands and exchanged a last phrase, "Remember, Son, there will always be a spot waiting for you back here."

Jack released his father's hand and turned to board the bus. There would always be a spot waiting for him and he would never want it.

From his seat, he looked out the window as the bus began to move. He watched as the houses, lawns, and semi-chain restaurants of Middletown-ville, USA melted into the distance. All he could think about was what he was going to do next.

CHAPTER 41

"How far along are you?"

"4,000."

"4,000 what, dollars?"

"Yes, I'm offering you 4,000 dollars."

Jack and Sean sat across a table at a barbeque joint in Allston talking with Matthew Sutton. They knew Matt from school. He was what they needed. Matt's hands knew their way around a keyboard. Everyone at the table knew that $4,000 wasn't exactly 'market rate' for the type of website they were envisioning. Matt worked for a small firm building websites. This would require a 'friends and family' discount.

Matt thought about the dollar figure. "So, run me through this again."

Sean explained Flint. "We will be a platform that crowdfunds investigative reporting. The community proposes issues that they want investigated. People vote up or down the issues that they want to see covered. Popular topics rise to the top and people fund the projects they want. $5 here, $15 there, across thousands of people it adds up."

Jack nodded his head and added more. "Matt, we're breaking the mold. For the past century, journalism has been at the mercy of advertisers. Flint is a chance to stand up and say, 'No.' We can build something fundamental to society."

Matt laughed a little. Jack could tell that Matt was trying to understand why they had chosen him.

Jack went on to further sell his vision. "What happens when pharmaceutical companies sponsor 'independent' research? Who is contributing money to my congressman's campaign? We aren't reporting on *what* is happening, we are reporting on *why* it is happening. That's why this matters."

Steam from Jack's untouched pulled pork sandwich floated upwards. Matt finally spoke.

"You need more than a website. You have to support payments, accounts, and the distribution of stories—which all needs to run in the background. You're going to need something that looks really good. You don't get credibility with a half-assed website. If you want to be taken seriously you need to look better than *The New York Times*."

Jack smiled. This was the correct answer. "So, you'll help us?"

Matt responded. "10%."

"10% chance you'll help us?"

"No, I'll do it if you give me 10% of the company."

Sean and Jack looked at each other. Matt continued, "You could pay someone to build it, but what happens when it evolves? You guys have no idea what this will turn into. You need someone who can evolve with it on the fly. Even if you can find someone stupid enough to do all this for $4,000, you're going to have to pay them extra every time you want to branch out."

Jack smiled. He had hoped this would happen. They needed a technical partner, not a contractor. Matt could be their CIO. He just didn't know it yet.

"Well, Matt, it sounds like you want a job at our company. Why don't you come to my place next Saturday and we can talk business? Make a mockup of what you think you'd want to build and we will give you a proper interview."

CHAPTER 42

14 Slade Street Apartment 2, Allston, Massachusetts—Flint Media World Headquarters

Just as he had been engrossed in working with Anton, Jack became engrossed in starting Flint. Matt had come on board to join the team. Matt and Sean worked on nights and weekends. Jack worked just about all day, almost every day. Jack was working as a bartender at a restaurant down the street three nights a week. The money wasn't great, but it was good enough. He figured he had five month's rent before he had to resort to couch surfing, finding a better job, or moving back home with his parents. He didn't like any of those three options.

The early days were a magical time. Work began at 9:00 a.m. on Saturdays. Those first Saturdays followed a familiar pattern.

This was the start of something special. All three of them could feel it. Three laptops on the same table being stared at intently as they worked in a messy Boston bachelor pad—it was perfect. Periods of intense silence were broken by tales of fraternities, college exploits, and jokes. The commonality of purpose was supreme; Flint Media was the light in the night, and they've tossed themselves headlong in to reach it.

The guitar was never far. Discussions of equity and profit models rolled into songs. Stress was relieved by spontaneous sessions on the guitar. Sean would strum and Jack would sing. Cover songs, made up songs, horrendous riffs, and catchy rhymes flowed from the trio with the same zeal as their ideas. This start-up was held together by passion and the three knew no other way.

They praised the design of their website and then trashed it. They became excited as big ideas sprouted up and then cut them down. It was trial by fire, and they were throwing their hearts on the wall and hoping something stuck. Morning became noon and noon passed with only an acknowledgement of lunch. They talked about what they would do with millions of dollars and they wrote down how they would achieve it. Greatness was being born and the only witnesses were empty pizza boxes.

After dinner, the beers came out and the slow drip of liquid inspiration brought along spontaneous preaching about how they would change the world. Jack stood on his chair spilling out the story of Flint. Sean chimed in and Matt revised. The room became a sounding board for the origin story of the company. Each incantation tweaked the story until it became a carefully crafted tale of heroism and ingenuity.

The room was Jack's audience. He spoke words that were meant for the masses but were only heard by the two other members of his team. "Flint was born out of necessity. We looked at the world with the same eyes as everyone else. We built Flint to solve what everyone knows is wrong. Journalism is dying. Knowledge is power, but our ability to be empowered is fading. We need the press and the press needs Flint. So, we built it."

CHAPTER 43

"So how does it work?"

The irony of the situation was lost on neither Jack nor Anton. They sat in the very bar in downtown Boston where Jack's short career at the *Tribune* began.

"We've built a website for investigative journalism. People log in and propose things they want answers to. *How does the state actually use lottery funds, how much mercury is in my fish*—whatever question you want you can put out there to the world. Then you back the idea and try and get support. Users up-vote or down-vote the idea; the more votes the idea gets the more momentum it gets. It rises to the top and gets more popular. The ideas at the top will get there because they will be interesting to thousands of people."

They both paused. Jack watched the gears turn in Anton's head.

Jack offered, "The beginning stage is sort of like Reddit." Anton didn't get the reference. Jack continued, "But once an idea passes a certain threshold, that's where the fun starts. We're going to build a network of freelance journalists. Our journalists look at the popular ideas and make a pitch to cover the story.

Anton was following along, and Jack continued, "They propose how they're going to cover the story, why they should be the ones to cover it, and most importantly, how much money they think they're going to need to do it."

Jack paused one more time. He smiled and continued, "The crowd votes with their wallets. They back the stories and the reporter they want to see."

"You think people will pay for it?"

Jack didn't honestly know. "We'll find out."

Anton spoke. "You want me to be one of your journalists?"

Jack smiled.

Each raised a glass.

"I'll think about it."

He spoke again, "These stories will take a while. Think about how much time we spent on that last case. And we didn't publish anything."

The point was well understood. No one was going to subscribe to something that only published a story once every five months. He'd bring this back to Sean. They would figure this out.

"Well, that's why we need dedicated people. Like you."

The two sat and chatted. Jack missed the camaraderie of working with Anton. But he could also see the toll the case was taking on him. He wasn't strung out, but he was tired. Anton wasn't the same vibrant character that Jack had first met. "You look tired, Anton."

"When you give yourself to something, you need to be careful not to give too much, or else you might not get it all back. I haven't been careful, Jack."

It was time to go, and Jack stood to leave.

Anton raised one last point, "I've got one more question for you. How do you guys plan on making a profit?"

Jack laughed. "Why would I want to do that? Facebook, Snapchat, Instagram—they were all billion-dollar companies before they even thought about making money. If I had a revenue model, I would ruin our valuation."

Anton laughed.

CHAPTER 44

The three of them worked on Flint Media. They built the platform. They constructed a 'network' of five or so journalists, and they talked to everyone and anyone that would listen. Expenses weren't exactly high; they paid for a domain name and hosting. The journalists would get their money from whatever donations came in. While Jack didn't pay for labor in money, he paid for it in time.

Every day was one less day he could afford rent; every day was one more day that he ate leftovers for lunch. Jack had created 50 different profiles. He logged into Flint and constantly proposed different story ideas from each account and voted for his own favorites. Sean and Matt did this as well. The three of them made up a small, but living, community in their own world.

When you live every second in the present you have no idea what the next second will bring. Jack lived in fear that Flint would crumble; that all his time spent on it would be a waste. Every week was a rollercoaster. They would celebrate after getting a few hundred new users on the website. They celebrated when the first $25 dollars in legitimate funding came in for one of the stories—little victories were important.

The turning point came when they put their project and their first story on Kickstarter. It was a stroke of genius by Sean. Why not invoke the help of the community that gave rise to the crowdfunding revolution? So, the three of them put their idea out to the world on Kickstarter. They set a goal of $25,000 just to see what would happen.

It wasn't immediate, but it was close to it. The idea of Flint Media got picked up and circulated. People loved it. It was a 'new spin on journalism's new spin.' It was a crowd favorite. The money came, slow and steady; and then fast and continuous.

It was a Saturday afternoon and ten days into the Kickstarter campaign when it caught fire.

Jack, Sean, and Matt stood side by side looking at Jack's laptop monitor as the money ballooned each time Jack refreshed the page. First, hundreds of dollars, then thousands. Kickstarter put Flint Media on a featured campaign list and things accelerated even faster. The money was pouring in; hitting their goal was quickly becoming a non-issue. Matt ran to the fridge and came back with a bottle of Coca-Cola. He shook it wildly and opened the cap trying to spray it like a celebratory Champagne bottle.

That was the day that Jack first thought his idea might actually work.

CHAPTER 45

23 MONTHS LATER

For this week's *Pearson Magazine* 'Business Spotlight' I had a chance to catch up with Jack Ranger—CEO of Flint Media. Flint, as they call it, is one of a growing number of disruptive journalism websites. The 27-year-old CEO gave me a tour around the new Flint Media office. The office has everything you might expect from a fashionable startup in this day and age, no cubicles, no dress code, and of course a fridge stocked with beer. But my tour didn't end at the beer fridge, instead Mr. Ranger poured each of us his signature drink—a Jack & Coke. This is where the fun began. In our conversation, we talked about everything from his inspiration to start Flint to what a 27-year-old might do if he struck it rich. Enjoy:

Alexandra Cole: What was the moment when you knew you had something good?

Jack Ranger: Well, I mean we always knew it was good, but we just had to get it in front of enough people. At the beginning, we were scrambling to get attention any way we could. We actually ran a Kickstarter campaign, and we raised $25,000 in two weeks. That was the tipping point.

A. Cole: What was the hardest part of the early days?

J. Ranger: You mean besides being too poor to eat anything other than pizza? [Laughs] It was probably getting people to stop thinking I was crazy for sticking with this idea.

A. Cole: Why do you think Flint has gotten so much attention?

J. Ranger: Well, we're certainly not the first company to do what we do, but I like to think we do it differently. A lot of people crowdfund journalism projects, but no one sources the ideas like we do. Our community proposes the ideas and then votes the best ideas to the top.

Now our journalists already have a pool of ideas that are guaranteed to be popular. The journalists propose their own spin and why they are the best person to investigate the projects—now they go back to the community to ask for funding.

In the usual model people come up with their *own* story ideas and they try to convince people to sponsor them. That sometimes works great, but it's a lot harder for one person to be consistently smarter than a million people.

A. Cole: But you really didn't answer my question, why are you getting so much attention?

J. Ranger: I think a big reason is because even just the act of a story being nominated becomes newsworthy in itself. People see that there might be a story on something about their congressman and they get excited. The stories get legs; the proposals in a way become their own news story. Everything builds off each other. I think that's what drives a lot of our popularity.

A. Cole: So, I've heard you recently received some money from eFettro Ventures?

J. Ranger: Yes, very exciting. Most importantly it's helped us bring our founders on full time, Matt, and Sean. We've also used the money to make our website better, hire some amazing talent, and of course get a new office. This space here in New York City is a big upgrade over the table in my apartment.

A. Cole: You forced the recall of a drug from a major pharmaceutical company… from your kitchen table?

J. Ranger: Well, technically it was a studio apartment. So, bedroom table? But yes.

A. Cole: Many believe that Flint Media is just another over-hyped pipe dream pumped full of VC money. What do you say to critics who don't think your business model is sustainable?

J. Ranger: I don't think they get it. The new age of news belongs to subscriptions, and I think we do subscriptions better than anyone. Sure, you can subscribe to the *Economist* or the *Wall Street Journal* and get access to premium content—we do that too. But when you subscribe to Flint you get to do something really cool. You get to choose where the money goes. You distribute your 10 bucks every month wherever you want. You can put it to your favorite story, or your favorite journalist and you can change it whenever you want—no one else lets you do that.

Of course, we get a bunch of one-off donations from people interested in a particular story, but we always have that baseline subscription coming in. I don't think our critics understand how big a deal recurring subscription revenue is.

A. Cole: So, what does a 27-year-old do with his first million?

J. Ranger: Oh, no. No millions yet. The funding just lets me have a salary. We reinvest every dollar that comes in. I guess my stock is worth something but it's all just paper at the moment… I'll tell you one thing though. Once I make my first million, I'm donating half of it to my brother's charity fund. With the other half, I'm buying an Audi R8.

A. Cole: Why an Audi R8?

J. Ranger: [Smiling] Clearly, you've never seen one.

A. Cole: Are you afraid that you might upset the wrong people? We know you were almost expelled from college for writing about the university, but this is the real world.

J. Ranger: It's tough to change the world if you're scared. The day I get death threats from people will be the day that I know I made it.

A. Cole: Tell me about your motivation for this. You often talk about protecting the common man. Some who are close to you say that you're doing this for your lost brother. Do you think that protecting others is a way to make up for your failure to protect him?

J. Ranger: [Silence]

A. Cole: Jack?

J. Ranger: Thanks for coming, Alexandra. I think I better be getting back to work. Flint Media doesn't sleep. [Exits]

CHAPTER 46

Yes, the New York office was certainly beautiful. It was a shared space built for startups and Flint Media occupied a premium spot. It had offices, conference rooms, fancy desks, and an assortment of free snacks stocked on a weekly basis. The team had grown as well. Flint Media had hired a full-time staff to manage the operations, and they were adding journalists to their network at a steady pace. At the center of all this was Jack Ranger, the CEO of Flint Media.

The role of CEO suited Jack. He was learning to love it. He loved the chance to lead and the power to push his vision into reality. He was also learning to love the confidence that came with the position. But all the confidence in the world couldn't prepare him with the right words for what happened one otherwise normal afternoon.

He was leaning over the shoulder of one of the newest recruits, and he looked up at the doors as the elevator pinged and opened. Jack's pen slipped out of his hand as he saw the person he most wanted and least expected to walk through the elevator. With her perfect sundress, suntan, and sunglasses she walked through the glass door to the office.

Molly shrugged her shoulders, smiled, and waved. She lifted her sunglasses so that her blue eyes could take in the surroundings and she giggled. The air of refined innocence had never left her.

Do I hug her? Do I kiss her? Do I shake her hand? What does someone do when the one who got away wanders back into your life? What does the CEO do?

Jack took an early lunch that day.

"I miss you." The first words out of Molly's mouth at the restaurant were the first words out of Jack's as well.

Molly opened the conversation. "I'd heard through the grapevine that you were moving down here to the City. I wanted to see what the great 'Flint Media' was all about."

The two of them talked for a while. Molly was still working at her non-profit. "I love it. I didn't picture myself doing this exactly, but it's great." She paused. "It's a good feeling."

Jack picked at his food. He nodded. "Yeah, it's really something actually to make a difference for people."

"I like what you're doing, Jack. We help people differently, but it's admirable. You're making a difference. I'm glad I've found you again."

"How's your family?"

"Good, good. You know it's all the same. Dad can't quite figure out what I'm doing here in New York and my mom is running her 5K races and non-profit. Christopher is still busy being a 'star.' He's proud of that—or at least my dad is really proud of it."

"Doesn't sound like a lot has changed since school."

"True, but sometimes that's good. We should get together more. I mean, now that you're in the City."

CHAPTER 47

To say that Flint Media was making money wouldn't exactly be true. Not yet anyway. But they were making noise, and lots of it. The money from eFettro Ventures was the spark they needed. eFettro Ventures was the strategic investment arm of its namesake parent, the legendary tech giant eFettro. An investment from them meant credibility and exposure.

Jack stood alongside Sean and Matt. The three of them had been together on a wild ride. New York was still new to them; success was still new to them. It was exhilarating to be a part of something that was bigger than themselves and it was clear Flint was becoming something much bigger than each of them. They were getting nearly a million visitors to their website every month; they had new journalists asking to be a part of the network on an almost daily basis. But, more importantly, they were making waves at a magnitude that they struggled to comprehend.

Jack remembered conversations he had had with Professor Ray and remembered all too well the paranoia that came with being tailed by the police. When you mess with people and their livelihood you'd be naïve to think that they won't strike back. Flint Media had published pieces that ruffled a lot of feathers.

Flint Media was becoming a hub for *the people* to raise concerns. Those topics that were voted to the top, those that were voted on by tens of thousands of people, were a goldmine for the journalists. Of course, many of the proposed topics were bogus, and others were the products of jaded individuals with an axe to grind. But when a topic was fully vetted, and proposed on by a seasoned journalist, there was no better fuel for the slow-burning fire of public opinion.

News stories ran against Flint Media, calling into question its integrity. Politicians bashed the 'severe lack of journalistic morals' and larger companies sued. Jack counted four lawsuits already in the young life of Flint Media. But that was the benefit of eFettro. The legal resources of the multibillion-dollar company gave Flint Media the muscle it needed. As long as eFettro footed the bill, and they were willing to do just that, Jack didn't mind being sued.

The second lawsuit against Flint Media was Jack's personal favorite. After publishing a report showing ties between a Congressman, a major defense contractor, and some questionable contracts funneled their way—the Congressman sued for defamation of character. Jack's response was simple. He put the lawsuit on the front page of the site with a simple message: "Help us help you."

Millions saw it, and many people started proposing new topics. Within a month, Flint journalists had published additional reports exploring questionable ties to lobbyists, a history of ear-marked bills, and a connection between campaign financiers and the congressman's voting record. This got picked up in the mainstream media. The retaliation to a lawsuit itself was a storyline, and the public loved it. Jack took it upon himself to collect a hard copy of all the reports and personally mailed it to the congressman. His note was equally as simple as the message he posted on the website. He wished the congressman well and asked him to please enjoy the recently published companion pieces to their original investigation.

The success of Flint's response was more than just a satisfyingly cold dish of revenge. It was a warning that Flint would not stand to be bullied.

It was an attitude that Jack tried to pass on to all the employees at Flint. Every Tuesday they held a town hall style company meeting. The entire office gathered in the conference room and discussed the week ahead. Attitude was just as important as anything else and Jack wanted to make sure he set the tone every week.

CHAPTER 48

"And so, this is the…"

"Conference room." Jack finished the sentence and regained his tour. Jack walked slowly gesturing to each corner of the office. It wasn't often that he got to play tour guide, and so he rather enjoyed it.

"It's a great space. Better than I imagined. It's cool to see a couple of guys from school making it big."

Jack turned. "Thanks, man."

Today Jack was leading a one-man tour of Flint Media for his old friend Caleb.

Caleb was a year younger than Jack, but when they met in college while working at the school newspaper they had hit it off almost immediately. They bonded over the long hours of working on stories that they knew students would barely read. They both put in big-time hours for small-time impacts. It was the type of work that you would only do if you believed it served some sort of higher purpose. They forged a bond of common suffering in the form of missed parties and early mornings that they wore as a badge of underappreciated honor.

They continued the tour through the final part of the office. "Ok, so this isn't much yet…" They turned a corner and Jack opened a glass door to a half-filled room. The CEO-turned-tour-guide spread open his hand as if he was showing a multimillion-dollar property. "The game room."

The room was unimpressive, presently consisting of a ping pong table, a pop-a-shot basketball game, and Sean. Jack's co-founder sat facing the door with the chair reversed under him. He had his hands and face resting on the back of the chair and he smiled like he was waiting for something.

"Sean, I thought you were in Chicago today?"

"You think I would trust someone else with all the money I just spent? I'm waiting on a delivery."

Jack laughed. He didn't know what that meant. "Sean, you remember Caleb, right?"

He stood and walked over to Caleb. Sean extended his hand and smiled with his confident, magnetic smile. "Of course. Right on, good to see you again."

There was a brief pause. "So, Caleb, I'm assuming Jack is in the middle of recruiting you to work here?"

"Uhhhh."

Caleb looked at Jack's face to get a hint as to what the answer might be. He hadn't put the pieces together quite yet. As far as he knew he was just catching up with an old friend.

The two Flint executives looked at each other. Jack's head bounced up and down slightly with a grin.

Sean picked up where he left off, "Come on, Jack's been talking about you for the last two weeks."

Jack joined. "We need someone who's good, Caleb. The money we got, it lets us do a lot of things. We're expanding, we need more people. We need more *good* people." After the sentence, he nodded at Caleb.

Sean put his hand out in front of him; half clenched his fist and shook it. "Well, we don't have that much money. But we are looking to spend it smartly. We want to spend it on people who have balls. Jack tells me you have big balls."

All three laughed. "So, what do you say?"

Sean put up both arms and slowly spun as if he was taking in the awe of the Sistine Chapel. "Have we not impressed you yet?"

"Right here? Now? I mean, I have another job."

"Caleb, you're telling me that you'd rather live at home and work at that deadbeat paper covering high school sports and pie eating contests, than be a part of this?"

Jack knew why Caleb was hesitant. He'd picked up on Caleb's social insecurities in college.

Jack knew that Caleb wasn't a socialite, but he was a kid who funneled his pent-up social anxiety into fierce reporting. Just as importantly, Jack knew that Caleb was loyal to the few people and causes that he believed in. There was some sort of big and little brother connection between the two, but neither had ever verbalized it.

Caleb hesitated.

Jack evaluated Caleb as he stood making his decision. He was a short guy who wore glasses long before they had become trendy. His glasses, or rather his overall look, could be described in a word as 'meek.' He wasn't a star athlete, he didn't hang out with beautiful people, and he never walked into a room and commanded attention. Although that's not to say that Caleb didn't draw attention when he entered a room. He had a birthmark on the right side of his face that extended from his eye to his jawline.

From their late-night conversations in college, Jack knew that this had been the cause of much adolescent turmoil for Caleb. He confided in Jack that he was the kid who went through high school knowing full well why girls didn't flirt with him. He had told Jack that the birthmark left him perpetually self-conscious.

But Jack knew that for all his outward projections of 'second fiddle-ness,' Caleb wasn't someone who ever quit. He saw things through to their conclusion. Flint needed people like him. "You just can't teach that." Jack had told Sean those very words earlier in the week.

Sean's cell phone rang. He picked it up, muttered some words, hung up, and smiled. "They're here."

Both Caleb and Jack stood confused as men with uniforms worked their way out of the elevator carrying an assortment of awkwardly large boxes. Sean motioned them in.

"What's this?" Jack was looking at Sean, who returned the response with a coy smile. "This is your employee morale budget at work."

"I wasn't aware that was a line item."

Sean's smile widened. "It is now."

The movers made several trips. Three gigantic bean bag chairs came through the door and Sean directed the movers to put them in the far-right corner. A dart board, Nerf guns, and what had to be the box for a foosball table eventually made their way into the room.

"Did you know there is a company whose sole job is pimping out startup offices?"

Jack shook his head, but he couldn't stop the smile. "Series A Leaches Incorporated?"

Caleb was visibility perplexed.

Sean went to one of the unopened boxes. He ripped off the tape and took out a pair of boxing gloves. "I've been waiting for these all day."

He took the gloves and tossed them over to Caleb. "Since you're our guest of honor, I think you should take the first crack at it."

"What?"

"Put them on."

Sean walked over to the corner of the room. There was a large object covered in a sheet. "Jack, you remember when you told me that we needed a way to keep our employees engaged? Remember when you told me that we needed to give everyone a 'greater purpose' to work here?"

He grabbed hold of the top of the sheet.

Jack had seen the object when he first walked into the room and had dismissed it as one of Sean's as-of-yet unannounced schemes. Jack nodded.

"Well, I found the perfect way."

In one stroke, Sean ripped off the sheet to reveal a punching bag. Clanging on its chains and bumping into its support pole, the punching bag swayed back and forth in the corner of the room.

"It just came in this morning."

It was obvious this wasn't a normal punching bag. It had a wig. It was a wig of long yellow locks flowing from the top of the bag which neatly outlined a logo where its face would be. Embroidered on the punching bag in bright bold letters was 'Sallie Mae.'

Sean stood holding the sheet in his right hand.

Sean motioned to Caleb. "Take a crack."

Caleb put the boxing gloves on and walked to the punching bag dangling in the corner.

"What could be better for employee morale than giving someone the chance to punch the biggest bully in America?"

CHAPTER 49

Beer. Music. People.

It was as good a way as any to shake off the last 48 hours. Flint Media had informally rented out the corner of a bar and invited all 27 of its employees for a Wednesday night out on the town. Jack had made an executive decision for a team-bonding event.

It was getting late and the crowd was thinning. Jack supposed his employees didn't want to stay out too late for a variety of reasons. They ranged from the desire to be functional tomorrow morning to a fear of being 'that guy' at the company party. No one liked 'that guy.'

The usual suspects remained. It was the co-founders and a few other others including, to Jack's surprise, Caleb. But he welcomed that. Caleb had wasted no time in joining Flint. He wasn't technically on board yet, but at the first of the month, he would officially be one of the team. On a whim, Jack had texted Caleb to meet up with his future coworkers. He hadn't expected him to join, but he did. He must have been more excited than Jack thought.

They stood in the corner around a pool table.

Caleb raised his drink in a cheer. "Good to be one of the team."

Matt clinked glasses. "Here, here. Happy to have you, man."

"11:30 p.m. on a Wednesday?"

Jack wondered how many other cities in the world would have this many people still at a bar in the late hours of a weeknight.

Sean's surprise was slightly magnified by a twinge of drunkenness. "And it's still buzzin'." He took a sip of his beer. "Man, this city is great."

Matt raised his glass "To New York."

Jack swigged his beer. "New York."

They played a few games of pool. The alcohol was doing its job, the games dragged on. It became more of a game of knocking balls around than it did getting any particular ones into pockets.

"Hey, you idiots ever gonna give up the table?"

Apparently, their sloppy play hadn't gone unnoticed. A group of three guys and two girls were waiting on the fringe of the table.

Jack looked up to observe a tallish kid in a flannel shirt who had just directed his words at Sean.

A clearer minded Sean would have diffused the situation with well-timed words and a disarming smile. This Sean had no such smile.

"Ask me again like that and I'll shove this cue up where it belongs."

Sean's words were accompanied by an elongated gesture.

CEO Jack was summoned up to the surface of Jack's bubbly consciousness. Time to nip this in the bud. Maybe it was the confidence of having negotiated millions of dollars to fund his company, maybe it was the bravado that comes when 26 others call you 'boss', or maybe he just wanted to impress his colleagues—in either case he would be peacemaker.

"Guys, come on. We're just finishing a game here."

Giggles from the girls. A whistle from Matt, and nervous shifting from the two other unnamed pool players in-waiting.

Jack continued. "Give us a few minutes and the table is all yours."

"We're not leaving," Sean spoke up. "I'll stay here all night before I give up this table to this flannel dickhead and his cronies over here." He pointed his cue in the general direction of his verbal assailant.

CEO Jack hadn't solved the issue.

Caleb had been quiet thus far. He laughed. One of the girls laughed, too. Their laughter was an ego blow to the flannelled instigator. There was a tension mounting. The moment teetered for a few brief seconds.

"Who's this guy laughing over here? That little guy in the corner is laughing while his friends do all the talking?" He had turned his words to Caleb.

He continued. "Tell me, Bud, what do you think is so funny?"

Caleb froze.

Jack instinctively spoke up. "Leave him out of this."

The moment the words passed through Jack's mouth the target was set. The stranger saw the nerve and he struck it.

"Why? Is he helpless? Does he say anything?"

Caleb stammered. He just stood there and shifted his gaze, hoping to get a cue from someone about what to do.

Jack spoke again. "I said leave him out of this."

"What's a matter with your little scarred friend over there?"

Why was he pushing the issue? The whole scene didn't make sense. Why here, why now? Some people are just a certain way.

The group's tormentor stood with an obnoxious grin. He clearly got some sort of rise from instigating in front of his friends. Again, he focused his words at Caleb. He put his left hand to his face and traced an outline of Caleb's marked face on his own. "Why don't you speak? That scar makes you ugly, not mute."

Sean was passing the pool cue back and forth in his hands. He was leaning back on the pool table staring at the newcomer. Matt was trying to make himself invisible and clutched his beer while slowly peddling backwards to the wall. Caleb and Jack stood next to each other with the pool table between them and their antagonist.

"Tell me, do you keep this kid around to make you look better when you stand next to him? Because he sure doesn't like talking." There was a brief pause. One of the previously silent friends tossed in a sentence. It was more to his group than directly at anyone. At least one of the girls was clearly uncomfortable with where things had gone.

Tension hung, but no one was willing to push it any further. The newcomers were losing interest and turned back to the general crowd of the barroom floor.

Sean turned back to the pool table. "Your turn."

Jack picked up his cue and proceeded to resume his game. "What a douche."

Matt crept back from the shadows of the corner and drank his beer as if nothing had happened.

Caleb agreed with Jack's sentiment. His body language was different. Caleb lost the smile and had a slight hunch in his shoulders. Instinctively, Jack put a hand on his back in a silent form of reassurance.

There was no doubt that testosterone was elevated, but the four of them returned to what for them was normal conversation.

Matt began. "So, Jack, now that we have that money, can we finally hire some new developers?"

Matt had a habit of complaining about needing more help. Jack didn't mind though. He supposed that was Matt's job. It was no secret that Matt was overworked. He was almost single-handedly keeping the website afloat. Scaling their website to go from ten visitors a day to tens of thousands of visitors a day with flawless performance and top-notch design was not easy. Although, Jack admitted, the complexity of exactly what Matt did was lost on him.

"Hah, talk to Sean. He's the ops guy."

Matt cracked a grin. "Oh, I forgot. You just give interviews and talk to rich people all day."

Jack laughed, too. "It's tough work. Somebody has to be the face of this company and it sure ain't gonna be you."

Sean banked a shot into the side pocket then looked up. He was in a good mood again. "Well, Matt, that depends on our burn rate. Developers are expensive and we don't exactly make money right now."

They went back and forth on this topic. "Well, we'll never make any money when our website crashes and we don't have a decent mobile presence. Do you know how many hours I worked to get us the bare minimum?"

Jack chimed in. "User experience is essential."

Matt and Sean continued without acknowledging his comment.

Jack laughed and elbowed Caleb softly in the ribs to get his attention. It was a way of saying "Watch me mess with these guys." This clash was not unusual. Jack assumed that it was a common theme in any company. Tension isn't necessarily inherent between people who don't understand each other. But tension is unavoidable when competing agendas are involved. Sean and Matt were in a constant tug-of-war.

"So, it's okay to blow money on bean bag chairs, but not on building our product?" Matt's voice was raised.

Jack looked at Matt and offered the devil's advocacy: "It's tough to attract good talent. We need perks."

Jack got a kick out of egging each one on.

Sean wasn't letting this go. "That was one-tenth the cost of hiring a developer and it benefits every employee." He pulled out his phone and his fingers fluttered on the screen. He had opened the calculator app. Sean held up the screen for Matt to see. "289. Do you know what this number means?"

Jack laughed to himself. Sean had a flair for making a statement.

"Do you see this?"

Matt put up his hands in confusion. "Yeah."

"Good." He put the phone back in his pocket. "We have 289 more days until we are dead. We have 289 days until our money runs out."

Matt took another sip of his beer.

Sean continued. "If we don't start making—or raising—more money we are screwed. We'll be begging for coins on the side of the streets wondering why your precious team of seven new developers won't work for IOUs and your mom's chocolate chip cookies."

"Your mom does make great cookies though." Jack winked at Matt. The three of them laughed.

Jack glanced at Caleb. His brow was furrowed, as if he were trying to get up to speed.

The soon-to-be Flint reporter looked at his soon-to-be CEO. "You're giving me a job at a place that doesn't even know if it will be in business next year?"

There were a lot of things that Caleb didn't know yet. Jack wasn't scared about money.

Matt raised his glass.

Sean added, "It's more fun this way."

Jack addressed the group. "Matt is right…all I do is give interviews and talk to rich people. But lucky for you three, I'm actually good at it."

Caleb looked at his glass. It was empty, which prompted a survey of the other three glasses. Everyone was running low on beer. "I'll go grab a pitcher this time."

Caleb walked to the bar. When he was out of earshot Matt spoke. "I like him, good kid."

Sean laughed, "I think I scared him. Maybe next week you can tell him that we've got the next VC round in the bag."

Jack agreed. "Yeah, I think he's opening up a bit. Getting more comfortable with us."

The normal hustle and ambient noise of the bar settled in.

Then there was a disruption. A few gasps and the rattling of something rolling along the ground. They looked over and saw Caleb flailed on the ground, arms outstretched, feeling on the ground for his glasses. A near-empty pitcher was rolling in semi-circles along the barroom floor. There was laughter, too. Jack navigated around the pool table and came closer to Caleb. He saw the same flannel-shirted tormentor from earlier pointing and laughing. His friends were joining in on the fun as well. The ringleader kicked the pitcher towards Caleb. Remnants of the foamy beer splattered on the back of Caleb's jeans. Jack bent down to get Caleb's glasses. Caleb refused help, stood, and brushed himself off. It was a pointless exercise; his shirt was soaked with beer and dotted with whatever dirt and spilled drinks covered the floor.

He muttered so only Jack could hear. "That douche tripped me."

Jack knew who he meant. This time the girls he was with were laughing, too. The bar was the perfect amount of busy to maximize embarrassment. It was slow enough to the point where everyone could notice Caleb's fall, but it was still busy enough to ensure that a snickering crowd surrounded Caleb.

"Watch where you're going."

Jack looked up and found the unsurprising origin of the remark. He raised his voice. Jack's language was an outburst that was more of an instinctual snap than a thought-out response.

He stepped up and Jack moved closer. The smallish crowd converged; they could sense the sudden escalation. Would there be a fight? Out of the side of his vision Caleb noticed a bouncer inching closer trying to see if his services would be called for.

Jack stood face-to-face with the flannel-wearing tripper. He was breathing heavily and tensing his muscles. The thought of Caleb crawling on the floor looking for his glasses boiled Jack's blood. They were in each other's faces. Several looks were exchanged but few words. "Do you have a problem?" Jack could feel warm breath hit his face.

The kid sized Jack up. "You've got a scar on you, too. Good thing it's on your hand and not on your face like your little buddy."

The crowd was rising with anticipation. But Jack was stepping away and they could feel that whatever was coming next was anti-climactic.

Caleb was in the background. "I'm just gonna go home."

Jack turned and walked with Caleb. By now Sean and Matt had moved closer to see what was happening. Jack looked up at the two of them. "Let's get going, guys." They began walking to the door.

"Walk away, pussy. Have fun leaving with your friends."

These were closing words that were meant to end an event that societal rules dictated must be resolved peacefully.

As he walked to the exit, Jack looked at his hand. He felt the scar with his fingertips. He felt the pain of walking away through his scar and within his body. He had walked away before. The raised scar tissue reminded him every day of what he had walked away from. Walking away left him with pain and nothing to show for it. Walking away let things stay exactly the way they were.

Sean and Matt walked out of the bar. Jack started to follow them, but stopped.

Caleb paused when he noticed Jack wasn't following. He looked back to see Jack standing still, as if he was thinking. No one seemed to notice. The crowd had dispersed, and the ambient noise returned. Laughter, jokes, loud voices, and music. The heat of the last few minutes had vanished.

"Hey, man, hold up." The words from Jack's voice were oddly high pitched. He walked back towards the stranger. Jack waved to get the stranger's attention.

Jack's tone was conversational. "Look... sorry about that. I think we got off on the wrong foot."

The stranger and his friends looked confused as an affable Jack approached them and extended his hand for a shake. The stranger turned and grinned. He had won, but the olive branch was icing on the cake.

Jack began his sentence, "I just wanted to say..."

The smirking flannel-wearer instinctually reached out his hand to meet Jack's.

Jack couldn't help but muse on the arrogance of the ignorant.

With a sarcastic smile, Jack used his left hand to grab the stranger's right arm above the elbow. He swiftly pulled him forward. In the same motion, he swung his fist and connected with the bridge of the target's nose.

The stranger's hands went to cover his newly bloodied nose. As they did, Jack grabbed him, clinching with his arm around the stranger's shoulder and neck. He delivered two knees to his stomach in quick succession. As the stranger doubled over, Jack twisted his clinched hands and rolled the stranger to the ground.

The paper-millionaire CEO of Flint Media placed his foot on the neck of the stranger and pushed his face into the sticky floor.

Jack glanced up. His breathing was primal.

It seemed that the stranger's friends understood not to move closer. Beyond the group, there was an audience looking nervously onwards. The spectacle had become center stage and the spotlight focused on the twitching right foot of Jack Ranger.

Jack looked down to observe the pool of blood growing on the floor.

"I just wanted to say, that you're a prick."

He pushed down slightly with his right foot before removing it from the stranger's neck.

Two bouncers were converging on Jack. He held both arms in the air as if to announce to the crowd and the bouncers that his business was finished. He began to walk away. But before he could he was grabbed by both bouncers. Jack didn't resist as he was thrown against the wall, smashing the back of his head on wooden paneling.

The bouncers, each grabbing Jack's arms, dragged Jack to the exit doorway. They shoved him to the exit and made some indecipherable comments as Jack watched the door close behind him.

Jack clutched his head and then shook out his right hand as he tried to orient himself. Matt and Sean were already near the street waiting for a ride home. Caleb stood by the exit. The look on his face suggested that he knew exactly what had just happened.

To Jack, it was clear that Caleb had seen everything.

Caleb opened his mouth to speak. "Thank y…"

Jack raised his hand to cut him off. The two made eye contact and Jack gave a firm nod of his head. Caleb returned the gesture.

They understood each other. Words were unnecessary.

Jack and Caleb walked over to Matt and Sean. The two were killing time with small talk. Oblivious and bored, they complained about being hungover at work tomorrow and wondered when it got so cold outside.

Sean asked Jack, "What took you so long, man?" But he was busy calling an Uber on his phone. He didn't care about the answer to his question.

Jack was straightening out his shirt and responded without looking up. "One of us had to close out the tab."

CHAPTER 50

"Dinner was good."

The two walked up the stoop towards Jack's apartment. City living in New York was much different than his old apartment on the outskirts of Boston. Among the differences, Jack now had a set of stairs at which he could linger awkwardly before heading into his apartment.

To say that Jack was falling back in love with Molly wasn't quite right. He wasn't sure if he ever stopped loving her. Tonight, they had laughed. Her laugh hadn't changed; it was soft, gentle, and deliciously inviting.

"Yeah, I liked that place. We'll have to do it… What's this?"

Jack was working through his keys with Molly behind his right shoulder when he saw the letter. It was wedged in the door in such a way designed for maximum visibility.

Molly watched in curiosity as Jack opened the letter. She watched his eyes scan the letter from top to bottom, and she watched his hand shake ever so slightly. She watched as Jack read and reread the letter. Time passed and Jack didn't speak. They were still standing outside.

"What does it say?"

No words. Jack passed the paper to her hand.

The page held a neatly typed letter. It was short and to the point. No words were wasted in this one-sided exchange of words. It was a threat.

Molly read the letter and handed it back to Jack, again without words.

The rest of the night was a forced charade as the two of them tried to pretend that the letter didn't matter. But of course, that's all that mattered.

"What will you do?" Finally, Molly brought it up.

The problem was that Jack didn't know. It was just a piece of paper, but behind it was a real person—or people—that didn't like what Jack was doing. Molly sat on the couch in Jack's apartment. Jack laid his head on her chest. He stared at the ceiling and then closed his eyes.

Jack hadn't decided if he thought he was in danger or not. But the directness of the note, something about it, got to him. "I think it's starting."

He moved both hands to his face and exhaled. Jack knew Flint Media would create enemies; he hadn't forgotten about his case with Anton. Truth be told, he was scared what Molly would think more than anything else. She couldn't be with him—Jack Ranger, a dead man walking. It wasn't fair to bring her into his life, not like this.

"I can't ask you to stay; I know that."

"What do you mean Jack?" Her hands stroked his head.

"With me. I can't ask you to stay. Not when I'm like this. This isn't the last threat I'll get. It's not even the biggest threat I see right now. Who knows how Flint will do. We're bleeding cash, getting sued left and right… what if the other guys get death threats? What if we fold?"

Jack lowered his voice. "If I'm not dead, I'll be broke. I can't ask you to be with me."

Molly's necklace fell against his cheek. It distracted him from the tension and fear, but he wasn't sure that was a good idea. Maybe he needed to be on edge. Maybe he needed to be more guarded.

"I didn't come running back to you when I saw you had a fancy new office. I didn't show up because I heard you got money from some flashy company. I came back because I missed you. You've grown up, Jack. I can see it. Flint's not about you, it's about something bigger."

She spoke softly, still running her hands through Jack's hair. "I don't plan to go anywhere."

Jack sat up and looked at her. She meant it. "It's not going to get easier."

The two paused and shifted their focus for a moment.

Molly leaned against Jack's stomach.

He winced.

She frowned.

Molly's hands lifted Jack's shirt. She stopped as her hands traced two fresh bruises on his stomach. "What's this from? It looks like you got in a fight."

Jack pulled his shirt down. "I guess I bruise easily." He took her left hand in both of his. "I'm glad we're here together."

Molly smiled, "I love you."

With the threat hanging over him, her words seemed so terribly out of place. It was difficult to think about or even feel love. The air of Jack's future was thick and hard to breathe, filled with uncertain success and certain pain.

And yet amidst this all, the words remained. They were a promise as much as anything else.

Jack's mind raced as he played through the thousands of different futures that were possible to him at this moment. Death, fame, fortune, humiliation, pain, vindication, greatness, and wasted potential.

Jack put his head back on her chest and closed his eyes. He lay there listening. He lay there listening to her heart beat its steady rhythmic throb. Her chest rose and fell with each breath, and Jack placed his hand on his chest. He lay there listening to her heart and timing the beat of his own—desperately hoping that the pulse in his chest would match that of the women he loved.

CHAPTER 51

Three days later was a Thursday and it became a day that Flint Media fundamentally changed. Jack called an unexpected company meeting. He gathered everyone in the main bullpen.

They had grown fast, and the 27-year-old CEO was proud of what they were building together. Jack stood on a chair in front of a congregation of Flint Media employees.

"Some of you may have noticed the new pictures hanging behind me on the wall." Jack turned and made a sweeping hand motion to the wall behind him, newly filled with three small portraits.

"I felt like we needed a little inspiration."

"Behind me are three greats, each from a different generation. Ed Murrow, Bob Woodward, and Michael Hastings. If you don't know them—you should. These men risked their lives and reputations to push the world forward. These men have toppled congressman, presidents, and army generals. All three of them are legends. Two of these men are now dead, and only one of them died of natural causes."

Jack paused. His employees were standing in the hallway looking at him. Jack met Sean's eyes from the small group in front of him. Sean was nodding. There was silence in the audience. Jack could feel them hanging on his words.

He was at home up here in front of his people. This was where Jack knew he was meant to be.

Still standing on the chair in front of the Flint Media staff, Jack pulled out an envelope from his pocket and removed a single piece of paper. Jack read the letter that he had shown Molly only a few days before.

Mr. Ranger.

Your ambitions are noble but do not underestimate the trouble that the publication of your newest story will cause us. We trust that you know to which story we are referring.

We are giving you the opportunity to stop publication. If you do, no harm will come your way. If you do not, we will ensure that you will wish that you had.

Mr. Ranger, there are two motivations in this world: fear and money. As you consider our offer, please know that next time we will not provide you with a choice.

Everyone in the room was quiet. The reality of the letter was becoming clear. Some suspected the story that was in question. A proposed topic was making its rounds on Flint's homepage and gaining support to the point where it was getting noticed in other mainstream news outlets. It was about the persistence of organized crime in certain American cities.

Jack spoke again. He held the paper in his right hand up for everyone to see. "Ladies and gentleman this is a threat. But I have news for Mr. 'will not provide you with a choice'—we are not going anywhere and we will not be intimidated."

Jack raised his voice, "Effective immediately, whichever journalist takes up this story will have the option to publish under my name."

Above the portraits was a quote, now painted on the wall. Jack began speaking again pointing at the quote. "This is our mantra; this is why we do what we do. Flint Media will live and die by the people in this room. We will not fail if we remember why we are here."

Jack stopped before repeating the quote that everyone had been staring at. *"Sunlight is the best disinfectant."*

With his left hand, Jack reached into his pocket and pulled out the same lighter he had used so long ago. He held the flame to the letter until it caught. The first dancing fits of fire flowed upwards. For a brief moment, everyone stared as Jack held up the burning letter. He let go and watched it fall, half consumed by flames, to the floor. Jack stepped down from his chair and walked away. The rest stood watching the paper turn to smoke.

CHAPTER 52

Months passed. The organized crime story had been a success. There were no more cryptic notes aimed at Jack's personal well-being and the general media had held the story up as a supreme act of journalism. Things were going well for Flint. Everything was going well except for the fact that they didn't make enough money to pay their bills.

187 days.

That was Sean's official count until cash flow became a big problem. And by big problem, Sean meant the sort of problem where you couldn't make payroll, and you asked your staff to accept IOUs instead of paychecks. Flint Media was burning money. Hiring developers, hiring reporters, and just about everything else cost money; a lot of money.

Sean and Jack had discussed their options a number of times. The money that they thought they would raise wasn't as 'locked down' as they had hoped. Ramping up the profit-making engine was always a possibility. It was possible to turn Flint profitable, but it would come at the cost of their long-term future. They would have to slash the workforce and close their most interesting projects. Yes, they could make profits this year, but it would mean they would be irrelevant in two years. Profitable, but irrelevant was not an option. They could take out loans, but the interest rates for cash-bleeding internet companies was not cheap.

As a first response to the imminent crisis, Sean and Jack began making the rounds to the various hubs of startup capital across the states. Together they crisscrossed the country from California to New York, Massachusetts, and Chicago. They made their pitches, sold their dream, and hoped it would all work out.

The offices of the venture capitalists were far less opulent than Jack had anticipated. When he first started making the rounds with investors, he was surprised by the non-descript buildings, nice-but-not flashy offices, and the relatively standard boardrooms that they contained.

Jack and Sean strolled into one such office today. The meeting began just like any other. They shook hands, exchanged cards, and made small-talk. When Flint Media was still a nobody these meetings took on a very different vibe. Pitching a VC was a bit like playing basketball; you must be mindful of the shot clock. In the early days, they were lucky if they got 10 minutes—if they even got a meeting at all. But now, Flint Media was somewhat of a known commodity. Meetings are a lot easier to get when you are a household name—even if you are a household name that doesn't make any money.

The presentation began. It was a two-man pitch-team. Jack led off and spelled out the vision. Sean followed with the numbers: readership, influence, growth, and of course money. Jack swooped in and drove the message home.

"I like your team. I'm a fan of what you've done."

A younger man in jeans and a blazer sat tapping his hands on the desk. He was mulling over his reaction.

"There's a chemistry with you two. I like that."

Sean and Jack nodded.

Another voice, this time from a woman in a checkered blouse. "The growth is impressive. What's your hiring plan look like in the next six months?"

The discourse continued. The meetings were friendlier now, but friendly or not, this type of crowd didn't waste time with easy questions.

"Honestly, this would drive me crazy. There's no accountability. You say a story will take two months to complete and then it doesn't see the light of day for half a year. It doesn't seem like you're very good at managing your team."

Sean started to answer, but Jack put his hand on Sean's shoulder and answered first.

"I get the frustration. It's a tricky balance, but investigative work isn't like manufacturing. You don't know exactly how the story will end up. Schedules are good, but if you uncover something unexpected and meaningful you need to explore it."

There was a pause as Jack searched for additional words.

"Look, Sean runs a tight ship on the ops side. Just ask anyone. Ask eFettro or check our books. It's like clockwork. But we can't run our investigative side like that. If you want great results you need to run it more like an R&D team. You need to pay smart people to explore and make mistakes. We give our journalists the reign to do the best job possible, and sometimes that means pushing out deadlines."

There was soft laughter. The VCs had heard the 'special snowflake' argument before. It was standard practice for companies to coddle their 'creative geniuses.' Whether they are software engineers, creative designers, or in this case journalists, companies bent over backwards to keep those employees happy. But there was a balance that needed to be struck. Creativity must coincide with profits at some point.

The woman's laugh was like a parent reflecting on the naiveté of a child.

A follow-up question. "So, tell me exactly what you need the money for."

Sean took this question.

"To grow our subscriber base and to publish content more consistently." He continued, "Right now, to keep costs down we have a core of full-time journalists that act as project leads and a pool of freelance journalists. We flex up and down, staffing each project with as many freelancers as the project lead needs. But to grow our subscription base, we need more content more often. The only way to do this is to bring on more full-time journalists and support staff, like developers, to scale the platform."

A third put his pen down on the table. He had been taking notes. "It's not for me guys. Sorry."

The man in the jeans and blazer shook his head before asking another question.

"I didn't see it in the deck. What's your board structure right now? I assume eFettro has a seat?"

Jack responded. "It's simple still. Just three so far. eFettro has one, seat and we have one seat for each of the founders."

Jack motioned between himself and Sean.

"Got it. Small is good. If we came on we would need a seat, too. Obviously."

Sean gave a nod. "Of course."

The investor continued. "We'd probably push for an outside independent fifth director as well. You know… as a tiebreaker."

Sean was visibly interested. "Tiebreakers are good. It sounds like we might be moving towards something?"

The investor adjusted his blazer. "I'm not sure. It's interesting, but I just don't like the smell of it. Why isn't eFettro back in this deal?"

Sean rebutted, "We haven't gone back to them because…"

The man waved his hand and interrupted Sean. "It's cool. I get it. They're bullies. I don't want to be wrapped into another cap table with them anyways. Once is enough for me. How much of your soul did they take in exchange for the money?"

Jack stepped up. "None, it's a good deal."

"I smell a little desperation. Man, you're either in bad shape, or they really screwed you over on the deal."

Jack tried to continue but was caught off-guard by the comment.

The first investor chimed in. "Just don't drop the soap… I mean ball… they'll get ya."

There was light-hearted laughing from those at the table who possessed the money. Jack spoke and addressed the third partner in the room. "Surely, you can appreciate what we're doing here."

There was a pause as the final partner leaned back in his chair. He was thinking.

"Mr. Ranger. Mr. Cosatiri. I admire what you're doing. I really do. But the numbers just don't add up for me. If companies could run on idealism, then I would invest. I'd probably dump the entire fund into Flint Media if that was the case. But idealism doesn't fix cash flow."

The meeting started and ended just like all the other ones before it. It was a long flight back to New York City.

CHAPTER 53

There were 176 days of funding left in the Flint Media bank account.

"Rachel, I'm glad that you could fly out here on such short notice."

Fresh from the airport, Rachel Warner walked into the Flint Media conference room trailing a small rolling suitcase behind her.

The usual pleasantries ensued. At the conference table were the four largest shareholders of Flint Media. Jack, Sean, Matt, and Rachel as the eFettro proxy.

"How are things at eFettro HQ?"

Rachel sipped water from her cup and smiled. She had a smile that was as infectious as it was devious.

In taking the investment from eFettro Ventures, Flint Media agreed to surrender both equity and a board seat. The board seat was currently occupied by Rachel. Jack liked Rachel. Perhaps, in a different context, they would be friends. She was personable, down to earth, and tactical—just like her business.

When she was younger, Rachel had climbed the ladder quickly at eFettro. Eventually, she was tapped to nurture its venture capital arm from its infancy and turn it into the juggernaut that it was today.

"So, to what do I owe the pleasure of changing my flight so that I have a stopover in New York City?"

Matt looked over to Sean. He was nervous.

Jack nodded. It was a risk they had discussed amongst each other. The headlines in the press would be great fanfare. The Flint Media employees would cheer. *"Flint Media raises another X million dollars from tech giant eFettro."* But the founders knew the risk. Every dollar they took came with a string attached.

Rachel was nice enough. eFettro was keen on Flint Media.

Sean took the baton first. "We were holding out as long as we could, but we're going to need a new capital infusion."

Rachel's eyebrows moved upwards in surprise. "Oh really?"

Jack followed up, "Doing what we're trying to do is difficult. Journalism is old. You can't reinvent it overnight."

Rachel continued the silent thoughts in her head. Then she spoke. "You know I can't do that, right?"

There was a pause in the room. No one was certain about the truth of that statement. It seemed like an easy out. Sean tried to make a rational appeal. "It's really just about bridging our cash flow gap. We're not constrained by opportunity; it's just resources at this point."

"How much do you need?"

Both of Sean's hands were palms up on the table. "$30 million."

"When do you need it by?"

Awkward silence. Jack bit his lower lip and shrugged his shoulders. Sean looked at Jack, Matt fidgeted. It was like a toddler who sheepishly told his mom that he'd broken the rules. No words, just facial expressions.

Rachel looked surprised. "It's that bad?"

Sean just nodded. There was reluctance in Rachel's body language.

It was Jack's turn.

Jack thought back to the first time he had met Rachel. She had taken a leap of faith with Jack to bet on Flint Media and together they'd been on a wild ride. Rachel had been a great advisor along the way, she helped make partnerships, and she opened the right doors.

"Look, Rachel, what we're trying to do takes time. This little cash flow thing… you can make it go away with the snap of a finger. It will let us make Flint Media the established player it deserves to be. We're going to do for journalism what Airbnb did for travel and what Netflix did for movie lovers. The best journalists in the world aren't going go to work for *The New York Times*. Rachel, they're going to work for us."

She wasn't interested. Jack could see that. But he couldn't let her walk out the door. Flint Media needed this too badly.

Jack stared across the table and looked at her directly in the eye. "Rachel, please." His tone was low, he was serious and pleading. "Don't let us lose what we've done. Don't let everything we've done fizzle out."

There was a sigh. She leaned back in her seat. Jack moved his hands to his face. The emotional tightrope is an exhausting line to walk.

"Okay. We can work something out, but it's not going to be cheap. Jack, if you need this money so badly you're going to need to really show us something."

There was a pause in her words before continuing. "When eFettro doubles down, we don't lose. We don't want lifestyle businesses. We need 15x or 20x returns. Do you know what I mean?"

Jack wasn't sure what she meant.

"We'll make you a new deal but it's going to be contingent on you showing me a better plan. This company needs to make twice the noise, twice as fast, and it needs to start making money."

"Know this, Jack. If you take this deal I'm going to push you. eFettro is going to push you. You are going to have to grow up fast. Flint Media isn't an idea anymore. It's a business, and right now, it's not a very good business."

This was a challenge. But he didn't have much of a choice in whether he could accept or deny it.

Jack exhaled and pushed his chair back. He stood up. "Thank you." The words finished his long out breath.

Sean took the cue and stood as well. He extended his hand to shake Rachel's.

As Rachel stood, she pulled out her phone to check the time. "Guys, look. I'm going to send you some new terms tonight. I don't need an answer today, but this money won't sit around past the end of the week."

Sean answered. "Okay, we'll let you know our thoughts, and then we can finalize."

Rachel smiled. "Your thoughts? No, no. There won't be any negotiating this time around."

Jack's ears perked up. He looked at Rachel. It was clear that she knew what he was thinking. The price was going to be steep.

"In the meantime, Jack, I'd suggest that you and your team think of ways to blow this thing out of the water and start breaking some bigger stories."

CHAPTER 54

It was like the good old days. Jack and Sean both sat with glasses in their hands, leaning back, and talking about the future. Only this time around the chairs were replaced by bean bags, and the trusted surroundings of the college apartment were substituted for empty office space. It was late at Flint Media. It was dark outside, but the game room was unnervingly bright, flooded by the artificial fluorescence that only exists in the American office. A bottle of Jack Daniels was on the floor. It was mostly untouched; the CEO needed his wits about him tonight.

It seemed like every important decision between the two of them happened in a similar manner. Why break tradition?

Sean exhaled and leaned his neck back as if breathing towards the sky. His collared shirt was unbuttoned, his sleeves were rolled up, his hair was ruffled. Today had been a long day.

"That deal is rough."

There was an affirmative sound from Jack. The details of what eFettro proposed were none too pretty. Rachel made good on her promise. The good news was that there was an additional $30 million in it for Flint Media. But the price was steep. Every dollar came with a contingency. The $30 million came at the price of another 15% of the company and an additional board seat. They made their displeasure known. They called, and they tried to negotiate the price down. But there was no room. eFettro would not budge. Rachel was a woman of her word.

Jack looked over at Sean. "Does it say who the new director is?"

Sean thumbed through the papers he had printed out and stopped on a page with a photograph and biography.

"Some guy named Dean Allen. Never heard of him. Apparently, he's a big deal according to his bio."

Jack forced a laugh. "I'm sure he's smart."

Jack kicked a soccer ball that had rolled near his feet. "So, do we take it?"

The ball bounced off the far wall and dribbled into the hallway.

Sean sipped his drink. "We don't have much of a choice."

Sean was right. They didn't have much of a choice. How many pitches had they done? Too many to count. Jack swirled the amber liquid in his glass and watched it splash around the edges.

There was a certain inevitable truth before them. Sitting here in their glorified arcade only delayed what had to be done. "I started this so we didn't have to answer to anyone, and here we are."

"You can't take dollars from the man and expect to run your own show."

Jack looked at his friend. He raised his glass, and they both took a swig. "Here's to that."

But Jack wasn't ready to give up just yet. There was still liquid in his glass, and he would postpone as long as he could.

"Hey man, even Zuckerberg owns less than 30% of Facebook." Sean was right, as usual.

Something else was troubling Jack too.

It was about control. Not control of the company. That's not why Jack was in this business. It was about control of something deeper. Jack took the last drink from his glass. Ceding control of his future was not an action that he took lightly. He had put it off as long as he could, but he knew the time was now.

"Hey, a smaller percentage of a bigger pie is usually a good thing, right?"

Jack didn't enjoy that logic. It wasn't about the size of the slice. It was more about the dilution of his dream.

"I'm never doing this again." He'd made up his mind. eFettro was a great jumpstart for Flint Media, and it would soon become a necessary bridge, but he was never cutting anyone in on a deal like this again.

"We need to think bigger. We need to get to the point where we never take money…ever."

Sean was, at this point, still lying back in the beanbag chair. His arms were hanging over the sides as if he were making the world's laziest snow angel. "Well, Mr. Bigshot. How do you propose we do that?"

Jack sat up and pulled his phone from out of his pocket. He knew he would be making two phone calls tonight. He dialed Rachel. It was late, but she picked up. Jack couldn't help but think that she was expecting the call.

Jack barely spoke.

Rachel sounded confident. "So, you're in. Great. I'll have my team draft up the paperwork."

He hung up the phone and sat quietly for a moment.

Sean rotated his body to look at his co-founder. Jack looked over at him and took a prolonged breath before looking down at his phone and scrolling to the top of his contact list. He initiated the call and listened to the rings until a familiar voice answered.

"Jack?"

"Hi, Anton."

CHAPTER 55

The two men shook hands. It was the first-time Anton had been to the Flint Media office.

Jack looked at his old boss. How long had it been? Two years?

For his part, Anton looked more or less the same. He looked around the office with bemused satisfaction. "So, this is what my understudy left me to build?" He put out his hands and clapped them together. How could his smile be so mischievous?

Jack gave him the tour of the office. He walked him to the writer's bullpen, the conference rooms, the kitchen, and the game room. "You millennials do it differently."

Jack missed the banter. "When we were designing this, I had one fundamental principle. Think of whatever the *Tribune* would do, and then do the opposite."

Anton lingered in the writer's bullpen. "There's an energy here. I can feel it."

He took a deep breath through his nose as if to take in as much of the office as he could.

"Can you feel that, Jack?"

Jack nodded.

"That's what the freedom of press feels like." Anton closed his eyes. "This is new, but you're too young to know that this is old." He held up his finger and bobbed his head like he was listening to a song. He was moved by the beat. Anton took his pointed finger and curled it into a fist. He brought it to his chest and tapped it twice.

"This is what it feels like when you have to power to change things."

Jack's former boss was smiling ear to ear. He reached out and hit Jack on the back of his shoulders.

Jack walked into the main conference room. "Come on in and grab a seat."

Jack sat down and watched Anton. Memories of pain, torture, intrigue, and unfinished promises walked with a slight limp through the threshold of the door. Jack had invited him in.

Anton circled around the table and sat opposite of Jack.

"How have you been?"

"I've been keeping myself busy." Anton had kept himself very busy. Consulting, writing, private investigations—he was a man of many connections and many talents.

Jack had a flashback to the countless hours he spent in the passenger seat of Anton's car as they talked through the investigation. He could taste the bile in his mouth as he thought back to dry-heaving at the sight of Ronnie's dead body. He could see the vivid crystalline white of the bags that showed up at his door with Samuel. The scar on his hand burned.

Anton leaned back and put his feet on the table. "So why am I here, Jack?"

There was a pause as Jack put his thoughts into words. He explained the situation at Flint Media. The success and the troubles. "We need to break this thing wide open, and I need the best people in the world to help me do it."

Jack pointed across the table at Anton. "That story was huge. Murder, drugs, and corruption. Nothing we could do would be a bigger story than that."

Anton laughed. "It still is huge."

Jack hadn't forgotten the laugh. Called for, or uncalled for, the laugh was always the same. Anton's worldview was different than anyone else's out there. But nevertheless, he was the ticket. He was the gimpy knight in shining armor who had just so happened to choose a pen as his jousting weapon. Sitting with his legs up on the conference room table was the man Jack needed to help fulfill his dream.

Jack got more serious. He leaned in over the table. "Anton, I need you to help me take Flint Media to the next level."

Anton waved his hand. "Jack, I get it. This is about an excuse to finally get back at the people who did this to you." Anton twirled his right hand in the air.

This was about Flint. This was about getting out from under the corporate thumb; this was about building something that could give the world what it needed.

"It's about more than that."

"Sure, Jack."

And then Anton laughed again. He stood up and slapped the table. He was energized. "Let's get started."

CHAPTER 56

Bright natural light made its way into the fourth floor of the office building that housed Flint Media. Rays of the light slanted across the conference room table. Jack and the 15 others who were part of the core journalism team sat at the table. It was early in the workday and coffee cups still steamed with their morning warmth. This morning was the day that Jack was selling a new story to Flint Media.

"10x. That's our mandate. I want each of you to be thinking about how we make Flint Media 10 times what it is right now."

Enthusiastic nods affirmed his employees' willingness to follow their CEO.

"We talk a big game, but what have we done? Sure, we've exposed some little scandals, and yes, we've set a few things right, but think of what else is out there."

He paused. "Bigger. Bigger stories, bigger enemies, bigger impacts."

It was an interesting pep rally. There were a handful of soft objections and two questions about what the company's strategy would be. Jack needed his company to feel the vision. Bringing back this story wasn't something that he took lightly.

Prior to this meeting, Jack had made sure to clear the idea with Sean. Jack was uncertain how Sean would react when he learned that Jack had never told him about the bulk of his work with Anton at the *Tribune*. But, it turned out that getting Sean on board was easy. The look on his face when Jack told him about the dead body he found in a car was proof enough that Sean was in.

Jack gestured across the table. "It starts with Anton."

Until yesterday, there were 14 members of Flint Media's core journalist team. Now, with Anton, there were 15. Anton stood and leaned over to hit the power switch on the projector that was sitting on the middle of the conference room table. He only had one slide to show for this presentation. It was a slide which contained no words. On the screen in front of everyone was a giant portrait of the Governor of Massachusetts. Anton looked around the room.

"Can anyone tell me who this man is?"

Hands were held loosely in the air.

"This is the man who has caused me and Jack over here—" Anton nodded in the direction of Jack. "A whole lot of trouble."

Anton bent down to pick up a glass of water and take a sip before continuing.

"This is not a good man."

Anton continued. "Corruption, drugs, murder. This is the story that you dream of getting."

There was the start of a buzz. Anton was mostly an unknown to the group within the conference room. Jack suspected that some of his team would be skeptical of an outsider like Anton, but right now Anton was commanding a presence.

"I have records of known drug traffickers being brought in by the police and released after a day. I also have recordings of the chief of police giving orders that make him directly complicit in the cover-ups of murders and the distribution of hush money."

These were dark words for a sunny room. Anton's showmanship was alive and well. He knew where to pause, when to raise his voice, and when to look into the audience's eyes.

"And I have seen, with my own two eyes, a murdered man whose assassination was not only scrubbed from police records but which was almost certainly meant for me as well."

Murmurs.

Anton looked up. "If you don't believe me ask your CEO. He was there, too. Go ahead. Ask Jack what it's like to see a man slumped over his steering wheel with three bullet holes in him. Or ask him what it feels like to doubt that you would still be alive if you had been somewhere 10 minutes earlier."

The group turned to Jack looking for a confirmation. He acknowledged without words, just moving his upper body back and forth. Now Anton reached into a briefcase and pulled out a collection of papers and files. He passed them around the room.

"Case files, police logs, transcripts from recordings. Merry Christmas, Flint Media, here is your jackpot."

A shuffling of papers and some mild comments followed. One of the reporters spoke up. "What's this have to do with the governor?"

Anton smiled. "What you have before you is a start. But here's where it gets interesting. This isn't some small drug running operation. I'm talking about the systematic distribution of cocaine throughout New England and the profits it makes. Millions of dollars, but the bulk of that money isn't going to the police force. The police are getting some of it, but that is just "grease the wheels" money. The real money is going to the Democratic Party. Elections and campaigns are all being funded with this money. The governor and state legislators are fueling campaigns with dirty money."

The room broke out in comments and questions.

"How do you know this?"

"Do you have a source in the police who can verify this?"

"Even if they could pull this off, how would they get the money clean enough for campaign funding?"

If Jack had been hearing this for the first time he would have felt similarly to each of his employees in the room. But this was not the first time he had heard the news. Last night Anton broke down the details of what he'd been up to during his absence from the *Tribune*. Anton laid out the flow of illicit money from the bottom to the top. Everyone's hands were dirty.

"This is where I need your help." Anton panned the room. "They are laundering money at some point between the drugs and the political donations. I have rumors and circumstantial evidence, but I need hard proof. Half the Massachusetts Democratic Party is getting donations from a single group. The 'American Progress' PAC."

The elder reporter held up his hand to emphasize the importance. "This is the key. Crack this, and we'll have the trail for dirty money."

Jack asked the question that he hoped was on most of the reporters' minds. Perhaps they would have asked it, or perhaps Jack was just too anxious to advance the conversation. "Since when is a super PAC funding campaigns unusual? That's what they do."

"Perhaps. But I'd be willing to bet that most super PACs aren't run by ghosts. As near as I can tell, John Durston, the chairman of American Progress, is a ghost. For the figurehead of an institution that controls the flow of millions of dollars, John Durston keeps a remarkably low profile. You can Google him, you can find him on LinkedIn, but he doesn't have a birth certificate, a house, a car, or even a lover."

Anton's face broke into a coy smile. "Trust me, I checked."

He resumed, "My money says that he is a fictitious figurehead that serves a useful purpose. Can anyone guess what that purpose might be?" He appealed to the Flint team.

One of the reporters offered up her answer. "To move money around."

Anton smacked his hand on the table. "Yes. A puppet with strings that makes it easy to funnel 'donations' wherever the true man behind the curtain wants."

Anton reached for another piece of paper. He pulled it out and started reading off names. "This is a list of recent people and institutions that have benefited from American Progress's generosity in the last calendar year. There's one institution that I found particularly interesting to be on this list. It's a company that Jack and I both know well."

Jack finished the thought. "The *Tribune*."

This point settled in and the team in the conference room digested the implications.

Sips of coffee.

Ruffled papers.

A question from the table. "So, what do we do?"

Jack posed his answer. "We start with what we have. There is enough to make noise and stir the pot. And while we do that, we dig. We dig until we can link the governor definitively to the drug ring he's created. We dig until no one can deny the truth that Flint Media exposes to the world."

Jack's voice was rising. "This is how we 10x Flint Media, by bringing down the untouchables—by doing what no other news outlet on the planet can do."

There was one more question directed at Anton. "If you've got so much, why didn't you publish before?"

Anton nodded, acknowledging a fair point. "I *did* try to publish this before." He extended his arms as if trying to embrace the room. "But here, with you, we have a much more interesting mountaintop to shout from."

CHAPTER 57

Selling the story to the team at Flint was easy. Selling the story to Molly was more difficult. The two of them sat across the table from each other. The candle on the table shifted reflections on their wine glasses.

Molly was more cautious. "I don't know."

"Listen," Jack pleaded, "We can do something great."

"Haven't you already?"

"Not like this. This is bigger. *The Tribune* fired me for this story. This story is about more than corruption and drugs. It's a haymaker to old media."

This point appeared to be interesting to Molly.

"The *Tribune* is propped up by the pocketbooks of certain groups. There are stories that they just *can't* run. But *WE* can. We will run this story for the people. It will be funded by the people."

Jack looked across the table at Molly. Why wasn't she happy? Jack wanted nothing more than for her to be happy. This was the moment where Flint became the people's best sword in their constant fight for truth. Flint was the model on which a new era of social accountability could be built. It would be an era where normal folk, bound by a single cause, could stand toe to toe with those who, prior to this, had no fear of the common man.

And yet, at this very moment, at this restaurant, Molly just leaned in closer and tried to read what was behind Jack's eyes. The difference in understanding was pulling on Jack's stomach. He put both of his hands on the top of Molly's upturned palm of her left hand. "We're changing the world. I want to do it together."

Molly shook her head. "Together is what I want too, Jack."

She continued, "You don't need to move mountains to make the world better. You're not doing this for 'truth,' Jack. You're not doing it for me, and you're not doing it for your brother."

Molly moved her hand from under Jack's. Biting and sarcastic. He hadn't heard her voice like this before. She continued. "Don't fool yourself. I know this about you, it's about showing how unique and special you are. Don't flatter yourself thinking this is for the greater good."

It was a flash of truth.

Jack held still. His mouth anticipated the words he might say next. But Molly was the first to speak.

She looked shocked by her own self, shocked at her truth. She spoke softly as if the warmth of her next words would counter the chill of those spoken before.

"What you have is amazing. Don't wrestle with things you don't understand for a gain you don't know. Flint is great; Flint will continue to be great. You've done more already than a lot of people do in their entire lives."

She moved her hand to touch a tear below her left eye. Molly cared, that was easy to see now, but the pull-on Jack's stomach didn't go away. "I want to do this together, Jack. I just don't want you to be so obsessed with trying to change the entire universe that you end up losing yourself in the process. It's not so bad just being normal."

She continued. "This all makes me uncomfortable."

His response was simple. "I have to."

Molly looked at him. "I know."

CHAPTER 58

In the elevator staring at the doors. Waiting for the floor. Jostling the chicken Caesar salad in one hand and holding his stomach in the other. Late lunches make a hungry man. Feet tapping, why won't the elevator move faster?

Second floor.

Third floor.

Finally, the fourth floor.

Doors receding and muted noise. Light emanating from the glass entryway shielding the office from the elevator lobby. Giant bold orange letters staggered along the wall staring down every visitor. "Flint Media"— the letters scream with the audacity of their purpose. *Those are a nice touch.*

Left hand on the door, pushing through the lobby and into the office. Noise. Conversations, ideas, dreams filling the air and finding their way into the consciousness of the room.

Nod to Janice. Half-hearted salute to Taz.

Time to say hello to the troops in the bullpen. Every step brings noise. Laughs, chirps, whispers. More steps, more noise. Bullpen is cleared—unusual—it's past prime lunch time.

Scanning the room. Long tables and no cubicles—Jack wouldn't have it any other way. *Ok, it's not empty—just redistributed.* Everyone is congregating at one computer; whose station is that? Doesn't matter, it's still weird.

Walking. More noises. Walking up to join the crowd. Hand on Tim's left shoulder, trying to look over the group of people. "What's going on?" No response, just concentration.

Another try. "Hey, Tim." He was turning. Excitement and distraction. A group breath. The collection of people as a single living thing, acting and reacting as one. Then a voice, from the group.

"It's happening."

CHAPTER 59

That might have been the most successful lunch break Jack could ever remember. There were a lot of holes in Anton and Jack's plan, but step one was going better than they could ever have hoped for. They had published the first pieces of the story and the world was finding out about it.

"*TechCrunch, LA Times, Boston Globe.*" Matt rattled off names. "They've all written big pieces on us."

"Will we crash?"

"No, we're good. We can handle it."

The two of them sat in front of Jack's computer. Matt pointed to a chart on the screen. "Here's when the spike starts. This thing is huge. I mean huge. We've never seen anything like this."

The story was on fire. The world was loving it. The Flint Media reports were out in the wild. Testimonials, police records, and Anton's own summaries with supporting evidence were all made public. It was the beginning of the story that Jack never thought would be published. Flint Media was experiencing traffic overload; thousands of people were proposing and bidding on follow-up stories. The comments and emails screamed for more; in-boxes were overflowing.

The entire Flint Media team was alive with excitement. The hive was swelling and bursting with enthusiasm. This was real; they could feel the passion.

Jack looked at Matt. "This is the tipping point. Can you feel it? This is our moonshot."

It had been three hours since this story caught its stride and it was breaking every record they'd ever had. It felt good. It was a high that Jack couldn't explain, it made him exhilarated and yearning for more of the same.

How big could this get?

Jack's phone began to ring. It was a number that he didn't recognize, but he answered.

"Mr. Ranger?"

"Yes, who is this?"

"It's Alexandra Cole from the *Pearson Network*. Are you free tomorrow afternoon?"

CHAPTER 60

Dog parks in New York City are a funny thing. They are a green oasis in a concrete desert. The next morning Jack found himself holding the leash of Molly's newest companion. Mikko was his name. He was a short, gray-haired mix of a dog that Molly had adopted from the shelter.

Jack recalled trying to identify Mikko's heritage without success.

"He's a what?"

Molly had shrugged. "They don't know exactly, but his mom was a bird dog."

Jack took his turn guiding the dog around the winding pathway. It was obvious that Mikko was a mutt. He had the lean build of a dog who liked to run and his oversized paws hinted that there was still room for him to grow.

Molly beamed at Mikko. "Isn't he adorable?"

The dog was bouncing back and forth along the pathway. He was a puppy on sensory overload. His cuteness was undeniable. Boy and girl walked side by side occasionally holding hands and laughing just as they had years before.

The energy in Jack's mood was spilling into his conversation. An outsider would be hard-pressed to tell which was more excited, Mikko or Jack. Jack was carrying with him the enthusiasm of yesterday's high. Molly could feel it as if it were radiating from his body. She would have asked about it, if Jack hadn't told her first.

"It's happening, Molly. The break I've been waiting for."

"The story around the governor?"

"Yes, it's amazing. It's finally happening."

There was a pause in her response. Outwardly there was no indication of agreement or disapproval. Just a maddeningly obvious pause.

Jack raised his eyebrows at her to elicit a response.

Her smile had faded, but it returned. "That's great, Jack."

The smile. Was it fake? Was it forced?

Jack pushed these thoughts away. He was too far into the excitement to let Molly's cryptic social cues bring him down.

A tug from the leash drew Jack's attention to Mikko. He had lunged at a squirrel and spun upwards against the restraint of the leash. "He's feisty." He laughed. "Poor little guy just wants to run free. It's a shame he needs to stay leashed."

Molly laughed along with him. This sounded more real. Jack found something wonderful about her in her laugh. He couldn't place it exactly. But, whatever it was, Jack loved being around it again.

The walk continued until the looping pathway approached the origin of where it began.

Molly brought up Flint again. "Be careful, Jack, you know how dangerous this can be." Her tone was resigned, like a mother warning her son, knowing that he would not listen to her.

He nodded. He heard her, but he wasn't listening. He was focusing on his day ahead.

The path looped into itself. It completed the circle. They had finished where they started and Mikko was tugging on the leash for more. Jack pulled out his phone and checked the time.

He leaned in and kissed Molly on the cheek. It was the universal, "I gotta run, but see you soon" gesture.

He put his phone back in his pocket. Molly started to walk back towards her apartment and asked a final parting question. "Where are you off to?"

"I'll see you in a bit. I have an interview."

CHAPTER 61

"Thanks for agreeing to this on such short notice."

"Anything to give the people what they need."

Alexandra Cole walked into the coffee shop and shook Jack's hand. "Quite the stir you've been making." She looked around the café as if remembering an old apartment. "I'd been waiting for a reason to come back here." Jack shrugged and smiled sheepishly. She replied: "You can relax, you're not on the record yet."

The CEO nodded. He remembered his first interview with Alexandra. A lot had changed since then.

"Shall we?" Alexandra smiled back.

"Before we start, what's this for exactly? Another column?"

"No, hard news. Way less fun."

The two of them talked about the recent happening at Flint Media. Alexandra was keen to pick up this story. "It's the start of something new," she said. "It's contagious, and I'm going to help it spread."

Alexandra's questions started easy enough. "So, what's it mean for a piece to be popular?"

"I thought this was a hard news story. Why's that matter?"

She raised an eyebrow and laughed. She looked up from her notes. "Maybe, I'm just interested."

And so, they began to talk. The process itself did not take long. "So, you didn't answer my question. How do you know when a story is popular?"

Jack explained. "Popularity could be any number of things. Donations, proposals, views, etc.... but it all really comes down to 'buzz.' It's hard to measure exactly, but once we start seeing it discussed in online forums, or start getting additional tips from outside sources we know that we have something good.

"Here's what I don't understand. This is a story about drugs and murder, and you're getting coverage from outlets that don't cover that sort of news. Why do people like TechCrunch care?"

Jack had a theory here. "I'm not sure that they do. But I do think they have a vested interest. I've read their articles; they focus on the part about the donations to the *Tribune*. That's what they keep emailing me about anyways."

Alexandra was interested.

Jack continued. "I mean it makes sense, right? This story is also a jab at the old guard. 'Old institutions are corrupt and can't be trusted.' That's what they want. They want to say 'hey we don't take money from Super PACs... read us instead. Out with the old, in with the new."

Alexandra asked a question. "Do you believe that?"

Jack paused.

"Not really. Let me be clear. Good institutions like the *Times* and the *Journal*... I think they're the most important private institutions in America. But there's a lot of other places that pander to their advertisers or benefactors."

They continued. Jack told her about his time at the *Tribune*. "And when I saw this man dead, murdered, in his car, that's when it really set it in."

Alexandra still carried a pen and paper, but she typed her notes on the laptop while recording the conversation live. The economy of her words and the efficiency of her typing were supreme. She'd done this hundreds of times before; Jack could feel the answers being coaxed out of him. She made him feel happy to give her the answers.

She asked about theories. Who was to blame? Do you have more? Are you scared? Alexandra wanted every detail. Jack kept to the script of what they had published, but Alexandra prodded for more.

"But to be clear, you have no definitive proof that the governor is involved. You imply it heavily, but you have no hard evidence?"

Jack sat silently. This question was sharper than its predecessors.

"You are making serious allegations, Jack. You're influencing millions of people, and you only have circumstantial evidence?"

Jack didn't move.

"So, I'll take that as a no? No hard evidence."

Jack tilted his head towards his right hand. He placed it palm down on the table. "Off the record."

The scar tissue showed clearly. Alexandra's eyes widened. She understood what Jack meant, but she couldn't possibly know if he was telling the truth. She nodded and looked back at her computer screen. Professional skepticism was at work.

"Will more stories be following?"

Corporate Jack responded. "We have several reporters investigating different angles. I can't comment on the specifics now, but you can expect a steady release in the near future."

"What sorts of angles? Are you trying to get specific evidence on the governor? Will you be publishing the names of the police officers who have been receiving bribes?"

"As I mentioned, I can't comment on that right now."

A smile, "Oh, and the guard is up." She laughed. How many people had she disarmed with that laugh?

The interview ended. Alexandra packed the various tools of her trade into her bag. She leaned over the table. "I can tell you have more. You're going to slam this guy, huh?"

Jack smiled, "I'm just returning the favor. Men like him don't deserve to get off free."

There was a brief pause. Alexandra looked firmly into Jack's line-of-sight. "I'll help make you famous. It's stories like these that will make your company's dreams come true."

He thought about this point. He thought back to his last conversation with Rachel, and he could hear Sean screaming about cash flow. There were some pretty big dreams that needed to be fulfilled. He would take all the help they could get.

She was lingering, so Jack asked one last question. "Don't you just do things like this over the phone now?"

Alexandra smiled. Was there something more behind the smile? "There are some things I like doing better in person."

CHAPTER 62

New York City (Pearson Network—News Division)

The Massachusetts Governor and State Police department have come under fire in recent weeks amidst allegations of criminal misconduct regarding the trafficking of cocaine and distribution of illicit funds. The story was first brought to light by investigative journalism firm Flint Media.

A former senior official of the Boston police department familiar with the situation agreed to comment under conditions of anonymity saying, "In recent years the magnitude of this activity has become too dangerous to ignore. It became clear to me that there is an organized effort to profit from drug distribution networks throughout the state."

The official alleges that he was forced to quit after raising issues with the practice. In addition, he claims that significant threats were routinely made, and in some cases, acted upon towards officers who disagreed with the efforts.

The organization raising the allegations, Flint Media, has released first-hand accounts and documentation, including, what they believe to be, doctored police records that corroborate the story. Flint Media CEO, Jack Ranger, claims to have personal experience with this case while he was a reporter at the Massachusetts-based news outlet, *The Tribune Co.* Mr. Ranger said, "I covered this case closely during my time at the *Tribune* and saw first-hand the level of corruption and distorted extension of power exhibited by the state police and higher officials."

For his part, Mr. Ranger claims that his firm will continue to uncover evidence and make it public through its publications saying, "We [Flint Media] have a number of reporters currently investigating every relevant angle."

This is not the first time the governor has come under fire for alleged misconduct. Eighteen years ago, while serving as a senator, he came under scrutiny for illegal distribution of federal grant money to preferred constituents. Following a public debate and harsh criticisms from the media, he was later exonerated and charges were dropped. The governor was not available for immediate comment on this story, but his office issued an official response saying the allegations are "patently false" and that "the governor welcomes this line of questioning and will prove to the Commonwealth of Massachusetts that Flint Media's accusations are little more than headline-grabbing antics."

Also, enduring scrutiny is Massachusetts based Super PAC 'American Progress' which is alleged to be complicit as a vehicle for distribution of the drug trafficking related funds. Flint Media has raised concerns about the distribution of this money to political constituents in the form of campaign financing. American Progress could not be reached for comment at this time.

Pearson Times Network correspondents Alexandra Cole and Sean Zhang contributed to this report.

CHAPTER 63

You would have thought they had won the lottery. Champagne bottles abound. Today was press release day.

"Crowd-sourcing journalism platform, Flint Media, announces $30 million follow-on investment from tech giant eFettro."

The headlines were exactly as Jack had predicted. The deal had been made weeks ago, the money had already hit Flint Media's bank account, but the official announcement was made today.

The office was swarming with excitement. Sean had given a rousing speech. Smooth words paired well with funding announcements. It was like a fine wine and cheese. "This is a vote of confidence in what we do. This money is a validation of what we already know; that the people in this room have what it takes to change the world."

Instead of renting out a bar, Sean had suggested that the funding party come to Flint. Sean had ordered two half-kegs for the office.

"One of the nice stuff, and another of the cheap stuff to remind us of our roots." Sean smiled as he maneuvered the kegs of beer into buckets of ice.

Jack taunted Sean.

"Sean, just because we're cash-strapped doesn't mean it's ok to be a cheap-ass on the beer. Today is supposed to be about celebration and convincing everyone that we won't go belly up next week. We're celebrating $30 million dollars, and we give our employees this?"

Jack continued. "We deserve better. Miller Lite is, from now on, banned from our office."

Sean and Jack both laughed. Anton entered the room. He reached into his pocket and knelt down in front of the two kegs. He pulled out a sharpie from his pocket and scribbled on the two kegs. He labeled the first keg, 'Boston Lager,' which it was, and the second 'Arrogant Bastard IPA'—which it was not.

He stood and wiped his hands. "Problem solved. Just make sure you don't wheel out this second one until the first is gone."

"You're a clever and deranged man, Anton." Jack looked on with a bemused curiosity.

Anton continued his smile and replied, "You're lucky I'm not your boss anymore."

The three of them stood for a moment reflecting on whatever common thoughts they believed they were sharing. "Jack, I'm stepping out for a second to get this party some last-minute refreshments. Care to join?" Anton looked at Jack and motioned to the elevator.

"Sure. Sean, I trust you can get this going."

And so, Anton and Jack walked to the elevator and made their way onto the New York streets. The two of them walked to the liquor mart on the corner. "Is it enough?" Anton turned the conversation to what was on his mind. He was talking about the story he had brought to Flint Media.

"It might be."

Anton paid the cashier for a small bottle. He paused as he put his wallet back into his pocket and looked on at Jack. "We need to blow this open. You know that, right?"

Jack didn't respond. There was no need.

They strolled back to the office. Anton had the same look about him that Jack could remember from his days at the *Tribune*. "What we've published has been good. But on the next wave of stories we need to bring it. We're throwing darts at the governor. We need bullets."

Entertaining this thought was a precarious avenue for Jack's mind to wander. There would be more. More stories were in the works already. It would be a surprise if the governor and his corrupt ring weren't already sweating and nervous. Of course, he wanted to grind the man's reputation into the mud, but he had a company to run. Balance is essential.

Mid-stride, Anton stopped.

Jack twirled around.

Jack focused on Anton. The busy rush of the city streets didn't stop for two men in the middle of the sidewalk. Like water flowing around a rock in a stream—parting and rejoining—people continued their evening walks to wherever it was that they were going.

All the buzz and commotion around Jack faded to the background as Anton reached out his right arm, rested it on Jack's shoulder and stared at him.

"Listen. When this blows up, and it *will* blow up, we need to be ready. We need an ace up our sleeve."

The sudden dramatic gesture caught Jack off guard.

But he asserted his stance, "What we have is strong and what we will have is stronger."

Anton shook his head. "Bullets, not darts. What you have isn't strong enough."

"And you have something better?" Silence, stone face, then a nod.

"But you won't like it."

In this moment Jack could tell that Anton had been holding back. "What do you mean?"

"I have your silver bullet."

"Anton stop talking in riddles. What does that even mean? Actually, you know what? I don't want to know."

Stress is an insidious weed that thrives in the dark corners of the soul. It slowly worms its way into the cracks, and every so often it exposes the raw nerves underneath.

Jack threw up his arms in exasperation. "I can't deal with you right now." Jack glared at him.

Anton's calm voice sent chills down Jack's spine. "You will have to soon. And when you do, I'll still have it."

The flow of people on the street continued, and Jack turned and joined their path. He was soon swept into the anonymous, faceless stream.

Back in the office, Jack walked in, picked up a cup and filled it with beer. He walked over to Sean, smiled, and shook his hand. They stood on the edge of the office watching it fill with life and optimism. Stories, laughs, and music. It was a beautiful thing to see.

Sean looked over at his CEO. "Look how happy everyone is. They have no idea how close we were to being dead in the water."

"I'm not sure any of us ever do."

CHAPTER 64

Jack shifted his workbag from his right shoulder to his left as he approached the door to his apartment. It was another exhausting day, but exhausting is good if you like what you're doing.

Exhausted or not, he wasn't too tired to notice something was wrong with the lock. The key wasn't necessary. Was it broken?

No.

The door was unlocked.

Jack never left his door unlocked.

He turned the handle and the door complied. The doorway opened, and Jack hesitated before entering. He walked through the entryway and turned the corner. He didn't know what to expect other than he knew that he should expect something.

The pulse in his chest spiked.

The lights were still off in the apartment. The day's fading sun illuminated a figure. Sitting at his kitchen table, half covered in the long shadows of the approaching evening, was a man Jack had never seen before.

The man sat with a serious smile on his face. He wore a hat and a windbreaker. He looked at Jack.

"Welcome home."

Jack stood facing his guest and put his work bag on the kitchen table. He took three steps toward the man.

"Who are you?"

The figure left his chair. The man placed something forcefully on the table and then walked toward Jack. The silence of the apartment accented each step.

The man kept his smile. Finally, he came to a stop an arm's length in front of Jack.

Jack stood his ground but took an involuntary nervous breath.

The man spoke. "Relax. I'm not the one who is going to hurt you."

Jack didn't move; their shoulders touched as the figure walked past him and Jack stared ahead without turning. The door opened, then closed as the man walked out. Jack didn't watch him leave because he was fixated by what the man had placed on the table. Seconds passed. Jack was alone. He walked to the table and picked up the message that was intended for him.

CHAPTER 65

"Jack, this is off the record."

Nearly every conversation with Rachel Warner he ever had was off the record. Usually, however, Jack's conversations with Rachel weren't at 11:00 a.m. on Wednesday mornings.

They sat together in one of Flint Media's glass conference rooms. Markers lay on each end of the center table. The glass doubled as a whiteboard. Story outlines and business ideas were sketched across the walls. Red, blue, and black—those were the colors in which each step of Flint Media was first conceived.

Rachel's brown eyes and cool expression betrayed nothing of her intentions, save for the fact that Jack would not be happy with them.

"Are you here to 'suggest' another board member?"

Rachel laughed. "No, no. Still just the two seats."

It wasn't often that a member of the board of directors just "stopped in" to check up on things. Luckily, most of the people at Flint didn't recognize Rachel's face. Jack would have preferred a meeting somewhere else. He didn't want a game of 20 questions from the team after they figured out who she was.

"Jack, we need to talk about the story."

He was feeling witty. "So, you came to congratulate me?"

"No, Jack."

"It's the most popular story we've ever done. Millions more people now know Flint Media. What's not to like?"

Rachel took a breath. She wasn't ruthless or distant or cold. She just had business to speak about.

Jack continued. "Are you upset that we're finally making money? Because I thought that was what your last recommendation as our 'advisor' was all about."

"The state of Massachusetts is threatening to sue you."

As he always did when he sensed the importance of a conversation shifting, Jack leaned in. "I don't see an issue."

"eFettro is not your piggy bank. We can't go to trial for you on this one."

They looked at each other from opposite sides of the table. Jack was still staring at her, Rachel sat tapping the fingers of her hand on the surface of the table.

"You can't or you won't?"

Silence hung in the air between them.

"We want you to pull any follow-ups to any stories pertaining to the Governor or Massachusetts State Police. It's too risky."

Something didn't make sense in the balance of power. "You *can't* back us in court, or you *won't* back us in court?" He repeated his question.

"Like I said, as long as you don't publish any follow-ups we won't have a problem." She paused, "because if there is a problem, we *will* pull the last tranches of our funding."

"Both of us know you can't do that."

Her brown eyes were intense. "No, only one of us *thinks* that we can't do that."

Rachel looked over each of her shoulders and leaned in to mirror Jack's posture. Jack couldn't help but wonder if it was a deliberate charade to change the nature of the conversation or an honest subconscious move showing solidarity. "Look, Jack, I like Flint—I love Flint. There's a reason I'm the one on your board. But we can't have the governor on our bad side. We're just the venture arm. eFettro, the parent company cares. Do you know how many offices we have in Massachusetts?"

Rachel let out a breath before belaboring her point, "Tax incentives, legislation, contracts—if the governor is furious with you then you don't get those things. Let's be real. The money we've invested in Flint is peanuts to us. We are playing a much bigger game here."

"How do you know the governor is paying attention?"

"He's made himself very clear to us."

It made perfect sense. The governor was a smart man; he understood how to fend off his enemies. Find the money, follow the money, stop the money. Jack absently bit his lower lip as he considered the options in front of him.

Rachel stood. Another meeting to attend? Or another charade to elicit a response? "I don't need an answer from you right now. But I would just advise you not to do anything stupid."

Jack stood as well and smiled a half-smile. "I'll take that into consideration."

She nodded to Jack, and he returned the favor. Their eyes met.

"You know," he said, "I always wonder what I could have done without your money. I'm not a fan of dancing with strings."

CHAPTER 66

Sean could tell that Jack was troubled.

Jack was staring at a blank spot in front of him. "All of this, it's just so much to handle."

They were side by side at the greatest urban hideaway of them all—the golf course. Jack and Sean were not the first two troubled city-dwellers who sought the solace of carefully cut grass and well-rehearsed muscle memory. They also certainly would not be the last.

"What do you mean?"

"Rachel came into the office yesterday."

They were on the mats of the driving range. Mindlessly hitting balls into the green expanse in front of them. Sean stopped mid backswing.

"Excuse me?" Flakes of animosity spiced Sean's two words.

"Rachel Warner."

"Yeah, I know who Rachel is. When were you going to tell me?"

"I'm telling you now."

There was a pause as Sean teed up another ball. His next swing was faster, a transfer of anxiety into the dimpled white ball.

Jack explained. "She wants us to pull all stories stemming from Anton's work. Everything on the governor, everything about the police, pretty much anything about Massachusetts."

"And if we don't?"

"It's one or the other. The stories get pulled, or our money gets pulled."

More swings. More golf balls sent screaming from their clubs. Before them was a moral pivot point for the company. They debated the seriousness of the threat. Could eFettro do it? Would eFettro do it?

Sean's voice was less confident than usual. "She knows the whole reason we started running these stories was so that she could get off our case about 'not thinking big enough' right?"

Jack shrugged.

Sean looked over at his business partner. "So, have you told Anton it's over?"

Jack was focusing on the ball on the fake turf mat in front of him. Out of the corner of his eye, he could see that Sean was getting nervous.

"You can't be seriously thinking about *not* pulling this right?"

More silence was followed by additional logic from Sean. "Do you have any idea what our bank account looks like without eFettro?"

There was a soft-measured counter. "I know, Sean, I know." Jack's tone was low and reluctant like he wished he didn't have to offer his words. "But, it's not about the money. It's about what's right."

It was a debate neither wanted to have.

"We can't let money dictate our actions. Or else we'll be just like everyone else."

"Sometimes you need to compromise. Sometimes you need to lose the battle to win the war."

"Is that the type of company we want to be? One that says it's okay to compromise your morals when the situation gets too sticky. No. It's either all the truth or none. There is no middle ground."

"Well, on the road you're taking us, it looks like 'none' is where we're going to be. Hard to report on the truth when you're busy in bankruptcy court."

"Not now."

How many times had they had this fight? Ideals versus practicality. The balance was what made the company work. It was a productive friction of checks and balances that kept them glued together.

Jack put his club down and looked straight at Sean. "We will not compromise the reason we created this company. That's a direct mandate. That is my decision. We will not pull these stories, and I'm going to need all the help I can get to make sure we make it through to the other side alive."

Sean was clearly angry. "Whatever it is that you think Anton has left up his sleeve, it better be good. You better make sure it's a slam dunk, or we're screwed."

The loudness of their voices and the temperament of their moods caught both off guard.

Jack broke the ice first. "Look, I'm sorry. It's just there's a lot swirling in my head right now. I got another threat."

Sean's eyes flickered up. "Rachel?"

Jack answered without sounds. No, it wasn't Rachel.

Jack's mind flashed back to the moment when he first saw the stranger in his apartment. "It was worse than the others."

Sean pressed, "What was it?"

"But I don't know what it means."

"It's not a coincidence." Sean thought aloud. "People in this line of work can't afford to believe in coincidence."

It was obvious that Sean was hoping for more details.

They walked off the driving range and to the clubhouse. Each shouldered his bag. Jack was looking around as he walked, as if he was looking for an answer somewhere.

As they walked, Sean looked at the profile of Jack's left side. He pointed to Jack's eye, "What's that?"

Jack touched his face.

"It looks like you have the start of a black eye." Sean tried to joke, but there was no humor in his voice. "Who punched you? Don't tell me Rachel did this. Jeez, how bad was that meeting?"

Jack released a fake laugh. At the clubhouse, Jack found a mirror. He gazed at his face. Sean was right; a faint bruise was forming. "Weird, I didn't even notice."

Still looking in the mirror, Jack's next words were as much to himself as they were to Sean.

"I'm calling it here, man. I don't have it in me to play a round today."

"But you already paid."

"Give it to someone else."

CHAPTER 67

Jack's head hurt, his whole being hurt. He had never had a stress migraine before, but this had to be it. The pressure from all sides of his skull numbed thought. He needed to lie down but he couldn't sit still. It was a long night lying in his bed staring at his ceiling.

This New York City apartment was smaller than his apartment at the fringe of Boston. Jack was alone. He had cancelled his dinner plans with Molly; he needed to rest and think. New York City was filled with millions of lonely people who lived right next to each other. Tonight, Jack joined their ranks; he lay alone in his bed counting the cracks in the ceiling above his head. He was up late that night and went into the office late the next morning.

His stress headache was like a hangover; he couldn't shake it, and he showed up to the office holding his head. That was one of the benefits of being the boss, though. When Jack showed up late people just assumed he had a morning meeting somewhere else; when he left early, they assumed he was off across the country trying to raise money. Even the CEO of Flint Media preferred for some truths to be concealed. At the office, Jack waited for Anton.

Sauntering and chewing some form of candy, Anton walked with an aloofness that would be contagious if it could ever be imitated. His gait was unique, happy, and purposefully flavored with his semi-limp. Anton turned the corner to see Jack sitting at his workstation rubbing his temples.

"Rough night?"

"Not in the way you're thinking."

"Sure, boss."

It was obvious that they were about to have a conversation.

"You told me there was a silver bullet."

Anton smiled a wide Cheshire Cat smile. He swallowed the candy and motioned with his head towards the conference room. Jack was slow to get up and walked with a deliberate pace. Anton shut the door and sat across the table from Jack. He looked down and pulled from his pocket the bag of Skittles that fueled his toothy grin. Jack sat and looked onward waiting for Anton to make eye contact. One side of the table was having more fun than the other.

Anton was digging in the bag of Skittles and laid two out on the table. Still, there was no eye contact with Jack. He lowered his face to the table so that he was eye level with the Skittles and pushed each one with his forefinger towards the middle. Jack didn't feel like processing Anton's motives with the candy, so he sat back, staring blankly.

"The red pill or the blue pill?"

"What?"

Anton was still looking down at the table. He repeated himself. "Red or Blue?"

Jack hadn't caught on yet. Anton looked up to finally meet Jack's eyes. "You say you want the silver bullet, but you don't know what it means. I would normally say that it's ok because there's no way you could know… but deep down I think you know."

Jack just rubbed his eyes and tried to make sense of Anton's riddles.

"I know you want to take this story to the next level. But I don't think you know what it will do to you. That's why I'm giving you this choice. If you choose the blue pill, we will carry on just as we did. If you choose the red, then I tell you the truth. But just keep in mind, that sometimes our pursuit of the truth can kill us."

Through his screaming temples, Jack put the connection together. "This isn't the Matrix, Anton. And those aren't pills—they're Skittles." With the back of his hand, he sent the Skittles shooting off the table and bouncing into the wall.

Anton didn't lose his smile. Jack spoke loudly. "This isn't a game." Then softer. "eFettro wants me to pull the stories."

Anton seemed unfazed. He didn't break the grin.

"And what say you to that, Mr. Ranger?"

"That it's not gonna happen. That man doesn't deserve to be roaming free, that…"

Anton continued the sentence for Jack—plugging in the words that Jack wanted to say. but wouldn't.

"That you'll never make it to the big time if you always surrender?"

Calm yourself, Jack. He slumped back in his chair with his left hand on his forehead and his right hand gripping the edge of the table. "I just need the truth, Anton."

Anton popped four Skittles into his mouth. He spoke aloud like he was announcing a sports game. "And the red pill it is." He slid the half-eaten bag of candy across the desk and watched it collide with Jack's hand. He chewed, and he grinned. "Let's go for a drive."

CHAPTER 68

It had been a long time since Jack had stepped into this office. The professor looked the same. There was more seasoning in his salt and pepper beard, but otherwise, his purpose of presence was just as Jack remembered it: deliberate, powerful, and quiet. To his right was Anton. Had the three of them ever been in the same room together? Jack didn't think so.

Coming back to the campus was a fizz of memories. It was fall, the most iconic time for colleges in New England. The quad was a scene ripe for a postcard. Several students were walking underneath the perfectly turned trees. Orange and yellow, a quiet fire, simmered on the trees as students in corduroys and sweaters held an assortment of books under one arm and laughed amongst each other as they walked to class.

Then there was Jack. He had easily navigated the grounds to the familiar office. He wasn't long past his time here. The stories, the escapades, the curiosity about the outside world—he missed it. Campus was a bubble existing somewhere outside of reality, and he was nostalgic to return.

Jack sat in his usual chair in his mentor's office.

Anton stood behind him, leaning against the bookcase.

"Good to see you, Jack." The professor greeted him.

"I hope I can say the same to you."

They didn't spend much time on small talk. Jack didn't drive all this way to charade through polite niceties. The CEO knew there was something more that he would soon understand. The troubling part was that he already had an idea of what it would be. He didn't like it.

"Change. That's what's going on. Momentous change and you get to be at the center of it." The professor spoke similar to how he always had. He looked at Anton.

Jack stopped him before he could start his next sentence. It was a burst of assertiveness that Professor Ray had not seen from his former student before. "Stop, just stop."

The three men in the room took simultaneous breaths.

Jack continued. "What's changing is that you're going to come clean on everything that you've been keeping from me."

The world was coming together piece by piece. Jack thought back to the three job interviews that had turned him down. He thought about the first time he met Anton. The premade business cards with his name on them—it was all arranged. Sitting opposite the desk was the maestro orchestrating Jack's life with a few phone calls and well-timed words.

Confusion and anger tangoed along Jack's face. The professor knew the conclusion Jack was reaching as his voice trailed and his words caught up to his mind. Jack whispered a thought aloud. "*The New York Times* was my dream. You *knew* that."

It had been years ago, but his mind could still recite the rejection letter. They were cordial and well-mannered when they broke Jack's dream.

The professor nodded and spoke.

"It hurt me to have to hurt you like that, Jack. But it had to happen. Getting you onto Anton's team was the most important thing. It gave you the chance of a lifetime."

Jack wondered if it had been easy for the professor to snuff out the dream of his favorite student. In practice, Jack supposed it was easy enough. A few calls from the professor and Jack's job prospects would never stand a chance.

Jack was still hung up on the point that he finally comprehended. He couldn't understand the justification for playing with someone's life. "Why?"

Anton entered the conversation at this point. "You know I was working on the story before you ever came to the *Tribune*. But I'm not

sure you ever knew how deep into it I was. I had hit the wall. I needed
help to push it through."

Jack thought back to his time at the *Tribune*. Anton knew all along
where the investigation needed to go.

Professor Ray added to the thought. "It was beautiful timing. You
were the best student I've ever seen for this."

The flattery was sickening. Jack sat there. Professor Ray stood from
his chair and walked to the window. He looked up at the clouds and out
over the college quad. "But you came here for the truth. So, I'll give you
what you came for."

"You have a most advantageous connection."

Jack knew what he meant, but he needed to hear it aloud.

"Christopher Bingham is the missing link." The professor walked
from the window and past his desk. He paced around the room. Next
to Jack. Behind Jack. The professor's voice was a narration to the cinema
playing in his consciousness. Jack sat in his chair staring straight through
the open window overlooking the quiet campus.

"But you already knew that didn't you, Jack? It was too obvious; the
clues are right there in front of you. It's not an accident that he's risen so
fast in the governor's party. It's no accident that business is booming for
his consultancy. It's fake money. His books are flushed with dirty cash."

Did he know it was true? Had he blocked it out? Yes. Christopher
Bingham's business was the gatekeeper for the drug money into the
political system. Molly's parents were right in thinking that their son
was a rising star. They just didn't know why.

Jack could hear the footsteps of the professor circling.

"Maybe that's why you were so attracted to that girl. She brought
you closer to your purpose."

The professor walked closer. Jack stood and slammed his fist on the
desk. The noise startled Anton.

Jack flashed back to his time at school. He had *introduced* Molly to the professor. He had been proud to show Professor Ray the wonderful person he was dating. If only Jack knew what that would mean, that his fate would be impossibly intertwined with hers. He was a pawn in a chess game between two masters of their craft, and the pieces were no longer black and white.

A soft haze descended on his senses. Everything was muted. Anger radiated with each breath he took.

Professor Ray matched the moment with an opposite force. He extended his arm and put a hand on the young man's shoulder.

A connection formed in Jack's mind. There was a deeper meaning behind this. Jack sensed that there was an old feud burning and he had been unlucky enough to stumble into the fray.

"What did he do to you? The governor?"

Professor Ray retracted his hand. "You're smart, Jack. I like that about you." He paused before continuing, "The governor is a bad man. It takes a lot of work to get to the top like he has."

Anton was still sitting, "This isn't the first story he has covered up. It's not the first time he's ruined a journalist's career."

The two older men in the room looked at each other and shook their heads. Jack understood. Professor Ray and Anton were chasing retribution. He was still breathing heavily. He stood eye to eye with the professor. The possibilities from the past came to the surface of understanding. Had Professor Ray been behind exposing the governor's past scandals? More importantly, is that what chased the professor from his career?

The professor spoke. "They went after my family. They sabotaged my career and threatened me with the life of my daughter."

Jack finished the logic, "And so you left journalism to teach."

The professor affirmed.

"But you never *really* left it behind, did you? You just played the game from a different angle. With other people's lives."

Jack didn't know what to think. Like it or not, his life was part of a decades-long feud.

Jack continued. "You played me. These are your problems, not mine."

The response from Malcolm Ray was not swift, but it was forceful. His voice rose with energy as if he were giving a speech. His words were carefully emphasized and artfully charged.

"Played you? You're upset about getting played?"

"This isn't about getting 'played.' This is about the opportunity of *your* lifetime. Yes, you can publish with what you have. And yes, it *might* work. But this isn't about *maybe* cashing in. You can use this connection. This is about serving it up on a silver platter, tying it up in a pretty bow, putting it on a tee, and knocking the biggest story this state has seen in ten years out of the park."

He paused for breath. "Yes, we set it up. Yes, we chose you. But it was the right thing to do. I'm sorry about your job and I'm sorry about your girl. I really am. But this is about doing what's right, and that's bringing the governor to justice. We all have to make sacrifices for what's right."

Anton completed the professor's logic, "We thought Christopher was involved and we knew that if that were true, then you would be able to exploit it."

For a second anger retreated and temptation took its momentary hold. This was Anton's silver bullet. This was the key. He could blow the story so wide open that it didn't matter what Rachel and eFettro thought.

He could get information from Christopher. Maybe not directly anymore, but there was a way to find out what he was up to. The eye contact between Jack and the professor was uncomfortable; they stood face to face only a few feet apart.

"Think about what you found. We thought it was dead. But you rose from the ashes and built a company. You built your generation's voice for truth. We didn't play you, Jack. We gave you the perfect opportunity. This is the moment you've been so desperately waiting for. This is how heroes are born."

Jack broke eye contact. Flint Media was already everything he could have hoped for. Why did he so badly want more? This could take the dream to an entirely new level.

Doubt. He couldn't do this to Molly. It wasn't fair.

"But, Molly never…"

Loudly—"She left you, Jack."

Jack shook his head. No, it wasn't like that.

"She left you, and she will leave you again."

Turning, he faced the professor's desk and partially bent as he placed both hands palm down. He didn't know what to think.

Softer now, the professor once again put his hand on Jack's shoulder. "She isn't like you and me. She can't understand you and she never will. Molly doesn't get people like us."

Jack turned his head to look at the professor and asked a question he already knew the answer to with a single word, "Us?"

"We aren't so different, Jack."

CHAPTER 69

Jack had a sudden undeniable urge to go back to the *Tribune*. He wanted to look at it and see it for what it was.

So, he drove.

The brick exterior was the same, the metallic letters spelling out the '*Tribune*' along the building's roof were unchanged. It was Saturday, and the office was partially filled. Memories came back to Jack. His desk, his editor, his passion. In some ways, he enjoyed much about the *Tribune*.

The streets were mostly quiet. Jack felt like he was at a zoo looking at an endangered species. The *Tribune* went about its daily routine unaware that it was amongst the last of its kind.

The bottom floor of the *Tribune* was a lobby, an elegant open space with an old printing press to the side. It was roped off with red velvet ropes as you might find in a museum. It was a beautiful antique, a relic of the past. From the street, Jack looked through the window into the lobby.

He saw his reflection in the pane of glass. Each Jack Ranger stood staring at the other. Did the Jack in the window know who he was looking at? Did he know that he was waging war against the world of Jack's reflection? Did this Jack know that he was looking into the eyes of the man who would be his downfall? No, Jack blinked twice. It was only a reflection.

CHAPTER 70

Glancing at his phone, Jack noticed for the first time the number of missed calls. How long had he gone radio silent? 36 hours? It was too long to leave a company unattended. He reflected on his instructions to Sean when he left to drive back to Boston. "Run things while I'm gone. I'll be back soon."

Sean's hands were capable hands with which to leave Flint Media. Yet it didn't stop an onslaught of unanswered questions that barraged Jack's voicemail.

But the unanswered questions would wait. He had made one last stop 136 miles north.

It was a new day. Jack inhaled slowly through his nose and exhaled through his mouth. His breath drew in crisp mountain air as he stood at the New Hampshire trailhead that he remembered. Somehow during all the changes throughout Jack's last few years, this trail was just as it always had been. The air was peppered with pollen and spiced with the sounds of rustling trees.

His eyes were closed as he breathed in the outside world.

In and out.

Jack's body was still, but his mind was racing. He was hoping to find peace.

He walked the trail that he and Molly had walked so long ago, only this time he was alone. The leaves on the trees were in full turn. This was Fall. The season was on the edge of the weeks where it was still comfortable to walk the trails. There was indecision in the air, almost as if nature had a say in deciding between the warmth of summer and the chill of winter. Nature debated, pondering if it had a choice other than the inevitable flow of the seasons. Jack wondered if the trees thought they had a choice.

Sitting on a rock by a stream, Jack tried to clear his head. There were decisions to make, things to do, and people to disappoint.

From his seat, he picked up a handful of stones and threw them into the stream.

Jack saw the darker side of his mentor now. He was a gifted man, a master puppeteer, who would not be denied his role in shaping the world around him. Jack was furious. If there was an irony in this realization, he didn't bother to figure it out. They say you can hate the things that are most like yourself.

In the professor's world, Jack was a pawn. A grandmaster goes great lengths to position his pawns and understands that they are often sacrificed for the greater good.

He watched the stones sink into the stream one by one. The clouds oversaw his debate. He threw the rocks further and faster. He tried to convince himself that there was no decision to make. But there were too many decisions to make. How did he get to this point?

Flint Media was his ticket out. It was his chance to rewrite the rules. When you're born in this world, you accept the rules as they are placed before you. Whether just or unjust, you must adapt to what others have decided. Precious few get to live on their own terms, and this was his chance to make his own terms. Flint Media was his chance to ensure that he wouldn't be a slave to the borrowed promise of a hollow future. Jack was rewriting the equation.

Except that he wasn't.

He understood that now. He had the illusion of control. The last few years of his life were the function of an ancient slow burning feud, and the future of his company was dictated by money as old as time. The late nights, the stress, the scar on his hand—all these inerasable marks on his life were the product of others.

He was a fly, stuck in a web, raging furiously to no avail. But there was a way to avoid the fate of the fly. It was the way of Professor Ray. He could exploit those around him to get the leverage he needed. Surely it could be justified.

The mountain stream at his feet held no solace for Jack.

But then there was Molly. He stood from his perch and continued to walk. How many years ago had it been when he and Molly walked this same path? Those were different times. They were younger then. Their problems were younger. Back then, they worried about what they might be. Today, Jack feared what he had become.

Red and yellow leaves dotted the path. Jack held his hand out hoping it would be taken by the Molly of the past. Innocent Molly. She would be wearing her gold wired sunglasses and laughing as they jumped from rock to rock trying to cross a stream in the path. She didn't deserve this decision.

Something about this wooded path coaxed old memories to resurface.

They lay laughing and sharing stories. They were together with all their friends at the lake. Again, he thought of the cabin, boat, and woods. He remembered swimming in the sunshine, and the cool twilight that followed the warm day. The campfire kept the darkness at bay and invited stories and laughter. In this moment, the fire illuminated the only parts of existence that mattered. He remembered lying on his back next to Molly, staring at the stars as they traced constellations with their fingers. While their friends slept, they talked.

A rustle in the woods. An animal, a falling branch? Molly stood nervously.

"Relax," he said. "Don't be afraid. There's nothing out there to be afraid of."

She settled and followed his hands pointing at the stars.

"Not much scares you, does it, Jack?"

"No."

"But something must. What are you afraid of?" She had asked.

He had looked at the stars and swept his hand across the sky. There was a long pause. He had known her for such a short period of time. He hadn't told anyone in his life about his only fear. Did he dare trust her?

He took her hand and raised it to the night sky and its milky white portals. He moved her hand as if she was brushing the night. "I am scared of being as anonymous as all of these."

"I understand," she said.

Why did this memory haunt him?

Another memory.

It was the night Jack sat shaking in his room fearing his expulsion. Sean had already left. It was just Molly and Jack sitting silently next to each other. She understood why the story about President Haleson was not published under anonymity. She had cried, and Jack shook. Jack had tried to put his feeling into words. It was difficult to describe. It was a primal feeling that had originated long before mankind had developed the words to explain it.

"I understand," she said.

"I know this won't be the last time you need to do something like this," she said.

He remembered feeling that his soul was exposed. It was more terrifying than any punishment that might await him. He was admitting to the person he loved the reason she should never love him. But she didn't leave. Instead, she embraced him.

"It's who you are. It's going to take time to figure out, it will be difficult— but I know eventually we will make it work. I'll wait until you're ready. I'll always wait for you."

They say that to love someone is to give them the power to destroy you while trusting them not to.

Jack had entrusted her with his demons, and she accepted him. Those words stuck with him. It was a promise. She understood him, and she said that she would wait.

That's why it felt like a piece of him was ripped open when she left him all those years ago. It had hurt him beyond his imagination. But she was back. Everyone makes mistakes. She was waiting again now, that's all that mattered.

His attention drew back to the trail.

A deliberate pile of rocks lay at the corner of a crossroads in the path. Here it was, the marker to the offshoot path that they had walked before. He didn't know why, but he needed to see the twisted metallic remnants of the plane crash. Jack took the turn. A mossy, rusted assortment of jumbled metal welcomed Jack to his decision. He reread the plaque on the ground.

He was the only person here on this day. Jack stared at the wreckage. When he first stumbled on the crash, he looked with a sense of wonder at the circumstances leading to that moment. How oddly fate can work.

He'd forgiven her. Could she ever forgive him?

It was time to leave the mountain. He left the tragic time capsule of the plane; he left the quiet woods, the clear stream, and the unassuming mountains. It was time to go back to New York. His company needed him, Molly needed him, and Jack's future needed him.

The choice was his love or his dreams.

The problem was that Jack loved his dreams.

CHAPTER 71

A giant American flag hung from the 20-foot-high ceilings of the old warehouse. It was lit by bright industrial lighting that took Jack a few minutes to get used to.

"What do you think?" The mouth guard distorted Jack's words as it partially hung out of the side of his mouth. He gestured around to the gym. The floor mats, pads, punching bags, and jump ropes were faded from years of dutifully doing their jobs.

Sean, Jack, and Caleb stood waiting for the lesson to begin.

Sean had never been here before. "So, this is where you've been sneaking off to?"

Jack laughed, "Beautiful, isn't it?"

Sean was right. This is where Jack had been sneaking off to on certain weeknights. It was also the reason Jack would show up at the office with unexplained bruises.

Recently, Caleb had been attending classes with Jack. It was their secret. Jack was never quite sure why he didn't tell his other Flint colleagues. Maybe he liked the idea of keeping it hidden from them, or maybe he didn't think the others would understand. But the reason he kept it quiet wasn't important. What was important was why he came.

The martial arts gym was a hidden gem in New York City. Some years ago, it had been repurposed from an abandoned space to a sanctuary for the frustrated. They taught Brazilian jiu-jitsu, muay thai, judo, and, of course, good old boxing. The gym was open nearly 24 hours a day. For almost every hour that it was open, it was filled with the sound of heavy rock music. The gym was never packed per se, but there were always people wandering in an out. Investment bankers, delivery men, lawyers, army veterans, bartenders, and CEO's of tech start-ups wandered in. The instructors were ex-military guys; they provided the rigor needed for focus.

In the ring or on the mats it wasn't the size of your paycheck that mattered. The gym was a point of pride for those who went. It wasn't necessarily patriotism, although there was plenty of that, it was a sort of nationalistic fervor for manhood. Today's world was one where the measure of a man had more to do with the skill of his hands on a keyboard than his skill as a craftsman. Today's world is one where the toughest, best-trained men can be indiscriminately felled by the simple twitch of a trigger finger.

Technology is the great equalizer. But, for the briefest of hours when a man steps into this converted warehouse filled with heavy music, heavy punches, and heavy sweat; technology has no bearing.

Men entered the gym, took off their neckties, removed their uniforms, and wrapped boxing tape around their carefully moisturized hands. The men that Jack saw on those weeknights came ready to transfer the punishment of the day onto their fellow comrades who awaited the pain with an enthusiasm that was impossible to explain to outsiders. This gym was a shot of testosterone. It was a vaccination against the ever-encroaching emasculation imposed by the modern world. Together the men in this gym raged against well-manicured chest hair, rows of cubicles, and the necessary substitution of coffee for adrenaline. Every night these men raged one punch at a time.

Tonight, he brought Sean. Jack's cofounder had been troubled since Jack's impromptu multi-day retreat. Stress was nothing new to Sean, but showing it was. Jack could see Sean was troubled. It had to be the pressure from the eFettro board members. Jack guessed that the Board was 'asking' Sean to persuade him to make 'the right' decision.

Tonight wasn't about that though. It was about the therapy of the gym. The three Flint Media employees wrapped their hands in boxing wrap. They talked and walked out to the main floor, eventually standing alongside five other men waiting for the lesson to begin. Tonight was an introductory lesson.

The instructor was off to the side chatting with regulars. He looked at his watch and walked over.

Jack reached out his hand. "Chuck, how's it going tonight?"

The instructor smiled and accepted his handshake. "Jack, welcome back." He nodded at Sean. "An intro lesson? To what do I owe the pleasure?"

Patting Sean on the back, "This is our friend Sean. I thought we'd show him what this place is all about."

Chuck was a lean man. You could see the veins in his forearms as he clapped his hands together. "Good stuff." He laughed. "Any friend of Jack is always welcome here. Welcome, Sean. We don't go easy on newcomers."

Everyone laughed, people were loose. Jack took in a deep breath. When he was here, he was alive.

The lesson was hard. The class started with basic drills and then finished with sparring.

It was easy to tell that Sean was enjoying the lesson. He methodically took to each new drill. He adopted the forceful execution of someone willing himself to improve. At the end, they sparred. Jack matched up with Chuck and Caleb paired with Sean.

After a few minutes, Chuck called for a pause. "All right, let's switch it up. Last five minutes of the lesson here. Everyone pair up with someone different."

As the men shuffled and paired off, Jack called out for Sean. "Let's see what you learned."

The two matched up with each other and the sparring began. They circled and traded blows. Jack's hands and feet were well practiced. Months of training gave his motion a fluidity that contrasted Sean's.

Jack took on the role of an instructor. He deflected Sean's strikes and called out when Sean did something well. "Good left! Again." Sean threw another left. "Again." Sean threw again. He grunted as he put more behind it. "Again!" Sean did it again.

Chuck called for an end to the lesson; time was up. But Sean and Jack did not stop. The others in the lesson started to notice and casually watched the ongoing motion. The sparring between Sean and Jack escalated.

Chuck didn't seem to mind. He crossed his arms and started repeating advice from earlier in the lesson. "Don't drop your hands." "Keep your feet moving." Each time Sean responded with more force and more focus. Sean was yelling as he delivered every strike.

Jack kept countering and daring Sean to pour more of himself into the moment. "Now hit me as hard as you can." Sean swung. "Harder." Sean swung again. "Good, now again." This continued for five more punches.

Dimly, Jack realized the true purpose of this match and why they couldn't quit. This wasn't a lesson in good form or proper strategy. This was catharsis.

Sean was dripping in sweat, and the group watched as he transformed himself with a singular purpose. Sean was releasing himself one punch at a time. Without warning, Jack broke from his mentoring defense. He deflected Sean's last punch and delivered a jab to Sean's chest. The force caused Sean to stagger backwards before dropping to a knee. For a moment he had lost his breath, but he stood and raised his hands ready to start again.

Chuck looked onward with a smile on his face. "Time!" He yelled. "Great work today gentleman. I'm impressed."

Jack dropped his hands and turned to find the instructor.

But in that split second between dropping his hands and turning, he felt an impact to the side of his head. For a moment, he saw blackness as his neck whiplashed to the right. A deep and immediate pain rattled his jaw. Now it was Jack's turn to stagger to a knee. He only needed a moment to comprehend what happened.

He looked up and saw Sean standing above him with his hand's hanging by his side.

In the locker room, they showered and changed. Despite the last punch to his head, Jack was feeling good. He always felt good after spending time at the gym. Jack looked at Sean. He was smiling. No doubt he was feeling the same. People don't realize how much they need the gym at first. It is a gradual realization. Day one is the lesson. Day two is for finding new bruises. Day three is where you begin to understand the sterility of the modern world. Day four is when you first feel the itch for more.

Sean, Caleb, and Jack stood and began to walk out of the locker room.

Caleb turned to Sean. "Why'd you do that man?"

"Do what?"

Jack pointed to his eye. There would be the first traces of a bruise tomorrow.

"I guess I just didn't hear Chuck say it was over."

Caleb snorted.

Jack glanced at Caleb then back to Sean. He shrugged.

The subject changed. "Caleb, Sean and I are gonna grab some food. You want in?"

Caleb shook his head. "Next, time. I'm good tonight. I'm not hungry."

Caleb's eye's lingered until the caught Jack's. Caleb's refusal had more behind it than the reason he provided.

Outside, Caleb hopped in a cab while Jack and Sean found a restaurant around the corner.

They sat at a booth until their food came. Sean pushed around the food on his plate. "So, are you ever going to tell me where you disappeared to? I tried calling you at least ten times."

"I was the off the grid."

"I noticed."

Jack took the first bite of food from his plate. "Sorry, Sean. It's been a rough couple of days."

Jack looked down. Even the magic of the gym had its limits. It could make you forget your troubles in the moment, but it can't erase the pains of your circumstance. The truth was that Jack didn't know how to feel. He felt handcuffed yet empowered at the same time. He could choose whichever pre-defined fate he wanted. Mostly, he was overwhelmed.

Sean eyed Jack. "Is it family stuff?"

Jack shook his head.

"Then, it's Molly. Is everything okay?"

"How do you know it's Molly?"

"I've known you for a long time. If it's not your family, it's Molly. She's the only person that makes you look like that."

It was true, and yet he hadn't talked to Molly since he left. Two missed calls and four text messages from her were still waiting to be answered, but he just couldn't bring himself to face her.

Sean was right as he so often was about this sort of thing. Molly's addition to the equation tightened the vise on Jack's emotional well-being. Here sitting across the table was an old friend. How many conversations had they had where Sean pulled Jack back to reality? How many dreams had he and Sean shared? He was a good friend.

But what to do about the stories? Sean brought this topic back to the conversation. "Jack, what we're doing is stupid. It's too risky."

Jack had thought about this. Sean was probably right. Why wake sleeping giants?

"We have a responsibility, Sean."

"Responsibility? Think of the people we have working for us. We have a responsibility to keep the company safe. The Board doesn't like it, Jack. I don't like it."

"Sean, we *are* half the board. It doesn't matter what eFettro thinks."

Sean let out a deep breath. "I don't see why you've let Anton's obsession become yours, too."

"This isn't about Anton."

The two paused. Jack ate more of his fries. The two of them didn't disagree on much. Jack searched for the words that might convince Sean otherwise.

"Look, Jack, you might be right. But is it worth it? This is a powerful man. Let it be. Let's fight another battle. Let's live another day."

Jack thought about the recording he first heard so long ago. He thought about the cocaine on Ronnie's dead body. Flint Media could succeed without running the rest of these stories, but it meant that this corrupt world would continue just as it always did.

"It's not too late. It's not like we can't call it off. We haven't crossed the point of no return, and there are a thousand other things we can do to start making us money."

It was a subconscious tick. Jack knew it was in his head. His left fingertips brushed the raised bumps on the top of his right hand. The scar flared up. It was like post-traumatic stress. A flashback to the car crash. He felt the slow motion of the impact and then the darkness that followed. His hand cringed as if reliving the burn. His body shuddered. The pain was still within him.

They just weren't on the same page. Jack's voice rose, "Are we going to stop publishing stories that might lose us money? Are certain things "off limits" because we might upset the wrong people? If we do that, we'll be just another cog in the wheel that keeps everyone and everything exactly as it is."

Neither had expected the conversation to get so contentious. This was a conversation that deserved much better surroundings than the run-of-the-mill restaurant they were in and much better food than their plates of burgers and fries.

Sean ducked his head into his right hand. He rubbed his forehead. He took a deep breath before he spoke again. "You've already made it, Jack. You've already broken out of your hometown and your thankless jobs. Think about it. What more do you want? You've already won. Cash out your chips and walk away."

Each stared down at his food.

Sean continued, "We built something amazing. Why risk losing it?"

How could he convince him? Jack was willing to risk himself for what he thought was right. Generations aren't saved by people who cash out their chips early. This is for a greater purpose.

Right?

Jack's mind lingered a second longer. What if it *was* about rising to the top? Could it be that he was the compulsive gambler? Could he be the man who never cashes out in favor of chasing bigger thrills? Could he be the fool who thinks he can beat the house?

He tapped the table. He looked left then right, then at Sean. "I'll think about it Sean. I can promise you that."

Sean reached out his hand. "I'm begging you, Jack. Think this through."

Sean was right. The risk/reward equation was out of alignment. But that wasn't the only thing that mattered.

"I don't know what they did to you. But it's not worth it."

Jack raised his hand signaling to the waiter, "Check, please."

CHAPTER 72

Sleep is the worst kind of friend. It deserts you at the first signs of stress or fear.

Jack was done with studying the ceiling in his bedroom.

He lay on his back looking upwards, thinking through his next move. Sleep was nowhere to be found. How had his life become so contorted? Jack was playing checkers and he needed to be playing chess. That much at least was clear now. He couldn't beat the governor or the professor at their own game. If he wanted to win, he needed to write his own rules to his own game. There is no winning when you play on some else's terms.

The choice was painful, but it was not difficult. It's not hard to choose your only choice. It was 3:32 a.m. but Jack reached to his bedside table, grabbed his phone, and sent the message he needed to send.

The night passed.

Later that day Jack stood on a chair in the Flint Media office. He was addressing the usual eager audience of Flint employees. "A few short years ago this company was nothing more than the farfetched idea of an unemployed journalist. Today—"

Jack paused and spread his hands out. He pointed to his employees and then motioned around the office.

"Today we are here. But, before we became the best collection of the hardest working people in journalism…"

Jack smiled and at least two of the employees clapped. Somewhere, Caleb gave a whistle. The mood felt like a miniature political rally. "Before we became what we are today, we were just a couple guys putting money into our own Kickstarter campaign." More laughs, then a break from the loud booming voice and a shift to commentary from Jack. "But seriously, I think at least half of our first donations were funded by my credit card."

Jack wondered if his employees would remember him as the CEO who stood on chairs?

"We've come a long way, and everyone in this room should be proud." He paused and then picked up, "A lot of you know this, but some of you newer folks might not. Today I want to honor the two men who have been with us from the beginning. Our business is a nasty one. Raise your hand if you've made at least one person angry through your work here at Flint."

Jack raised his.

Most of the employees raised their hands.

"I know *I* have… and I've got the lawsuits to prove it." More laughs and another whistle from the gathering.

"But our business is also an important one. Nothing worthwhile in life can be achieved alone, and our business is no exception. Today we're starting a new tradition here at Flint Media. We cannot change the world without the greatness of each of you and our unfailing commitment to each other. So today we will begin by honoring two of us who have been the cornerstone of everything that we have built together."

There was a small pause as the group understood that the moment was about to turn into an impromptu award ceremony. "Today we are starting the Flint Media Iron Man award. This award is to recognize those employees that go beyond the call of duty to help us build this great company. Every year I want to recognize the people that work tirelessly towards our dreams day in and day out."

He paused. "This year I'd like to recognize Sean Cosatiri and Matt Sutton as the co-recipients of the first annual Flint Media Iron Man Award."

There were cheering and applause. "I'm fortunate enough to count both men as among my closest friends. They've stuck with Flint from the beginning because they believe in our vision."

The cheering and clapping continued. The office was buzzing.

Jack looked into the crowd for Sean's face. He saw Sean's eyes widen for a moment. The moment passed, and Sean swapped his surprised countenance for a cool grin. He looked around at the rest of the crowd and clapped his hands along with them.

CHAPTER 73

The day faded and turned to evening. Jack found himself at the office near the end of the night with Sean. They didn't say much; the award was a surprise to Sean, but he had an idea of what it meant. "So, you're going to kill the stories?"

Jack nodded. He had done the math, and it didn't add up. "Sean, you're my best friend. I know you'd follow me anywhere."

It was obvious that Jack wasn't happy with the decision he had made. "It's the right thing to do. We can't risk losing everything that we've built."

Sean wore relief on his face. His shoulders pushed back, and he stood slightly taller; a weight was removed. Jack settled on the new plan for Flint media. He would break off the stories and appease eFettro and the governor. It hurt him to his core, but he had to do it. He owed it to everyone who had followed him this far.

"Have you told Anton yet? He's not going to like it."

"I don't care what that narcissistic idiot thinks."

Jack was not yet over the revelations of what Anton and the professor had shared with him. He felt no kindness for those who pulled the strings in the background of his life.

Both paused.

Jack stood. "We're going to be all right, Sean." Jack pulled his phone out of his pocket to check the time. "For the first time Sean, I feel like we're going to make it."

"The company?"

"Well, yes, the company. But I mean us. Once this is behind us and we get this ship sailing straight we're going to buy out eFettro's position. We're going to cut the strings and do things the right way."

Sean understood. "Be our own men."

Years had passed, the walls surrounding them were different, but the words were the same. They each thought back to the days of what first drew them together in college.

Jack turned to leave. "Are you going to tell Anton?"

"I will, but there's someone else I need to tell first."

CHAPTER 74

No one shows up to apartments unannounced anymore. Even fewer people do so with a bottle of Champagne in one hand and flowers in the other.

He rang the buzzer and spoke into the audio box at the top of the stair by the door. "Molly, it's Jack."

The response came. "Jack!" Excitement. The door buzzed and Jack walked in.

Anger and indignation soon replaced Molly's excitement.

"Where have you been?"

"I'm here now, that's all that matters."

They talked. She was mad at him for going silent for days. Jack didn't blame her. How could he articulate what he had been through? How do you explain to someone that they were so important to you that you had to ignore them?

"I'm pulling the stories on the governor."

The news was settling to Molly. There was no asking why, there was no push to understand the reason behind it. There was only immediate acceptance and relief. She smiled the smile that made Jack love her.

"That's why you brought the champagne?"

"Sort of, I brought it for us." He smiled and looked at her. They poured the bubbling liquid and made a toast.

Jack made his toast, "To starting fresh."

Molly followed, "To the demons we decide not to chase."

They both drank. Her strength of presence was remarkable. She did it effortlessly, but people always knew where Molly was in a room. Her presence loomed over Jack.

Jack tried to explain his thoughts. So much was swirling in his head. Why bring down the moment? Molly could read the thoughts pass through his eyes. "You bring a bottle of champagne over and look so upset?"

There was no easy way to do it, but it needed to be done. "Your brother." Then silence.

"I'm dropping the stories, but you need to know." He stuttered again, "It doesn't matter to me... He's part of a... I mean, look at all the success that your brother... that Christopher has... That's not by accident."

Molly wasn't saying anything.

Then it came out. A string of thoughts. A string of truths.

"The drug money. He's laundering the money. He and the governor don't play golf together just because they are friends."

Jack knew he wasn't making sense. But it didn't matter.

Molly started to cry. It was surreal, the two of them sitting across each other at a table in a small Manhattan apartment. The crying became heavier. She looked up and shook her head. "I know, Jack. I'm so sorry."

Jack stood and backed away, staring at Molly.

Neither spoke another word.

She knew.

Jack's mind was blank yet furious. He didn't understand.

What did she know? How long did she know? What did that mean?

The volunteering, the non-profit, the shunning of power—what was that? Were they Molly's ways of making up for the evils of her brother? Did Molly do this to even out the Bingham's score in the grand cosmic calculus of karma?

Words were even harder now than before. "I... I... thought..." Jack started and stopped.

Molly blinked. "I do love you."

Jack didn't respond. Not until she started to stand up. There was a thought that occurred to him. It was a singular, far-fetched, painful thought—but it could not be ignored. A jolt of memory from a few weeks prior, the man in the windbreaker in his apartment. Jack had collected what the man left behind on the table.

It was the most malicious of any threat that had come to pass. He had carried it on his body since that day, hoping its proximity would help him understand the motive behind it. He didn't know what it meant other than that whoever sent it knew enough about Jack to hurt him in the worst way.

"Do you, Molly?" Jack's voice was climbing.

He reached into his pocket. What he pulled out made Molly's bottom lip quiver. Jack placed on the table two halves of a ripped baseball card. A 1987 rookie card of Mark McGwire lay in two pieces on the table between them.

"This was waiting for me at my apartment."

Her voice was low, and her words were punctuated by tears, it was wavering and uncertain.

"It's not safe. You can't do it, Jack." Her voice cracked, "I've already saved your life once."

Jack's mind raced through everything he had been through. He didn't know what to say. What else did she know?

"Is this what you do to the people you love?"

"He's my brother."

The two let the words sit between them. The words were undeniably true. There could be no more discussion between them.

The champagne glass fell from the table. The sound of shattered glass punctuated the apartment's silence.

Molly's quiet crying was all that remained.

Jack stared at the broken glass on the ground. Then he walked out. He didn't close the door.

Molly's voice called for him to stay.

On the street, he was breathing hard. The earth was spinning around Jack. Molly's admission was the final thread to unravel the veil that covered his reality.

He screamed at himself: *Is there anyone else? Is there anyone else controlling my life?*

The dark night and cold air forced him to confront his reality. His visions for the future were less than illusions. They were delusions. Delusions of grandeur. Life is not so easily tamed, and yet he had fooled himself into believing he had done just that.

He knew what he was about to do. He recognized the pain it would cause and understood just how deeply it would burn who he loved. But he had no choice. He could set things right.

Jack took out his phone and called Sean. Sean picked up the phone. Anger, betrayal, and confusion, obscured everything except for a single purpose.

"Sean, there's been a change of plans."

CHAPTER 75

Jack had declared war.

The outside world didn't know it yet, but those in the Flint office got the message. Jack busted into the office the next morning with a backpack full of Red Bull. He walked around the bullpen tossing cans at every employee he saw.

"Drink up. We've got work to do and sleep is not an option."

The mood was infectious. People could feel the groundswell of energy. Jack tossed a Red Bull at Caleb. He nodded and cracked it immediately. It was 9:15 a.m. The caffeine addicts made themselves easy to identify.

Jack turned and threw, overhand this time, another can to a willing recipient. It was like a basketball game with a free t-shirt giveaway. Jack was the half-time show, and his fans eagerly awaited him.

Music accompanied his antics. On normal days blasting music in the morning was frowned upon, but today was not a normal day. Jack had scrolled through his playlist and turned up the volume. "Bombtrack" by Rage Against the Machine flooded the office. With each beat, Jack handed out another Red Bull, with each crescendo the energy grew. The lyrics of the chorus seemed oddly befitting of the circumstance.

Anton was at his workstation with his legs on the table. Jack approached him with the Red Bull. "You know, Anton, you never actually look like you're doing any work." He tossed the slim metallic can, and Anton caught it with one hand and popped the tab immediately. He took a swig.

"The elixir of productivity." He paused then continued. "You know Sean wants me to talk you out of this."

"It's been a long night, Anton."

"I can see that." He looked at Jack's face and noted the bags underneath his eyes.

"So, are you going to try and convince me out of this?"

"No. Let's burn him alive."

Jack couldn't help but laugh.

Jack wasn't sure if his animosity towards Anton was temporary or if it was deeper. Either way, it was still present. "You know I still hate you right?"

"Look, I get it. I'd hate me too. But it's going to be awfully hard to hate me after we get this first Pulitzer." He drank more Red Bull. "Use the anger. Channel it."

Jack nodded.

Anton didn't know it yet but he was going to be fired after this set of stories ran. Anton's manipulation could not go unpunished. This was his life and his company. There could not be another person pulling the strings.

Anton's desk was tidier than usual, but still messy. He leaned back further in his chair and put both hands over his head in the universal body language of relaxation. "It's all hands on deck. It's time to nail this guy."

CHAPTER 76

People respond differently to pain. In this instance, Jack responded with focus. Flint Media was going to war. The days after were intense. Of course, the company covered a variety of stories given their network of reporters and what the readership demanded; but the real focus was on the series that Anton had revived. The community was eating up the coverage. The momentum from last week spilled over with surprising force into the new week. It was time to add rocket fuel to the fire.

From the conference room, Jack set up camp. This week he wasn't flying around the country trying to raise money, attending networking sessions, or screening new hires. This had his focus, and he commandeered the company's main conference room to set up shop. "Mission control" he called it. To this point in time there were four Flint Media reports on the governor, the suspicious Super PAC, and the police force—but none of the stories had a by-line featuring Jack Ranger. Thus, far Anton and two other reporters in the network had been the public face. That didn't bother Jack. The more famous his reporters got, the better off Flint Media would be. Nevertheless, there was an opportunity. Never had Flint Media published a piece quite like the one Jack was working on. To date, everything published at Flint Media stuck to the facts and was presented with third-party objectivity; the investigative pieces presented evidence so that the audience could reach their own conclusion.

On Jack's computer screen was the start of something more than what Flint's readership had come to expect. It was more of a winding first-person narrative that connected the dots in a way that only someone who had lived them could. It didn't fit with Flint's model. There was no crowd-sourcing of this story, and there were no dollars attached to it from eagerly awaiting subscribers. It didn't fit, but so what? Sometimes it was good to be the boss.

His phone rang and he looked down. It was Molly's number. He didn't answer, letting it instead ring out to voicemail. It had been six days since Molly's confession and it had been six days since they last spoke. She had tried calling multiple times the day and night after, but nothing since. Maybe she was betting on the passing of days to cool Jack off. Maybe she just wanted to say sorry.

His body ached to see her. His rational mind knew it was over between them, but his body was a mess. Twisted stomach, difficulty sleeping, and the threat of sadness loomed constantly on his physiological doorstep. He refused to let the feelings in. He would not allow himself to pick up her call.

His distraction was his work.

Jack acknowledged that the case was weak in terms of direct evidence back to the governor. There were suspicious campaign contributions, but a clever politician seldom allows things to implicate him directly. The open questions remained around funneling dirty money, bribery, and extortion. Admittedly, Jack wished there was more, but it would be enough. Flint would do exactly what Jack had always hoped it would— light the fuse.

News outlets were reaching out to him directly. Alexandra Cole's last article had made the rounds on the *Pearson's* publication networks. It was a major boost; the third-party vote of legitimacy started the snowball growing bigger as it rolled down the hill. Maybe the governor would survive, maybe he would side-step a public execution—but maybe he wouldn't.

The computer screen glowed a milky white as he watched the blinking cursor beat its metronomic beat. He was halfway done writing what would soon be Flint Media's front-page feature.

Anton's words from a few days before held a tantalizing space in Jack's sub-conscious. Winning a Pulitzer was never even a consideration when he started Flint, but he sure wouldn't mind one now.

CHAPTER 77

It was to be a glorious day. Launch day. The 3,500-word story was a scathing account that used allegations of corruption, abuse, and chemical burns as punctuation. It was a story made from the fabric of his most painful memories that he threaded together using vindication as his needle. It was his offering to the world, and it sat in the publishing queue ready to launch at 12:00 noon Eastern Standard Time. He walked to the office in a trance, thinking about what would happen next.

On important days, Jack was usually first to the office. He liked to get in, settle down, and watch as his company awoke from its nightly rest. He loved the silence of the early morning when his own keyboard was the only sound that could distract him. It was like watching an animal stir at the first rays of sun. Employees would trickle in, and the noise would slowly escalate in a slow-moving wall of sound that eventually morphed into the full sounds of the midafternoon.

But today he was not first to the office. Today he was fourth.

The conference room was open. It was the only lit room in the office. The room emitted an eerie fluorescent seduction that backlit the silhouette of Rachel Warner standing in the open door. No smile, just a nod. "Can we have a word, Jack?"

Jack walked into the conference room. On one side of the table were three individuals. On the center of the table were two manila folders.

Here sat the Board of Directors of Flint Media.

Rachel from eFettro Ventures sat at the center directly in front of Jack. Dean Allen, the other director from eFettro sat to her left. But he wasn't looking at either of them. He was looking at the man sitting to her right. He was staring at Sean.

Jack answered with a coolness that contrasted his heart rate. "Care to share?"

Rachel spoke. "There are two folders on the table. Each folder contains a press release. We wanted to give you a choice."

There was no comprehension, just a blank stare.

Rachel continued "The folder on the right has a press release saying that you were let go because of a severe breach of journalistic integrity."

"But we like you, Jack, we really do." She pointed to the other folder, "The one on the left has a press release saying that you were forced to resign for personal reasons. Which will it be?"

Three individuals on one side of the table and Jack on the other. The ownership of Flint Media sat in this room, but the controlling votes sat opposite the CEO.

Jack understood the situation. He understood with a rush rising inside of him. "You want to fire me? We're trying to tell the truth, something everyone else is too scared to do, and you want to sabotage it?"

"So, personal reasons it is."

Silence.

Rachel was making direct eye contact with Jack. Sean was staring at the envelopes at the center of the table.

Jack spoke a single word. "Why?"

"You're dangerous, Jack. You can't be so cavalier with other people's money."

The answer was nonsense. Jack knew it. Everyone in the room knew it.

Jack shook his head in disbelief and looked at Rachel.

"Tell me, what did he threaten you with? What deal is he cutting you? I care more about this company than anyone else." Jack paused as his words trailed off into a plea, "You know that. I *know* you know that."

His words didn't alter Rachel's response.

"The Board does not have faith in you, Jack. Your highest-level employees don't either." Rachel made a head nod towards Sean. "The Board has appointed Mr. Cosatiri as interim CEO in your absence."

Sean was still staring at the folders at the center of the table. There was no denying Sean's role.

"How much did he pay you, Sean? How much of his drug money is going into your pocket?"

Sean said nothing.

Rachel pleaded. "Jack, please. Don't make a scene."

"No, I want to know. How much money does it take to backstab your partner? We built this together, Sean. How much money does it take to ruin your best friend?"

Rachel rose from her seat. "I think you should leave now, Jack. We no longer have a need for your services."

Jack stood. Rachel was right. He should leave. He still couldn't believe what was happening. The puzzle shifted in his mind; he tried to make sense of it. He was standing now.

"Jack, wait." It was Sean.

After saying the words, Sean stood. It was an impulse. He wavered, not knowing what to say next.

Jack looked at him. "You know, Sean. This was our chance to do something that mattered."

Sean looked back at Jack and shook his head. He had nothing more to add.

"We were right you know, all those talks we had about how messed up the world is."

Jack paused. He walked to an arm's length away from Sean. Then he added the final words he would speak to his friend.

"I just wish I had known how right we were."

CHAPTER 78

TWO WEEKS LATER

This wasn't how it was supposed to be.

New York City is a lonely place when you're broke and friendless.

Jack lay in his bed, once again staring at the ceiling in his tiny apartment. New York City was the hub of everything. It was the epicenter for money, connections, and opportunity. But what did that matter when your friends are gone and your family is hours away?

Molly, Sean, Anton—really anyone at Flint Media—was out; or more accurately, Jack was out. He had spent his soul trying to build something which he was no longer a part of. He was alone and betrayed.

He spent most of the first week on the couch playing through scenarios in his head. What could he have done differently? There was anger with a mixture of self-pity in the first week. Was the world so cruel as to conspire against him? Or, had he inadvertently twisted the crushing jaws of fate on himself? Whatever the answer was, it did not come.

Jack spent the second week trying to do something. He didn't know what needed to be done, just that something was better than nothing.

The Board, the investors, and even Sean didn't dispute the rumors that there were more than 'personal reasons' behind his resignation. Jack was toxic. The former CEO of a company would always be able to find a job if only he or she had the energy to do so. But for the first time in his life, the drive wasn't there. Jack was tired.

The only job he wanted had just been taken away from him. When he was at Flint, he was alive. The company was an extension of himself. He had hand-picked the people, he had dreamed about what it would become, he had lived the events that made it what it was. But there was no place for him now, and nothing else could ever be the same.

How do you tell news like this to your family? It's not easy to just casually call your parents about being ousted from your own company. Truth be told, for the first few days Jack thought that it all might change and he would be welcomed back. He fantasized that it was an elaborate prank. But, as the days strung together, his irrational hope turned into sober reality.

He had no doubt that people wanted an explanation. Reporters, employees, family, and friends—they all called. Sometimes Jack recognized the numbers; sometimes he didn't. Regardless he treated them all the same.

How many phone calls had he ignored? It was too many to count. He had stared at his phone as the calls came in. He didn't even silence the phone. Jack just stared at the blue luminescence of the screen watching it ring again and again.

By the end of the second week Jack was tired of sitting in his tiny apartment, looking at tired walls, and eating tired meals. He had worked hard enough for two people, and yet, here he was. He was hungry, physically hungry. It was a deep burning hunger that the frozen pizza in his refrigerator couldn't begin to address.

Jack called his father. His words weren't much and he didn't explain. He simply said, "I'll be home at the bus station in seven hours. Can you be there?"

And so, he left. He packed a single bag and walked out of his apartment without locking the door.

Penn Station was a marvel of people flowing in every direction; there were a constant ebb and flow of those fleeing and those seeking the allure of the city. Today, Jack joined the flow of those leaving the bright lights behind. There were thousands of people bustling in and out of bus terminals. How many, like Jack, were going home?

The ride itself was long and painful. He sat next to the window with his forehead resting on the glass, hitting the window with every bump along the way. With each rotation of the tire, Jack was one step closer to the destination he never wanted to have. It was ok to go home on a weekend or a vacation, but it wasn't okay to go home without a timetable to return to your other life. Round-trip tickets were good; a one-way ticket was unthinkable. Every bump along the way bounced Jack's forehead into the glass window, reminding him of his new reality.

His father was waiting for him at the station. He stood tall and strong, dutifully waiting for his son at the terminal. Jack stepped off the bus and gave his father a silent hug. The eldest Ranger understood what it meant for his son to be here.

CHAPTER 79

The ride from the bus terminal to the house was short.

"So, I assume you've read the news reports?"

"We've all read the stories."

Jack put his head against the passenger seat window.

Jack's father did not mirror his son's mood. Jack's father was smiling and happy to have his son home. "Jack, I know you're upset, but try and pull it together. We have people coming over tonight."

"People?"

"Yes, to celebrate."

"What?"

"To celebrate you."

That night there was a special dinner. Jack's grandparents and a few of his aunts, uncles, and cousins joined the Ranger household in an impromptu celebration.

They all gathered that night; there was wine, drinks, and delicious food. Veal was the main dish. It was his father's favorite. Everyone smiled and joked, and no one talked about what had brought Jack home.

The party had started early in the evening, and Jack's older brother Jason was late to arrive. Amidst the laughter and commotion, his car pulled into the driveway. Tired from his day of work he walked into the house.

"I didn't realize this was going to be such an occasion," he said to his father.

Jason saw Jack but couldn't understand the mood of the scene in front of him. He, too, knew the circumstances that preceded Jack's return. Why all this happiness?

Jason shook his head. The last time they were both in this house together his middle brother had begged for money. Since that day, Jack had run to New York City and squandered the savings his father had given to him.

Turning once again to his father, Jason put out his hand and motioned across the gathering of food and people in front of them. "I wish I got this treatment every time *I* came home."

His father laughed. "Relax, can't you just be happy your brother is back?"

With those words, Jack's father cleared his throat and raised his glass. The buzz grew quiet and eyes turned towards him. The immediate and extended family looked onward at the three Ranger men standing on the far side of the dining room.

Then came the toast: "I have two sons left in this world, and tonight the one who was lost has been found."

There was cheering and laughing. The celebration continued.

CHAPTER 80

He stood looking out the window of the mid-sized house in a mid-sized town. He was home now. Home, home.

Jack's father saw his son looking out of the window. He walked over and put his hand on his son's shoulder. Jack was melancholy each of the nine days that he had been home.

"I know it's hard, Son."

Jack looked onward out the window. He replied to his father without changing his gaze. "I'm just so angry."

"You can't be angry at everyone."

The son put thought to his father's statement. To Jack, it felt like he could be angry at everyone. Each day Jack played the scenarios back through his mind. What could he have done differently, what *should* he have done differently? He sat in silence for hours every day trying to figure out the answers. Sean was the frequent object of his thoughts. He was furious at him, but really, how could Jack be angry at him? Jack had pushed him too far. He saw that now. Sean was a pragmatic operator. When people are pushed to the brink, their decisions shouldn't be a surprise to anyone. People do what they are wired to do. When people are stripped down, there is no hiding their inner circuitry. The current only has one predictable way to flow.

His father continued, "I know you've never been a fan of rules, Jack. But there are some rules that are in your best interest to follow."

Where was his father going with this? He didn't know the answer, but he knew why failure was his tormentor.

He looked at his father. "It's not how it was supposed to happen. There was so much there. It was so close to making it. *I* was so close."

Close to what? That was the answer. His father understood now. There was a spark of recognition and a new purpose to his words.

"What will you do now? You've been home for a while. It's not like you to sit around."

"I don't know, Dad."

Jack had never watched so much TV as he had in these past nine days. He hadn't worked out and he hadn't put on real clothes. Nine days of sweatpants and television.

"I have a spot for you at the firm."

Jack looked at his father. "You know I'm no good at that sort of thing."

His father cut him off. "Not like that. We need a real business mind. Someone like you could help us out."

There was a sigh from Jack's father. "I'm getting old. Your brother is good. He's better than me. But he doesn't have that instinct like you."

Jack was sarcastic. "The instinct to get fired from your own company? No one wants me running anything."

The father put a hand on the son's shoulder. "With your brain, with your experience—you could really build what I've started. You and Jason could do it. He would do the construction and you could run the business side. I'm too old to get new clients; I don't have the energy. You're a marketing whiz. It would be perfect."

Jack knew he could do it. His father's company was a profitable business despite its lack of formal operations. He ran a good business. Jack could turn it into a great business.

He responded to his father. "You're probably right."

"It gives me purpose. It can give you purpose, too. Every time that I drive by a building that we made, I know that my own hands helped to create it. We built this community, and that's something most people never get to say."

Jack lingered on this point. He was right. There was a chance to do well. He would have an impact. Jack liked the thought of having a legacy.

He glanced at his father's face.

In that moment, Jack saw himself from his father's perspective. He was a father who saw his tormented son. He saw the same son who, ever since he was a child, thrashed wildly to rattle the cage of life. And for what purpose? Was it to do something great? No, it was slightly different. It was to *be* great. To prove that he could "win" on his own terms. He saw a son who sat here today—tired and broken—from throwing himself into the wall of life hoping that he could break through.

His father cleared something caught in his throat. "You're going to get there, Jack. It just won't happen as soon as you want it to."

His father walked away leaving Jack alone with his thoughts.

To build and to be burned. It was a tough way to go through life.

Absently, Jack twirled his phone between the thumb and forefinger of his right hand. Looking down at the glowing screen, he scrolled through the phone numbers in his contact list. Sean? Molly? Anton?

Delete?

Yes.

He lay on his bed and flicked on the television.

CHAPTER 81

The bulletin board in his room had a single piece of paper tacked to it. It stood as a focal point for attention. It was a printed copy of the press release that Jack had been dreading. "*Sean J. Cosatiri to assume interim CEO role at Flint Media.*" There was a sickening quality to this black ink on white paper, and yet he couldn't bring himself to throw it in the trash. It was perverse motivation.

Still, Jack stood staring out the window, feeling the ticking second hand of his bedroom clock tick within himself. He couldn't stay here. Every day was as painful as it was necessary.

Despite his emotional malaise, his time at home should have been pleasant. He had reconnected with old friends and they were all more or less happy. Some were still living at home, others were struggling with student loans and rent, but everyone seemed content with the gentle upward slope of their life.

But their contented nature did not rub off on Jack. Each morning was another opportunity for people to live exactly as they were supposed to. It was another opportunity to meet expectations. Jack wanted to be better; he wanted to be the outlier. But every day he spent here was another day spent reverting to the mean.

The doorbell rang.

It was the middle of the day and Jack was the only one home. He walked to the door. Waiting for him was Caleb. Life was on his doorstep.

Jack looked at Caleb with an awkward expression. Jack was in no mental shape to receive visitors.

"I'm happy I found you here."

"Where else could I go?"

They went to a coffee shop in the center of town. The New England air was crisp. The two walked in with few words between them.

The coffee shop's patrons included a smattering of retired individuals chatting with old friends and younger people dutifully scrawling in their notebooks or on their laptops. Sipping and browsing. Coffee and email.

They sat at a small circular table sun-kissed with slanted light. Windows showcased pictures of personified slices of bread, cupcakes, and coffee mugs that were made to look like stick-figured people. He loved how the smell of coffee filled this quirky hideaway. The atmosphere was lighter than Jack's mood.

"You really disappeared on us. What does it take for you to return a call?"

Jack put his hand to his head. He didn't know what to think about Caleb's arrival. He was bored at home, but at least there was no one to remind him of Flint. It was good to see Caleb. It just wasn't good remembering everything that came with it.

With a flip of his hand Jack changed the subject, "So why are you here?"

"I've been trying to get a hold of you for weeks. I figured my only shot was to come all the way out here."

Caleb laughed slightly and continued. "I quit, you know. A lot of us quit."

"Good for you."

It was obvious Caleb wasn't satisfied with that response. "What did you think would happen? We were all furious."

This time Jack didn't dismiss Caleb. "What happened?"

"That was the day we were supposed to launch that monster story. I thought it was weird when I didn't see you. We all did."

Caleb took a sip from his coffee. "It wasn't until the next day that we got a company-wide email from Sean."

"What did it say?"

"Not much. Just that the board decided you were unfit to lead and that Sean would be taking over."

Hearing the words stung. Jack made a whistling sound and then laid back in his chair. He closed his eyes and tilted his head back as his body relived the pain of that morning.

Caleb put his hand on the table and leaned in as if he was about to whisper. "I know what happened, Jack."

"It's a long story, Caleb. I don't really feel like…"

Caleb interrupted. "I know what Sean did."

"It doesn't matter anymore."

"Of course it matters, Jack. You *were* Flint. We were all following *you*. That's what we believed in."

Caleb paused. "Maybe you would know that if you ever bothered to check your email or phone."

"I'm sorry. It's just… I can't." It was unlike Jack to trip over his words, but he didn't know what to say.

Instead, Jack asked the most obvious question he could think of. "So, what are you doing since you quit?"

Caleb smiled. "That's why I'm here."

Caleb adjusted himself in his seat and leaned forward again. "Half the team left. Without you Flint Media is dead. It's just a matter of time now. But it's too important for us to let it die. You said it yourself. The world needs Flint Media."

This comment raised Jack's interest in what Caleb would say next.

Caleb continued. "We, everyone that left, want to keep working on this idea. We can make a new company. We can make it bigger. We can make it better. We've spent a lot of time on it already."

Now Jack was leaning forward over the table. The background sounds and smells of the coffee shop came back to his consciousness. He was beginning to grasp the meaning of Caleb's words. "A new company? When did you start?"

Caleb looked at Jack. "We won't launch for another couple of months or so. We are waiting on you."

Jack smiled and shook his head. "I love it. But I can't be that guy. Not now."

It was too much. It really was. The thought of going back to New York, the thought of trying to convince investors that he was worth their money—it was all too much. There would be threats again too. Here, at home, no one bothered to write death threats to Jack anymore.

"Look, Caleb. It was nice of you to come here. But I just can't go back with you."

Caleb must have sensed that he was losing Jack. "This is bigger than your feelings. That story needs to be told. People need to know. You were ousted to keep it hidden. Don't let them win."

Jack wasn't thirsty, but he took a sip from his coffee anyway. He placed the mug back down on the table.

Caleb continued his plea. "This company will be bootstrapped. No outside funding. We build it organically, and we never compromise. Ever."

Jack swayed his head as Caleb made his final persuasion.

"We already know what our first big story is going to be. We just need you to help us tell it."

Caleb reached into his backpack to pull out a series of folders and papers. "Everything that Sean and the others at Flint Media put on the backburner is right here." He patted his stack of papers. "All the hard work is done. We just need to build the platform to share it."

Caleb paused, seeming to gauge Jack's reaction. "Although, when we were putting everything together there are a few missing pieces that we couldn't find on the Flint servers before we left."

This brought a genuine smile to Jack's face. His mind flashed to the laptop sitting in the bedroom of his parent's house. "Sometimes you can only trust yourself."

The sunlight coming through the windows of the coffee shop shifted.

"Come join us, Jack. We need you, and I can see you need us."

Jack shook his head. He wasn't convinced. "I believe that *you* need me."

Caleb pushed back his seat and gave a sigh. "Don't let ego stop you from doing what's right."

Jack stood to leave. He was exhausted.

Caleb asked the only remaining question. "What are you going to do instead?"

"I'm not sure. But I'm needed here, too. I have an opportunity to build something that lasts. I can have a real legacy here."

Caleb stood. "Promise me you're going to at least think about this. We'll be waiting for you to give us a call."

Jack shook Caleb's hand. "I can't promise anything right now."

With the handshake complete, both men went their separate directions.

Back at his parent's house, Jack stared at the screen of his laptop.

He scrolled through the files from Flint Media. Jack learned his lesson from the *Tribune*. Each night at 12:01 a.m. his work files automatically backed up to his personal server. There was a lot of useful information here. Much of it had already been published. Much of it, however, had not. He opened the unpublished piece that he thought was destined for the front page.

He didn't want to invite any more pain back into his life. Jack's finger hovered over the delete key.

He would always have the memories and the experience, but he didn't want to relive them every day. Part of him wanted to move on.

Jack had already gone down this road twice. He wondered what a psychologist would say about letting go and moving on.

What to do with all this?

Something must be done.

But Jack was tired. He was too tired to do anything.

CHAPTER 82

It had been weeks since he met Caleb in the coffee shop.

There was a knock on Jack's bedroom door.

Jack looked up to see his brother Jason.

"Hey, I was just stopping by."

He motioned his hands around the room. "Come on in."

"I'm sorry about everything that's happened, Jack, I really am."

Jason walked further into the room and put his hand down on Jack's desk chair.

"And I'm sorry for all of the flack I've given you. I know this town isn't exactly what people dream about, but it's not so bad."

Jack sighed. "You're right. It's not so bad. I'm actually learning to like it."

It was an admission of truth. Jack had gained an appreciation for life here. He could see why people loved it and could see himself wanting the simplicity it offered.

Jason continued. His words came from an unresolved feeling. He looked sad.

"I guess, I just could never get over the fact that you wanted to leave me, Dad, and Mom so bad."

Jack didn't know how to explain it to Jason. It wasn't about leaving his family. It had never been.

There was a long pause as Jason took a good look at his younger brother. Jack stared out the window, but he could see Jason in the corner of his eye.

Jason broke the silence. "You ever still think about him?"

Jason had guessed what leaving was really about.

Jack sighed. "Every day."

"Yeah, me too."

Jack realized how deep this bond between them went, despite their differences. Whatever happened between them, they were brothers. And they would always share the love and pain of their memories of their youngest brother.

Jason stood. For the first time, he looked around the room. "Dad told me about your decision. That's exciting. You're out of here in a few days, right?"

Boxes, mostly full of clothes that he had accumulated in the last few weeks, were scattered across the floor.

"Yup, Dad is helping me move on Thursday."

"I'll have to check out the place once you settle in."

Jack shrugged. "It's nothing special. Just some space with an old friend. I just can't be in my childhood bedroom anymore. It's been getting to me."

Jason shrugged. "Yeah. I can understand that. Either way, I'm excited to see what you can do. It's going to be a challenge, but you'll get the hang of it."

Jason started to walk out the door. "Well, we'll catch up soon. I'm going to go. I'll let you get back to…" Jason thought, clearly not sure what Jack was up to. He finished his sentence, "work?"

His room had become his office. But Jack knew that it could no longer be that way. He needed to be more than just the CEO of his childhood bedroom.

Jack gave a short laugh. "Yeah. It's time to build a legacy."

CHAPTER 83

TWO MONTHS LATER

"Can you close that window?"

If the window was open, the apartment was too loud. If it was closed, the apartment was too hot. Jack went to the window and looked out at the city streets below. It was comforting to be surrounded by so many people again. Even if he didn't know their names as they drove by, Jack enjoyed knowing they were there.

He returned to the Ikea chair sitting next to the folding table that doubled as his desk.

Six of them sat throughout the apartment. Some on the couch, the rest at the same folding table as Jack.

Caleb looked up from his laptop and clapped his hands.

"Taz, how's that press release looking?"

"Looking good, chief."

Jack smiled. "Whoever's playing that music, turn it up."

On cue, the volume doubled.

Heads bobbed to the beat.

Fingers typed.

Work was getting done.

Caleb stood and walked up to a whiteboard on the far side of the room. On the left was a column of tasks. He grabbed a marker and crossed off the latest checkpoint.

His eyes shifted to the right side of the whiteboard. A hand-drawn calendar populated the space. Seven days away from today, two words were circled on the calendar: "Launch Day."

Caleb walked from the whiteboard to Jack. He put his hand on Jack's shoulder and looked onward at the computer screen.

"That's a lot of words, Jack."

"Well, there's a lot to say."

The doorbell rang. Dinner was here.

Jack went to the kitchen and brought out two bottles and an assortment of glasses. When he returned to the living room he found that someone had already replaced his laptop on the table with a stack of pizza boxes.

Jack mixed his drinks and passed them around.

Caleb raised an eyebrow. "A celebration?"

"Why not? We've made it this far." Jack paused for a moment.

He was sentimental for a Tuesday evening. Looking at Caleb, he started to say what he was feeling.

"Thank y..."

Caleb put up a hand and shook his head. Jack stopped mid-sentence. They both understood.

For the first time in these hectic weeks, Jack took inventory of where he was. The apartment was old, and the couch was second-hand, but he was surrounded by people driven with the same purpose.

Jack surveyed the room. The pizza boxes, whiteboard, and fake wood flooring added to the moment.

Jack heard the beat of the music, saw the energy, and could feel the future.

He took a sip from the glass in his hand. It was sweet, and it was smooth.

Jack spoke. Not just to Caleb, but to whoever was willing to listen.

"It's good to be back."

MORE INFO

I have put together the business plan for Flint Media and I want you to have it. It's what Jack and Sean brainstormed when they were forming the company and what they would have used to pitch investors. I hope one of you might just be inspired enough to build on this idea and make it your own.

You can download it for free at www.JimmyHaight.com/JC

ABOUT THE AUTHOR

Jimmy Haight is an author and entrepreneur obsessed with the intersection of humanity and the future. Jimmy was born in New Hampshire and draws inspiration from his New England upbringing. Always in search of the next adventure, Jimmy lives in Arizona with his fiancé.

Jack & Coke is his debut novel.

ACKNOWLEDGEMENTS

In the spirit of Flint Media, we crowdfunded *Jack & Coke* to take it from merely a manuscript to the published work that you are reading right now. This story owes everything to those that believed in it enough to give their time, money, and energy to get this project off the ground and into your hands.

Below are the names of those who contributed to the crowdfunding campaign. I am deeply thankful to all of you and I am convinced that I have the best family and friends anyone could ever ask for.

Yasi Abdolmohammadi

Shammara Al-Darraji

Matt Allbee

Annie Allbee

Roland Anderson

Drew Archer

Daniel Arsenault

Kay Arsenault

Lauren Augustine

Jessica Bahr

Brian Barnett

Jon Basha

Eric Bird

Katie Black

Jonathan Blackwell

Rebecca Blair

Kraig Bleeker

Megan Blier

Christa Boon

Brian Bossman

Kala Brgant

Thomas Brule

Ryan Burke

Bryan Cahoon

Mary-Margaret Cahoon

Timothy Carpenter

Irvin Castillo

Amandeep Cattry

Kevin Cecala

Willy Chang

Jen Chen

Ashley Clark

Joshua Clark

Victoria Cohen

Jeannette Conklin

Meghan Conklin

Kara Connolly

Lee Constantine

Aaron Cote

Michael Cunningham

Rachel Curtis
Ian Curtiss
Laurie Dahlstrom
Stephanie DeMatteo
Zack DerBoghosian
Adrianna DeRice
Nicole DeVito
Angela Diaco
Matthew Dishon
Burcin Dogan
Stephanie Dunbar
Crystale Dunn
Kelley Durgin
Amine El Housni
Chris Eldridge
Mariko England
Danny Erickson
Mary Fachman
Aaron Farley
Tara Fogarty
Kevin Forsa
Joe Frantel
Lyndsey Fry
Joseph Gabriel
Dan Gardner
Andrew Gauthier
Molly Gile
Peter Glynn
Monica Gonzalez
Kim Goody
Nick Gower

Deanna Grammenos
Megan Graves
Steven Graves
Susan Graves
Kenneth Griggs
James Guilmart
James F. Haight
Richard Haight
Stephen Haight
Hillary Hallinan
Claire Hambrook
Patrick Hambrook
Joseph Hark
Jonathon Harris
Sarah Harris
Alex Hasham
Ryan Herrion
Lindsay Houle
Jayde Huxtable
Pradeep Jacob
Colleen Johnson
Jordan Johnson
Ambra Jordan
Noah Kabbara
Andrew Kageleiry
Megan Panzer Kageleiry
Paul Kageleiry
Grace Karon
Ajit Karve
Matt Keeney
Mustafa Khan

Mandy Kiesl

Bryce Kuklok

Brittany Lafleur

Kevin Lapoint

Michelle Lauer

Mark Lawrence

Meaghan Leahy

Jeff Leshay

Hilary Leslie

Jeannine Leslie

Kent Leslie

Elliott Leslie

Dianne Leslie-Mazwi

Ian Levinsky

Brian Lofrumento

Helen Longvall

Stephen MacKenzie

Ellen Mader

Mike Maglio

Munirah Mahyudin

Cheryl Martin

James Mathieu

Samantha Mayer

Kathy McCarty

Chas McClure

Grace McCourt

Kate McLaughlin

Matthew Meads

Carley Mercier

Simone Michalek

Jesse Mills

Karen Mills

Ross Milne

Joey Milstein

Monica Mohan

Jeff Monk

Vienna Morrill

Brian Muelenaer

Patricia Mulqueen

Alexis Munson

Dennis Munson

John Munson

Julie Munson

Michelle Munson

Tom Munson

Kara Murphy

Liam Murphy

Pam Murphy

Patrick Murphy

Phillip Murrell

Mudassir Muztar

Glenn Myers

Jennifer Nahrgang Craig

Varun Nair

Prasoona Nalla

Joseph Nascembeni

Georges Nassif

Jansen Neff

Cindy Normand

Peg Nulle

Millie Oberlander

Charlotte O'Donnelly

Julie Pabian	Jeanne Sims
Manish Pati	Sankalp Sinha
Isaac Pease	Stephen Skidmore
Joel Penney	Michaela Sleight
Scott Pezza	Spencer Smitherman
Alex Pilitsis	Andrew Snow
Sally Platt	Sandra Somers
Mikaella Polyviou	Lindsay Spain
Abigail Porter	Kaitlyn Swist
Ariana Purro	Alex Temple
Rachel Quimby	Justin Temple
Gopinath Ramakrishnan	Yoko Temple
Hector Ramos	Joe Tenuta
Cory Ramsey	Elizabeth Terchunian
Justine Renadette	Aimee Tetu
Jacob Reuben	Dan Tetu
Toni Rhorer	Helen Tetu
Eve Richer	Paige Tetu
Tony Rizzo	Patrice Tetu
Ralph Rodriguez	Raph Thomas
Dan Ryan	Jennifer Thurlow
Miguel Santiago	Terri Tierney Clark
Joe Scheuermann	Cristina Torres
Amanda Schmitt	Joshua Tuttle
Maggie Schoening	Yash Vazirani
Jake Schwartz	Joe Visciano
Grace Seme	Jeanne Walcek
Shivam Senjalia	Karene Wallis
Nazanin Shahrokhi	John Warden
Prachi "Ralph" Shukla	Scott Wegener
Alexis Simontacchi	Dustin Weil

Jeff Weinstein
Jette Welch
Jen Whitten
Virginia Wong
Shirley Woodcock
Ali Serdar Yildiz
Angela Zeqollari
Paula Zuchetti-Frignani

Morgan James
Speakers Group

We connect Morgan James published
authors with live and online events
and audiences who will benefit
from their expertise.

Morgan James makes all of our titles available
through the Library for All Charity Organization.

www.LibraryForAll.org

Printed in the USA
CPSIA information can be obtained
at www.ICGtesting.com
JSHW022215140824
68134JS00018B/1073